fraud

a novel

PETER DAVEY

T0346998

SIGNAL BOOKS · Oxford

This edition first published 2018 by
Signal Books Limited
36 Minster Road
Oxford OX4 1LY
www.signalbooks.co.uk

A catalogue record for this book is available from the British Library

ISBN 978-1-909930-61-2 Paper

Printed in India by Imprint Digital

For Lyndy, Joe and Kit
and for Shelby and Carole

'O what a tangled web we weave when first we practise
to deceive.'
Sir Walter Scott, *Marmion*

Chapter One

'I'm going to confess. I'm going to confess everything.'

Maisy's charge was curled up on her bed, hugging a pillow and staring at the wall, which was ten inches from the tip of her nose.

'Confess what, my love?'

'That I'm a fraud. That my whole life's one pointless, meaningless lie.'

'I'm sure it isn't,' Maisy smiled soothingly. 'Now buck up, young lady, and get yourself off that bed. You've got a visitor at half past two.'

At first, Nicola did not seem to hear what the nurse had said but then, very slowly, she turned her head and stared up into her moon-like and relentlessly cheerful face. 'Is it Miguel?'

'No, honey, I'm afraid it isn't.'

She turned sharply back. 'I don't want to see them then.'

'He's from one of your fan clubs. Dr Lennox says he sounds nice.'

'Really?' she mumbled without interest.

'You agreed to see him, remember?'

'No I didn't.'

*

Dominic glanced at his watch. The traffic inching its way through the Blackwall Tunnel had stopped again. He sighed. He pounded the steering wheel with his palm. He had thought he had left himself plenty of time for this journey but now he was not so sure.

He still couldn't quite believe what was happening, that the letter he'd written three weeks earlier had produced a result. In it he had explained that he represented one of Nicola Carson's fan clubs and had organised a card and email campaign among their members to assure her they were all thinking of her in this difficult time. Might it be possible, he wondered, to hold a brief interview with her on the club's behalf and deliver them in person?

He hadn't held out much hope. But a week later, he had received a reply from one Dr Lennox – the clinic's medical director – saying that he had mentioned his request to her and she had agreed to see him. An interview involving any sort of recording equipment would be out of the question, however. He would be allowed a short, informal meeting with her but there could be no subsequent report of that meeting other than to convey her thanks to her fans.

He shifted under his seatbelt – six feet four and a half inches of anxiety was a lot to squeeze into one ageing Golf convertible. His armpits, which he had so carefully doused with *Guerlain Homme*, were two little pools of dampness seeping into his shirt. The traffic moved again.

Despite high hedges and an electronic gate, Malvern Hall did not look too threatening – like a minor stately home from some period drama on television, complete with sweeping drive and spreading cedar trees. The visitors' car park was empty but for one brand new Volvo estate. He switched off the engine and glanced again at his watch. Eight minutes in which to compose himself. He stared straight ahead at nothing.

What was he doing? What the *hell* was he doing? Did he really imagine that Nicola Carson – Oscar and BAFTA-winning star of *All about Me*, one-time Face of Chanel and darling of *Hello* magazine – would suddenly, in the course of a brief and no doubt painfully awkward meeting, simply open her heart and reveal everything? He wished he had never thought of this crazy plan.

The cavernous entrance led into space and coolness. The receptionist asked him to sign in and wait in the waiting room where he was greeted by Dr Lennox himself – a stocky, brindled Scot in a white coat and gold-rimmed glasses. 'I'll have you know you're highly privileged,' he said as they shook hands. 'I've turned away hordes of journalists but I'm letting you see her because I feel some messages of goodwill from her fans might do her good. And I was impressed by your website. Nice design with good definition in the photographs and a very evocative use of shadow. I'm a bit of a photographer myself.'

'Well, I didn't actually take them, of course,' Dominic laughed awkwardly. 'Just photo-shopped them a bit. But I'm glad you approve.' His shy, rather gawky demeanour seemed to be working in his favour on this occasion.

'I'll allow you a few minutes alone with her but I'm counting on you not to mention anything upsetting – especially all that nonsense about her book.'

It occurred to Dominic that the man was taking one hell of a risk – or a brave judgement call. He could be anybody – he could be some nutter who'd pull out a knife or a gun and murder her. There must be something about him that this psychiatrist – an expert in assessing human character – trusted.

'I promise,' he said. 'And may I just say that I thought all that stuff about her novel was nonsense too. Vicious nonsense.'

'Well, thankfully, it seems to have died down now. If you'd care to wait here, she'll be along in a moment.'

He returned to his office and Dominic, left alone, toyed with the idea of making a dash for it. Then he turned from the window at the sound of softly approaching footsteps and there she was standing before him – Nicola Carson, the girl who had dominated his thoughts for what now seemed an age. He stifled a gasp, unable to believe that this pasty waif of humanity in skinny jeans and navy top – her black hair cut in a bob to below her ears – was the star whose image he had seen a thousand times on screens, in magazines, on the sides of buses. Yet, despite her pallor and the shadows hollowing her eyes, he was astonished by her beauty – something he only now fully appreciated, seeing her in the flesh. He extended his hand and felt a limp, tiny hand within it.

'Miss Carson, it's … a real honour to meet you.'

'An *honour*? Jesus. Who are you, anyway?'

'My name's Dominic. Dominic Seeley. I represent one of your unofficial fan clubs – well, I'm sure you already know that,' he added with a laugh. 'We're based in … in Stratford, East London, but we have a major web presence throughout the globe. We're listed on Google on page … well, I'm not sure which page we're on but we're near the top.' Stop waffling, he told himself. Focus! 'I've brought you some goodwill cards and emails – just a fraction of what I've received – and I just wondered if you could spare me a moment of your time to share them with you.'

She contemplated him vaguely. 'Well, my diary's pretty full right now. I might be able to squeeze you in between rebirthing class and electro-convulsive therapy. You'll have to ask Maisy here – she's my PA.'

He glanced at the cheery nurse who had placed herself squarely at her side, then laughed a little too loudly when he realised she was joking.

'Have you got any fags?'

'Yes, I have, as it happens.'

'Let's go in the garden then. I'm gasping for a smoke.'

Watery sunlight was bestowing a gentle warmth on the wide stone terrace. It was mild for March. They settled on a bench overlooking the extensive gardens where a few patients were wandering dejectedly about, mostly alone, or were sitting hunched on other benches, gazing at the grass. Dominic, his fingers trembling, extracted two Superkings from his packet and offered her one, then took one himself and attempted to light them with the disposable lighter he'd picked up at the corner shop. God, this is so *typical,* he thought as he snapped ineffectually at the flint. The most important meeting of my life and I didn't bring a lighter that works. 'I'm so sorry,' he laughed. She smiled tightly.

A feeble flame finally flickered into life and he thrust it at her before it went out. She recoiled slightly then cradled it in her palm. It survived just long enough to get his alight too. They smoked in silence for a while, she clearly rejoicing in the first few drags and seeming unaware of his presence.

'It's really good of you to see me,' he said, then wished he had thought of something witty – or, at least, interesting – to say. 'You must get hundreds of visitors.'

'No, I don't. Not many.'

'Really?'

She lapsed into a long silence, drawing slowly but regularly on her cigarette as though hungry for the nicotine. He noticed she wore a Kaballah string bracelet and had something scrawled on the back of her hand with a biro – a phone number, possibly.

'My agent came, but that was just to check when I'll be ready to go back and earn him more money. And my mum came once. Or did she? Can't remember.'

'I'm amazed.'

'Yeah, well,' she sighed, flicking some ash onto the flagstones. 'You're no fun anymore, are you? When you're ill.'

A robin landed a few feet away and eyed them expectantly, its head cocked to one side. She watched it for a while. 'Those little fuckers come right up to you in this place. They're really tame.'

'That's so sweet, isn't it?'

'No, it's not *sweet*. It's because it thinks we've got some food. I was sitting here having a sandwich once and this blackbird landed beside me and tried to nick it off my plate.'

'You're kidding.'

'No I'm not. It's survival. It's probably got chicks somewhere. Everything wants to survive. And they'll do whatever it takes. Birds. People. They're all the same.'

They fell silent again then she suddenly repeated, in a nasal New York accent, 'Everything wants to survive, Brett. And they'll do whatever it takes. Animals. People. They're all the same. Oh God, I want so much to survive.'

He was disconcerted. Should he point out that his name wasn't Brett?

'That's a line from *The Beautiful and Blessed*. Can you believe I had to say that crap?'

'It won you a BAFTA,' he said.

'God, don't remind me. At least they had the sense to give the Oscar to Rachel.'

'Rachel Springer?' he said then felt like a fool. Everyone knew that Rachel Springer had won the Oscar that year.

'Yeah, dear little Rachel. She wanted it so badly, bless her heart. Is she still there?'

Dominic was confused. 'Who?'

'My shadow. My conjoined twin.'

He glanced over his shoulder to see her nurse installed on another bench about twenty yards away, ostensibly reading a paperback.

'Yes. She's still there.'

She turned and caught her eye, smiled and waved. Maisy waved back.

'They have to watch me practically 24/7 because I'm a liability. Plus they don't really know who you are so they're checking you don't start harassing me. Who are you, by the way?'

'Well, as I said, I'm ...'

'Yeah, yeah, I know, you're from the Surbiton branch of my fan club. Who are you really?'

His armpits were soaking again. His heart was thumping. 'I'm sorry?'

'Come on, I've met the sort of people who run fan sites. You're not one of them.'

'Well, we're ... we're trying to cultivate a more serious appreciation of your work,' he said hastily. 'You should see my ... our website. The graphics are amazing. A very evocative use of shadow.'

'So it's not just soft porn, then, like most of the crap on the internet?'

'No. God no.'

She took a deep drag on her cigarette and exhaled slowly. 'So what do you do when you're not running my fan site?'

'I'm a writer.'

'A writer?' She sounded surprised. 'You mean a journalist?'

'No, I'm a real writer. Trying to be.'

'A real writer,' she echoed slowly, savouring every word and clearly amused by the phrase. 'So, have you published anything?'

'No. No, I haven't. Not yet.'

She responded with silence. Dominic, heart still pounding, knew he had to push things forward before this one opportunity he had gone to so much trouble to engineer evaporated. 'I'm a great admirer of your writing, though,' he said. 'I really enjoyed *Loss*.'

'Of course, you could be verbally harassing me and she wouldn't know, would she? I guess that's a chance she's just got to take.'

The robin flew away. Maisy was approaching the bench to inform Nicola it was time for her counselling session with Maggie Burns.

'Can't she wait? I'm having a conversation here.'

'You know she can't. She's got other patients besides you.'

'Well, she shouldn't have other patients besides me. Christ, the way I'm treated, I might as well be in the Friary. I am a superstar, Maisy, in case I forgot to mention it.'

'No, Nicola,' she replied rather wearily, 'you didn't forget to mention it.'

'Okay, okay,' she sighed, rousing herself from her seat. 'Maggie Burns hath spoken and all the world must obey.'

She turned back as she was leaving. 'Thanks for coming, by the way. What was your name again?'

'Dominic.'

'Right. Dominic. Well, you can come again, Dominic. If you want.'

'Really?' he grinned, aware that he sounded like a little boy who had just been told he was going to Disneyland.

'Sure, why not? It passes the time. Coherent conversation's rather at a premium in this place.'

'When shall I come?' he asked, flattered that she thought his conversation coherent.

She shrugged and Maisy intervened. 'You'll have to phone beforehand to check that Nicola's free.'

'Yeah, and don't forget to bring your fags. And a lighter that works.' Then she smiled for the first time, that world-famous smile that tightened and puckered her lips very slightly – a quirk which added to her beauty its multi-million dollar dimension of pure sexiness.

After she had gone, he realised he had forgotten to give her his bag of messages.

*

Dominic was twenty-eight – two months older than Nicola Carson. Unlike her, however, his life had been unremarkable. Born and raised in Watford, he had obtained a degree in media and creative writing at the University of East Anglia before working for six years for a small but respected publishing house, The Dragon's Head, first as an editorial assistant and then as a fully-fledged editor. That job had ended four months earlier and he was now unemployed – or rather, he was employed in studying Nicola Carson.

Lying awake in his little room on the second floor of a block of flats in Stratford, he found himself reliving every moment of his meeting with her that afternoon. For years she had been a concept, a fantasy which had been at once beautiful and elusive but now, all of a sudden, she was a real person who joked and smoked and had a phone number scrawled on her hand.

He cast his mind back to the exhaustive research he had done on her over the previous months. Though she had always wanted to act and had given some memorable performances at university, she had not – like most of her kind – found fame through film, the stage or television but through writing. When little more than a student, she had published a vast and stunning novel entitled *Loss* – a teenage girl's odyssey in search of her biological mother – which had tapped into all the frustrations and insecurities of youth, becoming an instant bestseller and winning her the coveted Connaught Prize for début authors. It was only a matter of time before the book would be brought to the screen, the production company who held the rights (a subsidiary of the publisher) waiting for sales to flag before using the film to revive them.

He remembered clearly when *Loss* had burst on the scene. Close-ups of Nicola Carson's flawless face had been spread all over the Sunday supplements and Friday arts reviews; interviews by crusty old critics had coyly described how her raven hair tossed freely about her shoulders, her sudden, disarming peals of girlish laughter, her trick of stroking the sofa arm with the tip of her middle finger whenever she was discussing anything personal. 'If I have to look at that bimbo's face one more time I'm going to *throw up*,' Sonia

– a secretary at The Dragon's Head – had exploded at the sight of Nicola on the cover of *TLS*.

'She is a bloody good writer, though,' Greg, their resident geek, had mumbled defiantly.

'Yeah, well you would say that – you're a bloke. You keep your brains in your balls.'

Trawling through the internet, Dominic had acquainted himself with every detail of her subsequent flight through the firmament. While the world was waiting with bated breath for her second masterpiece, she met – on a book-signing tour in the States – a rotund arthouse director named Hal Birling who had a reputation for unconventional casting. Once, in film school, he had tried to cast Ronald Reagan as himself in the satire *Old President goes Nutzoid*, which he had been preparing for his graduation assignment. Nancy Reagan's private secretary had politely declined the offer on the ageing ex-president's behalf. When Hal met Nicola, he had been planning a feature called *All about Me* but had yet to cast the lead. Nicola, already a fan, had seemed the answer to his prayers but his backers had been apprehensive about how a twenty-three-year-old Englishwoman, who wasn't even a professional actor, was going to play a drugged-up, seventeen-year-old American drop-out. They need not have worried. She made them a fortune, was awarded an Oscar and moved Hal Birling firmly from arthouse into mainstream.

Thereafter, she worked with an energy which astonished and exhausted everyone around her – not merely juggling multiple acting projects but modelling designer labels and endorsing the coolest products – her agent cutting merciless deals with producers and her life choreographed by her scarily efficient PA, Alison Dwyer. Sleeping in snatches and seldom seeming to eat, the only concern of her coterie was how long any human constitution could tolerate such a regime. Dominic, lying in bed and staring at a fan of streetlight spanning his grubby ceiling, was aware that he was one of only a handful of people on the planet who knew that Nicola Carson's condition was not just a case of celebrity burn-out. It was far, far more than that.

II

His second visit to Malvern Hall followed much the same pattern as the first, although this time he made sure he was equipped not only with a lighter that worked but with a back-up. She was wearing jeans and a bomber jacket – as though already anticipating the outdoors – and he could not help noticing that she looked in better shape than at their first meeting. Then he noticed something else – something which made him catch his breath. She had applied a little lipstick and eye shadow. Maybe she had only done it because she was feeling better; but maybe, just maybe, she had done it for him.

They settled on the same bench and he lit the mandatory cigarettes. 'So, have you published anything?' she said.

He was disconcerted by the question. He was glad she had remembered he was a writer but surprised she had forgotten his telling her he was unpublished. Then again, she had more important things on her mind than him and his writing career.

'No. No, I haven't. Not yet.'

'Well, you will. Success is just around the corner for you – I can sense it.'

'I hope you're right,' he laughed.

'I'm always right. It's one my many charms. And you're so tall. That helps.'

'Being tall helps me to be a good writer?'

'It helps you to be a conspicuous writer.'

He wondered if she was mocking him, or the world, or something.

'So, have you always wanted to write?' she asked.

He thought about her question. 'For as long as I can remember. I wrote these stories as a child – with illustrations. Then I started a novel when I was fourteen – it took me eight years, on and off, and it changed beyond recognition in that time, of course.'

'Did you finish it?'

'Yes. Finished it, submitted it and had it rejected. By the person who's opinion I valued most.'

'That must have been tough.' She paused, blowing smoke

sideways away from him. 'I had loads of knockbacks like that before I met Hal.'

He was confused. 'You mean Hal Birling?'

'The very same.'

'But ... surely you'd already made it by then?'

'No, I hadn't.'

'I'm sorry, I thought *Loss* ...'

'Are you kidding? Okay, I was flavour of the month with that Londony lit-crit crowd for a while. But that's not fame.'

'No. No, I suppose not,' he murmured, aware he had strayed into sensitive territory.

'So how did you deal with your disappointment?' she asked.

It took him a moment to revert to the original subject. 'Drink and fags, mainly – you know, to dull the anger. Then I went out and did something about what had caused it.'

'What did you do?'

'I learnt to write.'

She laughed. She laughed properly – freely, openly. He had not meant to say something funny, he had simply told her the truth.

'So what are you working on at the moment?'

'I'm working on a novel. And I'm researching something else – a book.'

'Well, that figures, since you're a writer. What kind of book?'

'It's ... also a novel.'

I'm lying to her, he thought.

'And what's it about, this novel?' she persevered.

'You mean, the first novel or the one I'm researching?'

'I don't know, either novel. God, you're irritating.'

'Oh, you know, the usual stuff ... love, hate, betrayal ...'

'In other words, you're not going to tell me.'

'I ... I just feel embarrassed,' he stammered.

'*Why*, for Christ's sake?'

'I don't know.'

'Dominic, if you don't believe in yourself, how the hell do you expect other people to believe in you?'

There followed a silence.

'Not that I'm one to talk,' she added in a murmur.

'You have reason to believe in yourself. You've proved yourself.'

'Yeah, right,' she snorted.

'You have. *Loss* is brilliant.'

'Yeah, but which one of my many acting roles is *brilliant*?' she demanded, stabbing air-quotes.

'All of them. Especially *All about Me*.'

'How about *The Beautiful and Blessed*?'

He hesitated. 'Well, you were great in that too. But I don't think the character or the screenplay gave you the scope you deserve.'

'In other words, I was crap.'

'No, you weren't crap. You could never be crap. You're incapable of being crap.'

The conversation, that afternoon, lasted more than an hour, Dominic responding to her questions and talking mainly about himself – his job, his family, his dog, his years at university. He was flattered by her interest in him, though he sensed that it was to deflect the conversation away from herself, for when Maisy came and informed her it was time for tea, he knew little more about her than when he had arrived. Nonetheless, he had enjoyed their conversation and sensed that she had too. He was amazed how at ease he felt with her.

'Come again soon, Dominic,' she smiled as she was leaving.

*

That evening, Maisy found Nicola sitting on her bed, looking at the cards and emails Dominic had brought her. She sat down beside her and she handed her a few. She thought they were lovely.

'No they're not. They're weird.'

Maisy looked confused. 'What do you mean, weird?'

'I don't know. They're not like the usual stuff you get from fans. I mean, they are but there's something not quite right about them.'

'I wouldn't know. I've never had a fan. Except Kevin, when I was sixteen.'

'Please don't go there, Maisy.'

'No. Okay.'

'So what's his angle, do you reckon?'

'His angle?'

'His agenda. Everyone has an agenda, don't they?'

'Do they?'

'Course they do.'

Maisy thought about it. 'He just seems like a really nice guy to me.'

'So you like him, then?'

'Yeah, I think he's sweet. And I've always had a thing for tall men.'

'God, Maisy, you're so shallow. What difference does it make how tall he is?'

'It makes a difference to me, being dead shallow and all. I find being stared down at from a great height a real turn-on. So what do you think of him?'

'I don't.'

III

Dominic visited Nicola seven times at Malvern Hall. He became a regular feature, part of the landscape. As he was signing in, the girl on reception would smile and ask him how he was; Patsy, the old lady who was always sweeping floors, would glance up from her work to greet him, and Maria, the gigantic Jamaican nurse would call out 'Hi-ya, Domaneeck!' as soon as she spotted him across the hall. Dr Lennox, who was not conceited enough to believe his treatment the only path to improvement, could see how much Nicola enjoyed his visits. She looked forward to them and was always cheerful and positive after he had gone. He had no way of knowing what passed between them when they were together but he sensed that she was opening up to him in a way she found it hard to do during counselling and group therapy sessions – and she had a lot to open up about.

On his seventh visit, it was pouring with rain. Nonetheless she insisted on going outside. They scurried to the shelter of a cavernous veranda where some parasols and folded garden tables were stacked in a corner, though there were no seats so they had to sit on the floor with their backs propped against the wall. He offered her a cigarette but, to his surprise, she refused so he refrained himself. For a long time they said nothing. Dominic was enjoying sitting quietly beside her on that cold stone floor, listening to the rain popping on the perspex roof and watching it drive across the lawns and trickle down the strands of clematis. The vast, manic sprawl of south London seemed to have retreated to beyond that pale wet cocoon.

'It's nice here, isn't it?' she murmured. 'Peaceful. Even Maisy seems to have dematerialised.'

'Maybe she's finally trusting me to be alone with you.'

'Don't you believe it. She doesn't trust you around a corner. Nor do I.'

Her words – the first that had hinted that there might be more than just friendship between them – sent a wave of excitement sweeping through him. It was scary.

'Dominic?' she said, after a silence.

'Mm?'

'I was thinking ... if I left here, you could go on visiting me. If you want to.'

He turned to face her, astonished. 'Well, yes, that would be great. If you want me to.'

'I do.'

'Are you thinking of leaving, then?'

'Yes, I am.' She turned away, towards the mist-shrouded trees. 'I'm sick and tired of this fucking place. I know I haven't finished my treatment yet but all of a sudden I need to get back to the real world. And I reckon I can handle it now.'

'I reckon you can too.'

'Do you reckon I can handle it now?' She was facing him again, her eyes wide.

'I'm sure you can.'

His heart was pounding. He knew that if he said what he had to say at that moment, he would lose all chance of ever attaining his goal. But perhaps a different goal was looming, one he could never possibly have imagined. Either way, he longed to be honest with her as much as he longed to kiss her.

'Nicola ... I was wondering.'

'Yes?'

'Since I've been coming here ... These novels I've been working on ... I just can't get into them somehow. The timing's wrong. And I was wondering ...'

'Yes?'

'... if you'd mind if I had a crack at writing your biography.'

She said nothing. Finally she murmured, 'I knew it.'

'I'm sorry?'

'I knew you had an agenda.'

He was horrified. 'An *agenda*?'

'Yeah. Everyone has an agenda, don't they?'

'God, please don't think I had an agenda. The idea's just come to me since getting to know you ... since getting to know ...' He was going to say, 'what an amazing person you are' but held back, fearing her reaction.

'Okay,' she said at last.

The hiatus which followed was agonising.

'You're angry with me.'

'No, I'm not.'

After a silence, she said, 'I'd like to go back inside now.'

'Nicola, I really didn't have this in mind when I first came to see you. I just came to deliver those cards and emails. I was amazed that you even agreed to see me and I never expected you to see me more than once. You have to believe that.'

'Whatever.'

*

Staring at the world through the wedges of windscreen between the wiper strokes, Dominic felt numb. She knew he had betrayed her trust and that whatever frail bond had formed between them over the past few weeks had been destroyed. That was the problem with lying – sooner or later your lies are going to rise to the surface, like scum. The whole fan site thing had been crazy from the start and he'd been amazed that both she and Dr Lennox had bought into it. All the trouble he had gone to downloading that web-writing and FTP software, scanning photographs from magazines and snatching them from elsewhere on the net; then fabricating all those cards and forcing himself to write such nonsense as 'We love you, Nicola!!!' 'We're thinking of you, Nicola!!!' 'Get well soon, Nicola!!!' and littering them with hearts and flowers and kisses and smiley faces; then the emails he had concocted by opening Yahoo, Hotmail, Gmail and every other free account he could find, inventing all the screen names available then sending the messages back to himself and printing them out.

Now, as he crawled home past The Millennium Dome, he found himself bitterly regretting the idea which had seemed, at the time, so inspired; and, as he waited at a crossing, watching a red light weeping in the rain, he knew he would never see her again. As for his own career, he would just have to write a half-decent novel and find a more honourable way into print – just like everyone else. It was all academic anyway since, at that very moment, she would be sitting in Dr Lennox's office, informing him that the young man who had been coming to visit her was a fraud – the fan site was almost certainly a fake, a way of gaining access to her to obtain some dirt and turn the book he was planning into a bestseller.

*

The next morning he lay late in bed, too depressed to get up. Soon after nine, his mobile rang on his bedside table. It was Dr Lennox.

'Did you know about this?' he said.

He jacked himself up on one elbow, frowning. 'I'm sorry. Know about what?'

'Nicola's decision.'

Nicola's decision. Nicola had made a decision. Surprise, surprise.

'No,' he answered in a faintly tremulous voice, feigning innocence. 'What decision?'

'Her decision to … look, I can't discuss this over the phone. Can you get down here, as soon as possible?'

He was bewildered. If Dr Lennox was telling him never to come near Nicola or Malvern Hall again, why not just tell him then and there? Why did he need to see him?

On the drive to Bromley, he felt as though he were on his final journey to the gallows. As he was signing in, the receptionist – her normal cheery expression conspicuously absent – phoned through to Dr Lennox to inform him of his arrival. He appeared a moment later. 'Come into my office,' he said.

The room was large, comfortable, calm and orderly – a far cry, Dominic imagined, from what went on beyond its oak-panelled walls. Dr Lennox sat down at his desk, gesturing to the seat on the other side. The frame of the wide bay window behind him, with its view of the gardens, rendered the stocky Scotsman larger, almost godlike.

'So what's going on?' he said.

Dominic's palms were sweating. 'I'm sorry, but I honestly didn't plan this ...'

'So you know about it, then?'

'Dr Lennox, I'm not quite with you.'

'About Nicola leaving.'

His face formed into a grimace of mystification. 'No.'

'She's informed me she's discharging herself and wants to come and stay with you.'

Flabbergasted, a tornado of thoughts whipped through his brain. Where was she going to sleep? What do you give a superstar to eat? Why had he allowed the flat to become a tip?

'When?' he managed to say.

'Well, now, I think. She's packing even as we speak.'

Panic-stricken, he could think only of the pair of jeans he had discarded the night before – a pair of far-from-pristine underpants tangled into the crotch – and whether he had left them on the sofa or thrown them into the laundry basket.

'Dr Lennox, I swear I know nothing about this.'

'That doesn't surprise me. I suggested it might not be convenient for you and she said she'd go to a hotel. Either way, she's determined to leave – and she's not being manic, she seems calm and rational. Amazingly enough, she doesn't have a place of her own, she's always just hopped between hotels and rented properties. She seems to prefer a life of impermanence.'

Dominic barely heard him. He was still thinking about those underpants.

'So, what are your thoughts on the subject?' Dr Lennox asked.

'I ... don't know.'

'Well, I'm very unhappy about it, if you want the truth. I've tried my best to dissuade her but, when all's said and done, I have no choice in the matter. She's here of her own free will and she's perfectly entitled to walk out any time she likes. And if someone feels ready to go back to the outside world rather than live in a clinic, that's got to be a good thing. But she seems to be investing an awful lot in you and I just wonder how prepared you are for that. Not very, by the look of it.'

'No, I'm just in shock. She did mention wanting to leave but she never gave the slightest hint that this was what she was planning. But that doesn't mean I don't want her to,' he added hastily.

'So, what's your situation? Are you working? Apart from your website?'

'No, I'm, I used to have a job in pub ... in public relations. I had the offer of a job in the States but decided against it, so now I'm looking for ... something else.'

'Well, I have to say that Nicola seems a lot happier and more balanced since you've been visiting her. She's convinced people are only interested in Nicola Carson the star, not Nicola Carson the person, but you seem to have cut through that somehow. She trusts you. Please tell me you're worthy of that trust.'

'I ... I am.'

'And are you worthy of my trust?'

'I am.'

Dr Lennox scrutinised him for a moment. 'Okay,' he said, leaning forward and resting his forearms on the desk. 'You've probably picked up on a lot of Nicola's problems but let me explain the situation more fully. She suffers from a condition called bipolar disorder – which is essentially a mood disorder. The patient can swing between a state of manic euphoria where they believe they can fly, change the world, produce amazing works of art – you name it – and moods of utter blackness and despair where they can barely function. There's no cure for it and nobody knows what causes it. A large body of research has suggested abnormalities of the brain – possibly genetic – but there's no question it's also connected with life events and environment – childhood trauma, for example. My belief is it's a combination of the two. Life's a battle for all of us, isn't it? But things which you or I can deal with relatively easily can drive the bipolar patient over the edge, possibly even to suicide. My work with Nicola has revealed that she's experienced both states in the most extreme form, but by a combination of medication, counselling and therapy we've had some success in managing her mood swings ...'

'They often do produce great works of art though, don't they?' Dominic interrupted.

The doctor looked at him, a little put out. 'Yes. Yes, they do.'

'So, in a way, it has a positive side.'

'I suppose so. But it comes at a very high price.'

Neither spoke for a while.

'Anyway,' said Dr Lennox, getting to his feet. 'I'm going to keep her on the same medication for the time being and trust her to self-medicate – she's got the times and dosages on her medication schedule, which I'll give you, and I'd like you to make sure she sticks to it. I'll go through the precise details with you both before you leave but basically they're a combination of anti-depressants and mood stabilisers and it's vitally important she takes them at the right time of day. There'll still be mood swings, of course, but hopefully the self-harm is a thing of the past. Just the same, I'd like her to come back as an outpatient for her group therapy sessions and her counselling, and I'd like to see her myself, once a week, to monitor her progress. I can't force her to co-operate, of course, but I'd be grateful if you could encourage her to do so. And if you have any problems – day or night – I'm just a phone call away.'

'Thank you. That's good to know.'

When they stepped out into the hall, Nicola was there with Maisy, three suitcases and a number of bags. 'Dominic, if this is a pain for you, I can go to a hotel. I just need to get out of this place.' She spoke in a calm but resolute voice. 'No offence, Dr Lennox, or to you Maisy, you've both been brilliant.'

'None taken,' he said.

*

'I thought if we were going to work together on this book, we'd be better doing it at your place,' she said when they were on their way. 'I wouldn't be able to concentrate with Maisy peering over my shoulder all the time. But we couldn't tell them that, could we?' she added with a conspiratorial giggle.

'So you're okay with me doing my book?'

'With us doing our book. Yeah, I am.'

Only then did it strike him. Nicola Carson was riding in the passenger seat of his clapped out Golf convertible. Nicola Carson was coming to live with him. Nicola Carson was going to work with him on her biography. Nicola Carson was going to ... he didn't even dare to think it.

'I'm sorry about this car,' he said.

'Dominic, just relax! I love your crappy little car. It's so real.'

'I hope you feel the same way about my flat,' he snorted. 'That's pretty real too.'

'Trust me, if you could see some of the places I used to doss when I started out. I was wandering round London for months just crashing on peoples' floors and sofas – I couldn't even afford my own place.'

'Yeah, but you don't have to do that now, do you?' he observed, flicking up the indicator to take a right. 'That's the whole point.'

'Look, you could turn this car round right now and head up west, I could whip out my plastic and we could be living in some prime location with sauna, private cinema and a view of Park ...'

'That sounds okay,' he laughed.

'Yeah, but it's not what I want. Not right now. I don't want to be running into everyone in Julie's or Harvey Nicks and having to dodge the paparazzi everywhere I go. As far as they're concerned, I'm in Malvern Hall and if it ever gets out that I've left, they'll be looking for me in Chelsea or Knightsbridge, not in ... wherever it is we're going. Where are we going, by the way?'

'Stratford.'

'Well, that's fine then. What better place for an actress than the birthplace of the Bard?'

'Not that Stratford. The other one.'

'No. Really?'

The two flights of communal stairs up which he carried her bags had never looked bleaker. The lift, as usual, was out of order. He unlocked the brown, laminate door bearing the number 27, shot through to the living room and disposed of the jeans before she had time to see them. As he was transferring her bags to the living room, she strolled around as though she were a prospective buyer. 'This is okay,' she proclaimed, peering out of the window. 'Fabulous view of the bottle bank.'

'Thanks.'

'So this is the nerve centre of my fan site?'

He was caught off guard. Why weren't there posters of her all over the walls, if he was such a devoted fan? 'Well, that's ... that's all contained in hard drives and mass storage devices,' he mumbled.

'Thank God for that,' she said.

'Would you like a coffee?'

'Thanks.'

She followed him into the kitchen. 'So, have you always lived alone?' she asked.

'No, I had a girlfriend, but she left.'

'Oh dear, what did you do to her?'

'Nothing,' he laughed as he filled the kettle. 'We just had ... different plans.'

She responded with silence.

'This place was tidy when she was here,' he added wryly. 'I think I've got some Hobnobs but they may be a bit soggy.'

'I'll pass, thanks.'

They took their coffee into the living room and she settled on the sofa. 'I do believe you, by the way, about your reasons for coming to visit me.'

'That's a relief.'

'What I don't believe is that you can't find yourself a more interesting subject for your biography. Nobody cares about me anymore.'

'Rubbish.'

She rested her head against the sofa-back and closed her eyes. 'Dominic, I'm bipolar, I live in a nuthouse – or I did – and my idea of fun is drawing pictures on my arm with a razor blade. Plus I made a total ass of myself in front of the entire world at the BAFTAs. If that doesn't spell finished, I don't know what does.'

'You were given a standing ovation at the BAFTAs.'

'That's what they do! If you can't handle reality, give it a standing ovation. It's called show-business.'

'Nicola, I've followed your career and it's a recognised fact that bipolar disorder and other problems are often the flip-side of creativity. Genius, even. It's one of the things that gives your work depth and makes you fascinating – you're just in a different league to the others. Talent-wise, intelligence-wise ... That's why I want to write about you.'

'You and your flattery,' she snorted, after a pause.

'So is that your identity?'

'Is *what* my identity?' she retorted.

'If someone says "who are you?" do you say "I'm bipolar, I live in a nuthouse and I harm myself"? Or do you say, "I'm a seriously talented actress"?'

He was astonished by what he had said. He also seemed to have astonished her.

'I bet you say that to all the psychos.'

'I've never met any psychos. You're my first.'

She closed her eyes again. 'I'm really quite knackered all of a sudden. Do you mind if I go and lie down for a while?'

'Of course not.'

He was dithering over the sleeping arrangements when, to his horror, she simply went through to his bedroom and curled up on his unmade bed, grabbing a pillow and hugging it tightly against her stomach. He wanted to insist on putting on clean sheets (if he had any) but she seemed to have already fallen asleep.

He softly closed the bedroom door. Her withdrawal at least gave him the chance to tidy the rest of the flat and pop out to the mini Tesco for supplies. When he returned, the place was still silent and he collapsed in an armchair, suddenly exhausted himself.

Gazing out at the rooftops and drainpipes of Stratford, he knew everything had changed. He could never go through with his mission to write a book about the girl who lay curled up on his bed – not the book he had planned when he opened and read that copy of *Loss* which Katie had bought for their flight to America.

*

'So when do we make a start?' she asked as he was making spaghetti Bolognese – one of his specialities.

'Whenever you're ready. But tomorrow you're supposed to go back for your group therapy.'

'Oh Christ, am I? I can't face going back to that place.'

'I kind of promised Dr Lennox I'd make sure you keep up with your treatment. Maybe we should give ourselves tomorrow to acclimatise and start on the book the day after.'

'Yeah, okay,' she sighed. 'I can see you're going to be really strict with me.'

Later, over the Bolognese and Beaujolais, she asked, 'So, this girlfriend. What was her name?'

'Katie,' he answered, surprised by the question.

'And what was she like?'

He thought about it. 'Petite. Pretty. Ash-blonde hair. Beautiful blue-green eyes.'

'And perfect tits, no doubt?'

'Well … since you ask,' he laughed.

'You blokes are all the same. I ask you what she was like and you tell me about her tits. I want to know what sort of person she was.'

'She was ... honest.'

They ate in silence for a while.

'And did you part amicably?'

He set down his fork and sat back with a sigh. 'Not really. I mean, we didn't have a blazing row or anything. But something happened. Something I regret.'

She glanced up at his face. 'Sorry. It's none of my business.'

'It's okay. It was just ... my ambition to write. It got in the way of things. I think it might have been different if I'd published. If I were a real writer.'

'Well, you soon will be a *real* writer,' she responded, reaching for the parmesan. 'I've got some secrets up my sleeve that'll make our book a sensation. After that, you can write whatever you want and the publishers will be gagging for it.'

He turned and met her eyes. 'Seriously?'

'Seriously.'

He grabbed the bottle of wine and refilled their glasses as though for a toast. 'Maybe we should do a synopsis and come up with some sort of proposal. Start putting out feelers to agents straight away. Get them gearing up for a rights auction.'

She lowered her eyes, forking her spaghetti over and over with studied concentration. 'No. Let's hold off on that for the moment.'

IV

On their way home from group therapy, they stopped at the local supermarket to stock up on provisions. Since leaving Malvern Hall, Nicola had been dressing down in jeans and sweatshirts and a baseball cap and, with her eyes hidden by sunglasses, she seemed to have passed unnoticed. Only Sandra, Dominic's friend in the flat across the hall, had been taken into his confidence and she had sworn not to betray it. In the supermarket, however, he noticed, more than once, people glancing in their direction and whispering to one another. How long would it be, he wondered, before the tabloids got wind of her whereabouts?

'We should've done our shopping outside the area,' he murmured.

As they were queuing for the check-out, some teenage girls circled timidly around them like doves round discarded breadcrumbs. One was finally nudged forward and asked, 'Can we have your autograph please, Miss Carson?' whereupon Nicola gasped. 'You didn't think I was Nicola Carson, did you? Wow! That's really flattering.' The little party retreated in a confusion of giggles and mutual recrimination.

'And you say you've lost your talent,' Dominic said.

*

The next morning, they rose late and he was pleased to note that she ate slightly more than usual. A cup of coffee and a whole croissant was, for her, a hearty breakfast. Afterwards, they carried their coffee through to the living room, Dominic reckoning it would be more comfortable and conducive for work. He fetched a notepad and his Dictaphone from the bedroom and they settled down opposite one another, she stretched out on the sofa, propped on a pile of cushions, he in the armchair.

'Would you mind holding this?' he said, handing her the Dictaphone. 'You don't have to keep it up close to your mouth – it's quite sensitive.'

'I'm not talking into that.'

'It's just so I don't forget details. I've got a terrible memory.'

'You don't need a memory. You've got me.'

'I know, but ...'

'Take it away, Dominic. Right away. Put it back in your bedroom.'

He did as she asked, though he was surprised by her vehemence. 'Do you mind if I at least take notes?'

'Can't I just talk to you at this stage, not to your notebook or your Dictaphone? I need to get things straight in my head.'

'Okay.'

Instead, she lit a cigarette. Dominic sensed it was her security blanket.

'So what shall I talk about?'

'Anything. Start with your childhood, if you like.'

'There's nothing to say about my childhood. Except that it was crap.'

'Okay, that's something. Chapter One. Nicola's childhood. Crap.'

She smiled. 'Well, it wasn't all crap. Not until after Dad left.'

'Did you have a good relationship with your father?' he murmured, feeling like a psychoanalyst.

'I did. Until he abandoned me.'

'In what sense did he abandon you?'

'He fucked off.'

'Fucked off?'

'When I was seven.'

'You mean … he left your mother? For another woman?'

'No. He left me.'

Dominic hesitated. 'But … are you sure that wasn't just collateral damage?'

She turned and stared straight at him. 'Look, if you know more about my life than I do, why don't you write this book on your own? He *abandoned* me, okay?'

'I'm sorry,' he said. 'I'll shut up now and let you speak.'

'Good.'

He kept quiet and haltingly, little by little, she opened up. The bad bits about her childhood. The good bits about her childhood. Happy memories. Horrible memories. Then her teenage years, her posh girls' boarding school which she loathed and from which she would have been expelled on countless occasions, had the school not wished to hang on to the fees. From time to time, she would smile and launch into an anecdote – mostly about her triumphs in school performances. The sunbeams slanted across the green, threadbare carpet as morning became afternoon, the couple so engrossed in their work they forgot to stop for lunch.

'When did you know you wanted to be an actress?' Dominic asked.

She thought about it. 'I can't remember not wanting to act. Not that I was extrovert as a child. I was actually quite shy and introspective. Can you believe that? But I always loved performing, even in those silly little plays that kids put on for their parents, because I found that being in character – being someone else – was like an escape. I know it sounds corny but I felt kind of safe when I was in a role. The problems came offstage when I was trying to be me. I didn't know the lines and I didn't understand the character.'

'Did you feel the same about your writing? Was that an escape too?'

She turned and stared at him again. 'My writing?'

'Your prize-winning novel.'

'Oh, that. Yeah, I guess that was kind of an escape too. But I want to talk about my acting, not my writing. That's what matters to me. We'll talk about my writing tomorrow. Maybe.'

'Okay. I think we should take a break now, anyway.'

They walked to the corner shop to pick up some milk and a paper and, to his dismay, she seemed depressed. In the evening, he opened a bottle of Shiraz and made a curry. She picked at it for a while but left most of it.

'Sorry. It was delicious. I just don't have much of an appetite.'

They watched a film on DVD but he sensed her heart wasn't in it. When it had finished and he had turned off the television, he said, 'Is everything all right?'

'Yeah, fine,' she sighed. 'I'm just knackered, that's all. Reliving all that stuff … it's exhausting. I think I'll go to bed now, if that's okay.' But before leaving him, she did something she had never done since coming to the flat, that she had never done, ever. She kissed him – not on the lips but on the cheek. 'Remember the other day, when it was raining,' she said, running her fingers down his arm until they were touching his hand, 'and I asked you if you wanted to go on seeing me after I left Malvern Hall?'

'Of course I remember.'

'I said it because … I was scared.'

'Scared of what?'

'Of everything.'

'It's okay. I was flattered you thought of me in that way. Surprised but flattered.'

'You know if it weren't for you I'd still be there.'

'I'm glad to have been of use,' he smiled.

'Thanks for believing in me, Dominic.'

'It isn't difficult,' he said.

She went off into the little spare bedroom which he had used as an office and which she insisted on occupying, even though it was barely more than a cupboard. After she had gone, he settled before his laptop. Since she had not allowed him to use his Dictaphone, he had to get down as much as possible of what she had said before he forgot it. He thought of her reaction when he had asked her, tentatively, about her writing.

Eventually, he went to bed himself but couldn't sleep. His head was in a whirl, his brain struggling to absorb the information she had given him, trying to comprehend her, to comprehend the situation in which he found himself. Believe in her? Little did she know that the reason she was there was that he didn't believe in her. Or, at least, he didn't believe her. Yet there was something about her – a directness, an innocence, a vulnerability – that made it so hard to imagine she would ever commit a blatant and premeditated act of deceit. Why should she need to anyway, when she had so much talent of her own? And yet there was still the evidence he had seen with his own eyes: that manuscript which had turned up on his desk all those years ago.

Around midnight, or maybe later, he heard the door open and close and he could make out a shadowy figure beside his bed.

'Are you awake?' she whispered.

'Yeah. I can't sleep.'

'Me neither.'

She crossed her arms over her middle and, with one deft and graceful movement, pulled her outsized tee-shirt over her head and tossed it on the chair. For a moment she was a wraith in the half light, shaped by the shadows around her breasts and the hollow of her navel and the black inverted triangle underneath. Then she pulled back the quilt and slipped into bed beside him. He took her in his arms. She was shivering and he was astonished by her lightness and fragility. It was so long since he had felt the warmth of another's skin against his own and, all of a sudden, any doubts he had had about this frail, damaged creature seemed to vanish.

'Dominic?' she murmured.

'Mm?'

'You won't let me down, will you?'

Chapter Two

SIX YEARS EARLIER

Looking back, Ted Haymer often wondered if Tuesday the fourth of March, 2002, was the worst day of his life. Not because it was his fifty-fifth birthday, though that was bad enough – the sudden, sinking realisation that you are closer to sixty than you are to fifty, or closer to seventy than you are to forty; nor even because of what happened on that day, though that was bad enough too. It was because, in the long, dark hours of retrospection of which his life now largely consisted, he found himself, again and again, tracing back to that day the chain of events which had led to the loss of the only woman he had ever loved.

That day, oddly enough, had started out rather well – better, at least, than most of the other days over the preceding weeks, months, years – he had lost track of how long it was. The sun was shining. That was something. The collar doves in the garden beyond his bedroom window were endlessly repeating their monotonous, dreary call, suggesting that they, at least, thought it was spring. But it was more than that. Ever since surfacing into the daylight of consciousness, he had been aware that something was missing – that black despair which was normally squatting in his head like some warty, heavy-lidded toad, waiting to pounce before he had had time to mount a defence with rational thought. Its absence was so surprising and unfamiliar that it affected him positively, rather as the simple absence of pain is a 'high' for the migraine sufferer, once the headache has passed. He had almost forgotten what hope felt like, but he fancied that this could have been it – or something remarkably like it.

Anne was away. She had gone on a short holiday with her friend Linda, as she did every spring. This year it was to Bruges. Anne enjoyed being a tourist but she knew Ted loathed it and had long since given up trying to persuade him to go with her. 'Sorry about your birthday,' she had said as she was leaving. 'We'll celebrate it when I get back. Although I've hidden a little something for you in the house, for the day itself – I'll tell you where when I phone tomorrow, so you're not tempted to open it straight away.'

'You don't have to phone tomorrow,' he had said.

'Of course I do. It's your birthday.'

As he was shaving, Ted resolved to use her four-day absence to get his head down and finish the second draft of *Three Summers by the Sea* – his third novel. He would stick to a strict regime: five hours work in the morning, a sandwich for lunch, a brief nap then another four hours before rewarding himself with a Bird's Eye prawn curry and a couple of glasses of Shiraz while watching one of those artistically erotic films he used to improve his Spanish. Then a little practice on the clarinet before the evening news and bed. He wouldn't weaken once and go to the pub.

He made coffee and repaired to his study but spent a while gazing out of the window. He was relieved Anne was away, much as he loved her. Things had been tense between them lately as she had taken to suggesting – intermittently but nonetheless persistently – that they get an estate agent in to do a valuation on the house. It was crazy them rattling around in that place when the children had all left home. And expensive. She was right, of course – she was always right – but Ted loved their ugly Edwardian pile with its shambolic garden and this view across the lawn to the gnarled, collapsing Blenheim apple, its main limb propped on a post to give it the look of an old man with a walking stick. He sighed and switched on his computer.

He had been at his desk for an hour when he heard the familiar creak of the gate, footsteps on the path, the clatter of the letter-box and slap of letters hitting the doormat. Ignore it, he told himself. But he couldn't. He just couldn't concentrate while not knowing what awaited him out in the hall. Ted hated mail – it was always junk or bills or a postcard from some relative holidaying abroad, which would go in the rubbish after a cursory glance. But on the morning of March the fourth, 2002, there was another reason for his inability to concentrate. Back in January, he had sent off three sample chapters of *The Tyranny of Love* to a publisher called The

Dragon's Head, which he had happened upon one day while leafing dejectedly through *The Writer's Handbook*. The entry had seemed to call out to him: 'This excellent small publisher,' the editor had enthused, 'has somehow avoided going the way of the bigger houses. Founder and editorial director, Alistair Milner, is renowned for his "hands-on" approach with authors and is still prepared to take a risk with genuine new talent.' Ted, who normally had no belief in invisible forces, had fancied for a moment that his random rifling through *The Writer's Handbook* had not been random at all, that he had been guided towards that entry by some benign power, the patron saint of unpublished authors. Though he had never laid eyes on the man, he had sensed at once that he had found a friend and ally in this Alistair Milner, that he would be the one to guide him out of the wilderness he had dwelt in the whole of his writing life. Having been rejected by all the major agents and publishers, he had felt the flickering flame of hope flare up again, albeit feebly, as he slid his sample chapters into a jiffy bag.

He had taken immense trouble to do everything perfectly, the admonition of the Gods on Olympus ringing in his ears: 'We are inundated with submissions and if you do not follow these simple rules your work will not be considered.' The typescript had thus been double-spaced in 12 Point Times New Roman on pristine paper, along with his synopsis, cover letter and somewhat embellished CV. He had also included, on advice he had often received and always hitherto ignored, something called a 'marketing proposal'. This was supposed to indicate to the prospective publisher the book's 'target readership' and USP – its unique selling point. Ted had puzzled long and hard over what his work's unique selling point might be. It seemed a bizarre question. Every novel, every work of art, was unique if it was original and that should be its selling point. So, for want of anything more specific, he had finally put that as his USP – Originality. As to target readership, he had tapped his pen against his lips. Who the hell *was* his target readership? Power-dressed 'suits' needing something to pass the eight-hour flight to Dubai? The elderly trying to get through endless nights of insomnia? Suntanned singles sprawled on the beaches of Benidorm? He had tried to make his novel accessible to everyone because he wanted everyone to enjoy it. So he had shrugged and written 'Everyone' as his target readership. He had then tried, in a formal and professional manner, to point out what he felt to be the novel's strengths, forcing himself to overcome his natural modesty and blow his own trumpet for once, albeit tentatively. That was the only way to get ahead in the modern world, or so everyone kept telling him.

He knew from experience that publishers always took roughly six weeks to come up with a response. What they did with one's manuscript during that time he could not imagine, since he was sure they didn't read it. All they did was cast an eye over the first page – a task to which they might devote six minutes, if you were lucky. And, contrary to common belief, it was not quality in the writing they were looking for, apart from a basic grasp of grammar and syntax, it was something more subtle and transient – *marketability*. 'It's all about money nowadays,' he had complained to Anne during one of his many tirades about the publishing industry. 'Money, money, money! That's all they care about.'

'It's a fact of life in the modern world, Ted,' she had responded gently but rather wearily. 'You're going to have to get used to it. And it's no good just meekly submitting your manuscripts anymore. You've got to be pro-active. You've got to get out there and sell yourself.'

'Sell myself?' he had frowned. 'I'm a middle-aged, retired librarian. What's to sell?'

'You've got to do something to get yourself noticed. Like dancing naked in a fountain in Trafalgar Square.'

'I'd be more likely to get arrested than published.'

'Exactly. But you might get onto the evening news and then you'd be a celebrity.'

He had heaved a sigh. 'I don't know. When I look at those exotic girls with their Cambridge degrees and strings of literary awards ... and those blokes with that look of having worked ten years on an Alaskan oil rig that they've somehow acquired living in Wimbledon,

I just think, how the hell am I ever going to compete with *that*? My face doesn't fit, my background doesn't fit, nothing fits.'

Anne had not known how to respond. So, in the end, she had kissed him tenderly on the top of the head and gone off to start the supper. 'Don't worry, my love. You'll get there in the end, I know you will.'

'If only I'd been kidnapped by jihadists!' he had wailed. 'It'd be a different story then!'

'I know. Life's so unfair.'

Ted had always known that he and Anne – a solicitor – made an incongruous couple. He was scruffy, she was smart. He was reclusive, she was gregarious. His life was a shambles, hers ran like clockwork. He had once suggested she become his agent herself and she had replied, 'I would, if I weren't so busy looking after you.'

Ted's problem was that he loved writing but little else. His greatest joy was to shut himself up in his study and become as engrossed in his work as the monks of Lindisfarne in their fabulous manuscripts. When he wasn't writing, he wanted to be out in the world – incognito, a nobody – observing, absorbing, gathering material like a squirrel gathering nuts for winter. He knew that if he had wanted to be successful, he should have moved to London after leaving Oxford, been seen at the right parties and engaged in some serious arse-kissing. He was too old and cynical for all that now. Nonetheless, he was well aware that he should make more effort to get his work into print and felt guilty that he did not. So he had forced himself to write that marketing proposal and get it in the post, along with his sample chapters.

And that had been seven weeks ago to the day.

*

He suddenly rose from his desk, went out into the hall and scooped up the heap of mail from the doormat, sorting through it as he walked to the kitchen to make more coffee. There was the usual junk, a birthday card from his sister (he recognised the bubbly, schoolgirl hand that Betty still retained at fifty-two) and a couple of A4 envelopes. One appeared to be from the bank but the other was addressed in his own hand. It was the SAE he had sent with his sample chapters.

Tossing everything else aside, he tore it open and was surprised to find that it contained only his CV and the marketing proposal, not the chapters themselves. Maybe publishers didn't return the samples if they were interested in your work. He had never got far enough to find out. Clipped to the pages was a letter bearing a logo of a red dragon coiled around a triumphant Saint George who, sword aloft, was about to sever its head. He didn't pause to consider the symbolism of the image.

Dear Mr Haymer
Re The Novel: 'The Tyranny of Love'

Having read your sample chapters with careful consideration, I regret to say that, as a small publishing house, we are ill-equipped to take on a project of this magnitude.

May I take this opportunity to wish you every success with your writing career?

Yours sincerely,
Alistair Milner (Managing Director / Editorial Director)

Ted stared at the letter. And stared. And stared. *'As a small publishing house, we are ill-equipped to take on a project of this magnitude...'* He shook his head in disbelief. What the hell did it mean? Apart from rejection. Yet again.

Heart pounding, he stormed back to his study, crashed down into his revolving office chair and tossed the letter onto his desk. His fingers drummed furiously on its surface for a moment then he sprang forward, dragging open drawer after drawer, clawing aside papers and correspondence until he unearthed a lighter and a pack of Superkings containing four rather tired-looking cigarettes. He lit one with trembling fingers, even though he had given up smoking six months earlier. Fuck that.

After a few deep, calming inhalations, he sank back in a daze and stared into space. He knew, of course, what this was about. That marketing proposal. Putting 'originality' as his USP had come across as facetious and contemptuous of the realities of publishing; and putting 'everyone' as his target readership. The whole thing had seemed arrogant and unprofessional, and this letter was a way of taking him down a peg or two. The irony of it, he thought grimly, was that if he had never included that fucking thing his work might have stood a chance.

He angrily stubbed out his cigarette in his coffee dregs and lit another, breathing the smoke deep down into his lungs and blowing it into the cloud which was forming over the window. What did they expect from you, these stuck-up, judgemental bastards? It was a no-win situation – either you behaved modestly and professionally and were ignored or you tried to promote yourself and were accused of arrogance. As much as anything, he felt betrayed. For, despite the brutal commercialism into which publishing had descended, there was still an understanding that publishers and authors were on the same side – an understanding reflected in the tone of rejection letters, which had hitherto been polite and regretful, often containing a few genuine words of encouragement. Never before had he received anything like this. He looked again at the signature, which was apparently that of Alistair Milner himself, though it looked more like the scrawl of some retarded child. Alistair Milner. He would never forget that name.

He sat gazing blankly out at the garden, puffing away on his third cigarette, and in time his fury hardened into the old familiar black despair, blacker than ever. Okay, maybe his marketing proposal had been unprofessional. Maybe it hadn't struck the right note. But what really angered him was that those sample chapters were good; they were tight, pacey, funny – whatever that arsehole said. The truth was, of course, that he hadn't read them. In a way, it was reassuring.

Heaving a sigh, he resolved to put the whole ugly business behind him, to be Big, to be Mature and to get back to work. He added one paragraph to the text on the screen and stared at it while smoking his last cigarette. At lunchtime, he went to the kitchen, cut the crust off a loaf of bread on which he dumped a slice of dry, ageing ham he had found on a plate at the back of the fridge, then pushed it aside in disgust. If he had had a decent morning's work, it would now be time for a well-earned nap. He decided to take one anyway. He filled a hot water bottle, hauled himself up the stairs and clambered fully clothed under the blankets, curling up round the rubbery core of warmth, its heat helping to assuage his hunger and nausea. He pulled the quilt over his head. The darkness was comforting.

He drifted into a fitful sleep. Sometime during the afternoon, he was aware of the telephone ringing down in the hall. It would be Anne, no doubt, to wish him a happy birthday and disclose the whereabouts of the present. She could leave a message.

When he resurfaced, the room was in semi-darkness. Beyond the window, the tops of trees swayed against a stormy, rain-laden sky. The dramatic change in the weather seemed to reflect the change in his fortunes.

He rolled onto his back and heaved a sigh, then lay motionless, gazing at the ceiling. Maybe it was time to call it a day. Maybe it was time to put an end to this crazy dream and live like a normal person. All his life he had wanted to write – he could not remember a time when he had not. It was the dream which had sustained him through childhood, through school, through the years spent drifting like a ghost among the bookshelves in Eastbourne Library. Then had come the day, seven years earlier, when another envelope had dropped through the letter-box. It had contained a letter from a solicitor and a cheque for thirty thousand pounds – the legacy from his beloved brother Jack who had died of colon cancer. And Anne had said, 'I think it's time you gave up work and focused on your writing. I think it's what Jack would have wanted.'

He had looked at her in amazement. 'But it's only thirty grand.'

'It's enough. And the children are self-sufficient now. More or less.'

'What about my pension? I've still got seventeen years to go.'

'There are priorities in life, Ted. I'll just have to look for some more lucrative cases. Take on a bit less legal aid.'

He had smiled. 'So you're going to turn away all those single mums and battered wives and abused kids?'

'We'll manage.'

He had been forty-eight at the time. Finally liberated from work, he had decided to redraft an earlier novel – one he had begun in his thirties and abandoned when Julie, his adopted sister, had died. The rollicking adventures of its young heroine – all four hundred and seventy pages of them – had seemed to explode into being under the clattering keys of his computer, its mordant humour and witty first-person narration adding poignancy to the ultimate tragedy. It had never occurred to him that it would not find its way into print but, after years of submissions and rejections, of jumping through hoops to try to please agents and publishers, he had been stripped of all illusion and now, at fifty-five, he was still unpublished and Jack's legacy had all but vanished. He had let him down, he had let Anne down and he had let himself down. So maybe now – his fifty-fifth birthday – was the time, finally, to admit defeat. There was no chance of returning to his old job – it probably no longer even existed, sacrificed to the god of 'rationalisation' – but he could go back to freelance French and German translating, something he had done before to help the children through school. It was a prospect for which he could not muster a single grain of enthusiasm.

It was now dark. On days like these Ted welcomed the dark – it was so much gentler and less challenging than daylight. He weakened and went to the pub.

II

The Queen's Head – or simply 'The Queen's' as it was known locally – had been Ted's salvation on countless occasions. It was within easy walking distance and the moment he entered its low, eighteenth-century portal, he was embraced by the ambience of wood-smoke, home cooking and good cheer. Whatever his mood, whatever misfortune had befallen him during the day, The Queen's was always the same, always welcoming, always reliable. He knew most of the regulars, who greeted him cheerfully. They were all familiar with his moods – he was an artist, after all – and ignored them. He bought himself a pint before anyone could treat him, thus avoiding twenty minutes' discussion about the tyranny of fishing quotas or the recent resounding successes of the darts team. Brian Sexton, a local vet, plonked a large hand on his shoulder.

'Cheer up, Ted, old son. It might never happen.'

'It already has, Brian.'

'Oh dear. Another polite rebuff?'

'No. This one wasn't polite.'

'I'm so sorry, old man. I know how you must be feeling.'

No he didn't. He didn't have a clue how he was feeling. How could he? He was ten years his junior with a respected, well-paid profession, seven acres of land, four Labradors, two horses, a goat and a turbocharged Discovery. How could he have the faintest idea how he was feeling?

'Thanks, Brian,' he smiled feebly, wedging an arm and shoulder into the wall of backs at the bar to order his pie and chips. When he withdrew, Brian, thankfully, was chatting to someone else.

His commandeered his favourite table, tucked away by the inglenook. He was quite happy to just sit with his beer, gazing at the glowing logs and soaking up their comforting, throbbing warmth while allowing the murmur of conversation – punctuated by frequent bursts of laughter – to ebb and flow around him.

A waitress whom he had never seen before presently arrived with steak and chips and a salad, dumped them in front of him and demanded to know if he wanted sauces. Her manner was so abrupt that he found himself looking up at her in surprise. Her eyes were heavy with black and purple mascara, her lipstick was a glossy plum red and her jet-black hair hung straight as rods from a parting at precisely the top of her head. She wore pendulous ear rings in the design of a skull and her perfect breasts – which, on a different girl, might have cheered him considerably – seemed positively threatening. He must have taken a moment to absorb this bizarre spectacle because she repeated the question about the sauces with a note of exasperation, even menace, in her voice.

'Well, before we get onto the subject of sauces, I should point out that this isn't what I ordered. I ordered pie and chips.'

She sighed and snatched the plates away, clearly annoyed with him for having ordered something other than what she had brought. Ted noticed an elderly gentleman gazing longingly at the steak and trying to attract her attention, so he pointed him out to her. She took it to his table and disappeared, returning a few minutes later with his pie and chips.

'Right, so you've got what you ordered. Now to get back to the utterly riveting subject of sauces.'

'I'd like vinegar, mustard, ketchup and Worcester sauce please.'

'We don't have Worcester sauce.'

'Yes you do. I've been coming in here for twenty-seven years and I always have Worcester sauce. So would you kindly fetch it for me, please?'

Casting him a ferocious look, she flounced off, returning a few moments later clutching all the sauces he had requested. 'There,' she proclaimed, dumping the bottles down on his little table, 'Will that be all, *sir*?'

'A knife and fork might help.'

She murmured 'Shit' under her breath then set off in search of cutlery. By the time she returned, Ted's meal was getting cold. Just as she was making her escape, he asked her, 'What's your name?'

She turned back and glared at him as though he had made an improper suggestion. 'I'm sorry?'

'Your name. You know – the thing the police put on the charge sheet.'

Her eyes narrowed, as though she were assessing his motive for asking, then she answered, 'Nicola.'

'Well, I'd just like to say, Nicola, that I've had a terrible day, and I mean a really terrible day. And when I have terrible days I come in here to be cheered up. And, frankly, you're not doing a very good job.'

She stared at him, speechless with indignation. 'It's bad enough carting food around all night without cheering people up as well.'

'Just a smile wouldn't hurt, would it? It doesn't have to be sincere.'

'Yeah … well, I've had a terrible day too.'

'I'm sorry to hear it. But the sad fact is that I'm paying *you* to be nice to *me*, not the other way around.'

She hovered while he sprinkled salt on his chips, clearly frustrated at being unable to voice her opinion of him without getting the sack. Assuming she was a student who was earning some money to get through college, he suggested, 'A bit beneath you, is it? Waitressing?'

She considered the question. 'No. I'm just a bitch, that's all.'

'Well, thank you for warning me. I'd never have guessed.'

Melanie, one of the other waitresses, bustled past with a plate of food in each hand, casting her colleague an angry glance. Nicola mumbled, 'I'd better go.'

Ted had found his little tussle with the new waitress rather invigorating. And in spite of it – or perhaps because of it – he was in no mood to go home and have reality kick in again. The silence and emptiness of that house, the solitude which had engulfed him after dropping Anne at the station the previous morning now seemed unbearably bleak. He finished his meal and drained his pint, then bought a brandy at the bar. What the hell? Tonight he would stay awhile and maybe get just a little drunk.

'That new waitress of yours is quite a character,' he remarked to Ian, the landlord, as he was serving him.

'I hope she wasn't too rude, Ted.'

'Well, she could do with brushing up on her people skills, but I didn't really mind. There's something about her that amuses me.'

'I wish my other customers felt the same way. I've already had complaints. If she doesn't get her act together soon, I'm afraid she'll be seeing the door.'

'Who is she, anyway? Is she local?'

'Yes, she's Angela Pearson's daughter. Do you know Angela?'

'I can't say I do.'

'Her husband Bill used to be a mate of mine up in Croydon, before we moved down here. Made a fortune selling security systems to factories and office blocks but then he buggered off with another woman when Nicola was only seven. Knocked her sideways, poor kid. We've kept in touch with Angela ever since and, later on, she moved down here herself. It was she who asked me to give Nicola a job – well, begged me would be nearer the truth. Seems she's been drifting a bit since university and she's terrified of her going off the rails. When she came for her interview she looked like the Bride of Dracula. I told her she'd have to tone that look down a bit or she'd scare all the customers away.'

'Well, if that's the toned-down version, I dread to think what she looked like before.'

'Yeah, the shame of it is that she's a lovely-looking girl under all that crap. I remember her when she was little. I just long to scrub it all away and give her some normal clothes and a decent haircut. She'd be a stunner.'

'Maybe she's hiding behind it.'

'God Ted, don't get me started on psychology,' Ian laughed as he moved away to serve another customer. 'Life's complicated enough as it is.'

Ted took his brandy, installed himself on a barstool and sank into thought, trying his best not to dwell on the letter. Someone talked to him about fishing and someone else about the trials and tribulations of building and uploading a website. He forgot both conversations the moment they were over. As the night wore on, the pub began to empty until only a few gaggles of stalwarts remained, their conversation growing ever more impassioned and incoherent. The kitchen was now closed and Nicola seemed to be taking a break – she was sitting alone in the farthest corner behind the bar, staring at a glass of coke.

Ted took his drink and walked round to her. She glanced up. 'Sorry if I was a bit rude earlier.'

'I tell you what. You tell me about your terrible day and I'll tell you about mine. What happened?'

'Oh, I just flunked another audition. Over in Brighton.'

'Are you a singer or an actress?'

'Actress. Trying to be.'

Ted had the first intimation, then, of what she was feeling, since it must have been close to what he was feeling himself.

'What was the part?'

'It was in a play called *The House of Bernarda Alba* – you won't have heard of it. I was going for Adela, Bernarda's youngest daughter.'

'She commits suicide for love. It was one of Lorca's greatest works.'

She seemed amazed that anyone in Wemborne-on-Sea had even heard of the Spanish playwright. 'I was perfect, too. I rehearsed for bloody weeks. I really wanted a chance to do that part.'

'You'll get the chance – in the West End or on Broadway. Not in Brighton.'

She snorted with hollow amusement. 'I don't know. Maybe I'm just crap.'

He thought of all the platitudes he could offer her – about how you must never lose faith in yourself, how you must keep on trying, about the thousands of actors and movie stars who had struggled for years as waitresses or taxi-drivers before getting their break. But he could not bring himself to because they were exactly what people were always saying to him and they were never any comfort. And there was always the possibility that she was, if not crap, just not good enough to make the grade. It would be a long, hard road for her if that were true – or even if it were not. In the meantime, she had to come into The Queen's every night and smile at miserable sods like him.

He could not think what to say. So he just said what he felt. 'I'm sorry, Nicola. I'm really, really sorry. It's a shit world out there and they're all bastards.'

She met his eyes for the first time, surprised by the passion in his voice. 'What did you say your name was again?'

'I didn't. But it's Ted. Ted Haymer.'

'Well, thanks Ted," she said, as they briefly shook hands. 'You're a mate.'

Ian called last orders. The louts at the bar suggested a happy hour but he was not in the mood – in fact, he couldn't wait to get rid of them. 'You get off, Nicola love,' he said, knowing of her disappointment that day. 'We can manage.'

'How are you getting home?' asked Ted.

'Walking.'

'Alone?'

'Yeah,' she retorted with a hint of her earlier aggression. 'Why not?'

'It just seems a bit unwise – a girl on her own, late at night.'

'You're wasting your breath, Ted,' laughed Ian. 'I've offered to call her a taxi but she won't have it.'

'There's no point in working, if I have to waste all my wages on taxis,' said Nicola.

'I've told you, I'll pay for it. I get a special deal from B-Line.'

'I don't want you paying for it, Ian, don't you understand? But thanks anyway.'

'How far have you got to go?' asked Ted.

'Snetsham.'

'Well, I live that way myself, more or less. I could walk with you, if you like.'

'Yeah, but you might be an axe murderer for all I know.'

'Don't worry, Nicola,' Ian chipped in, 'In all the years I've known Ted, he's only ever used a cheese wire.'

'Charming. Okay then, but don't think I need protecting, because I don't.'

'The exercise will do me good.'

She fetched her jacket and bag and they left the pub to a raucous accompaniment from the bar – 'Don't forget the Viagra, Ted!' 'I'll tell your wife, Ted!' – to which Nicola responded with a roll of the eyeballs. Outside, the rain clouds had blown away, leaving the sky vast and clear, the stars glistening over a serene, silver sea. Ted took a deep breath. With such beauty in the universe, life could not be hopeless for long.

'Want a fag?' she asked, extracting a packet of cigarettes from her bag.

'I'd better not. I'm supposed to have given up.'

'Really? I'm totally hooked. I haven't had one since before I started work, which is probably why I'm in such a shit awful mood.'

She lit up, seeming to suck the smoke into every nook and cranny of her body, then raised her face to the stars and blew it out in what sounded like a huge sigh of relief.

'So, do you want one or not?'

'No, I'm okay. I won't deprive you.'

She shrugged as she tucked the packet back in her bag and they set off through the dimly lit, deserted streets, her heeled boots echoing among the houses.

'What really *pisses* me off,' she exploded suddenly, 'is that those fuckers who were running the auditions were so *snide*. And when I was doing my big rebellion speech, they kept chattering to each other. I reckon they'd already got someone for the part – some friend of theirs, probably.'

'Sod them. It's their loss.'

'I mean, I did loads of stuff at Edinburgh. My Ophelia was legendary. I mean, she was like the most fucked-up Ophelia ever. And then there was my Juliet. And I was in some fringe productions at the Festival. I even had a part on telly once. I could act rings around those fucking amateurs.' Her voice was rising to a wail and then she halted in her tracks. 'I only did it to keep my eye in.' Her hands covered her face, dropping her cigarette.

Ted turned to her in dismay. 'Hey, Nicola, don't cry. They're not worth it.'

'Sorry. It's just … everything.'

After a moment's hesitation, he slid his arms around her to comfort her, her leather jacket cold and unyielding under his hands. God, this was a weird day. Here he was under the stars, hugging the stroppy waitress with whom, only three hours earlier, he had been arguing about Worcester sauce. The louts, finally ejected from the pub, could be heard elsewhere in the sleeping town, pursuing their lonely and pathetic quest for fun, their drunken cries dispersing into the firmament.

He patted her shoulder as she drew away. Had they been in a film he might have offered her his pristine white handkerchief but, knowing the condition of his real-life handkerchief, he thought better of it.

'You must think I'm a stupid bitch,' she sniffed, dabbing her eyes with a knot of tissue she'd dug from her pocket.

'Not at all. I understand. And I'm not just saying that.'

'Thanks. You're a star,' she smiled wanly, 'even though you are a pain in the arse. I mean, who the fuck has mustard, ketchup, vinegar *and* Worcester sauce with their pie and chips?'

'I told you, it's been a lousy day. I needed to pull out all the stops.'

She squashed her dropped cigarette beneath her foot and they set off again.

'So come on then,' she said. 'What was this terrible thing that happened?'

'Oh, it was nothing. I'm making too much of it.'

'No, you're not. Tell me.'

'Well, first I need to explain that I'm a writer. I'm what's known in the trade as an NYP author.'

'What's an NYP author when it's at home?'

'Not yet published. It's a polite acronym for a failure who's crazy enough to keep on trying.'

He briefly painted a heart-rending backdrop of struggle, discouragement and rejection concluding with the letter, which he found he could recite almost verbatim.

'Bastard! Fucking *cheek*. How *dare* he? Excuse my language.'

'It's all right. Those were pretty much my words when I read it.'

'It puts my little knockback in perspective.'

'Not at all. What happened to you is exactly the same thing in a different form. That's why I mentioned it – to try to make you feel better.'

'Yeah, but I was just going for one little part in one crappy little production. I bet you've been slogging away at that novel half your life.'

She was right. And it was a life which was running out, unlike hers, which was all ahead of her.

'So what's it about, this novel?'

'The central character's loosely based on my adopted sister, Julie, who became ... well, surplus to requirements when I was born. She didn't have an easy time. I know it wasn't my fault but somehow I've never stopped feeling guilty about her.'

'So your parents didn't love her?'

Ted thought about it as he walked. 'It wasn't that they didn't love her. They just never managed to love her in the same way as their biological children. It was quite subtle, very often.'

'Did she mind you basing the character on her?'

'Not at all. I think she was rather flattered. I worked on it with her for weeks on end, going over old stuff. I guess she found it quite painful, but therapeutic as well.'

'So what happened to her?'

'She died at forty-two. Breast cancer.'

'*Shhhhit,*' Nicola murmured.

'I know. Unfair.'

'And did she ever meet her biological mother?'

'No, she didn't. Not after she was taken away from her as a baby.'

Ted felt he had cast something of a pall over the proceedings. 'So what about you?' he asked as they turned a corner into a gloomy avenue where the streetlights became less frequent. 'Are you in a flat-share in Snetsham?'

'Nah, I'm living with my mother. Temporarily.' She seemed disinclined to enlarge on the subject so he didn't press it.

Due to the rash of building in the fifties and sixties, Snetsham, on the north side of Wemborne, had fused with its larger neighbour, becoming little more than a rather superior suburb. They reached a bench at the entrance to Dunstan Crescent and Nicola suggested they sit down for a while. Ted wondered why, since they must have been close to their destination.

'I hate going home,' she said, as though reading his thoughts.

'Why's that?'

'Well, *these* are verboten for a start,' she laughed, unearthing her pack of cigarettes. 'Sure you don't want one?'

'Oh, all right, go on then.'

She lit them both and they sat for a while, smoking in companionable silence.

'I take it you don't get on with your mother.'

'That's the understatement of the century,' she snorted. 'She just makes me feel so tense all the time. I live in terror of staining the Laura Ashley sofa cover or spilling coffee on the fucking *escritoire*.'

'What about your dad?'

'He's dead.'

Ted turned and looked at her in surprise. 'I'm sorry to hear that.'

'Well, he's not really dead. Just to me.'

She flicked some ash onto the pavement. 'So, what about you? You married?'

'Yes.'

'Kids?'

'Three – two boys and a girl. And three grandkids – three and counting.'

'Wow. So won't your wife be wondering where you are?'

'She's away, so I've been let off the leash for a couple of days. Just as well, the mood I was in when I got that letter.'

'Must have been a bummer,' she murmured.

'It was. But, then again, it may have been a blessing in disguise.'

'How's that?'

'I'm thinking of jacking it in. Going back to some sort of proper job and getting my finances sorted out.'

'For Christ's sake, don't do that!" she retorted, facing him, 'This is your dream! Your lifelong ambition! And you're going to jack it all in because of one stupid letter from some little wanker publisher?'

'It's not just the letter. I've had dozens of rejections. Maybe that should be telling me something ...'

'Bollocks. They're all the same, these people. They wouldn't know quality if it crapped on them.'

'I appreciate the vote of confidence,' he laughed, 'but you haven't actually read it, have you?'

'Well, show it me then. I'll soon tell you whether it's any good or not – I read drama and English Lit at uni.'

He looked at her in surprise. 'Seriously? You'd like to read it?'

'Sure, why not? I can read, you know.'

'I just thought you might be too busy. With your job and everything.'

'Well I'm not.'

'Okay. I'll bring a copy up to the pub tomorrow, shall I?'

'Fine.'

Ted realised, to his surprise, that he was feeling almost positive again. He was enjoying his illicit cigarette, enjoying chatting to this strange girl on a bench in the middle of the night.

'Ah well,' she sighed, tossing down her stub and grinding it under her heel. 'I suppose I'd better go and face the music.'

'Have you done something wrong, then?' he laughed.

'Bound to have done.'

'Thanks for letting me witter on, especially when you've had such a lousy day yourself. It helped.'

'Works both ways,' she said as they stood up. 'So I'll see you tomorrow, yeah? With your novel?'

'Lunchtime or evening?'

'Either. I'm working both.'

He stood by the bench and watched her go. When she was about to vanish around the corner, she turned back, smiled and waved.

III

The church clock struck three. A propeller aircraft, high in the stratosphere, droned off into the distance like a bumblebee on a summer afternoon. Alone in his bed in his empty house, Ted listened to the sound as it faded away into silence. He began, yet again, to relive the day in memory, to open, once again, that tantalising envelope, to feel, once again, the fury and then that old familiar despair. And yet those emotions seemed strangely removed from him, as though he were watching himself experiencing them on film.

In the morning, he set to work promptly at his computer but, after half an hour, found himself gazing out of the window. He forced himself to work again, then lapsed again into thought. At ten to twelve, he remembered he had not picked up Anne's message from the previous afternoon, so he checked his voicemail, finding, to his surprise, that there were two messages. The second must have been left when he was at the pub.

'Bonjour, mes chéris! Just calling to see how you are. Call back if you have a moment. Je t'embrasse!'

He was glad he had missed her, since Marie never called just to see how they were – there was always an ulterior motive. Either she wanted a favour (which he, idling at home, was in a perfect position to grant) or she had made some vital contact he just *had* to meet to get his career belatedly off the ground. 'She means well,' Anne always said, but to Ted she was just a controlling busybody. Why, he often wondered, did she imagine that having the random good fortune to be the only child of a French perfume tycoon and wife of an American corporate lawyer gave her the right to be so relentlessly patronising?

Suddenly needing to escape the house, he took down one of four copies of *The Tyranny of Love* which were stored on top of the cabinet in his study, slid it into a Sainsbury's shopping bag and set off for the pub. He reckoned that lunchtime, when the place was always less busy than in the evening, would be a better time to give it to Nicola. At least, that was what he told himself.

It was a grey, blustery noon with fitful bursts of sunshine. He stopped at the corner shop to buy a packet of cigarettes, thrust it deep in his coat pocket then carried on through the suburbs. On reaching his destination, he was greeted by the comforting words, 'The usual, Ted?'

As Ian was drawing his pint, he glanced around, but could see no sign of the object of his journey. 'Nicola working today?' he asked casually.

'No, mate. She's gone.'

Ted stared at him. 'What do you mean, gone?'

'She's gone. Buggered off. Couldn't even be bothered to phone in. Her Mum had to do it for her. Reading between the lines, I'd say they've had another row. She was full of apology – Angela, I mean – but to be honest, Ted, I'm glad to see the back of her. I was willing to give her a chance for Angela's sake but she was more trouble than she was worth, that girl.'

'When did she phone, the mother?'

''Bout half an hour ago.'

'Did she say where she was going?'

'Nope.'

'Have you got a mobile number for her?'

'For Nicola? No, I just get her at her mum's.'

Ian went to serve another customer, returning to find Ted's pint abandoned on the bar. He assumed he'd gone to relieve himself.

He was retracing his steps of the previous night, still lugging his manuscript. He checked the main bus stops along the High Street but she was nowhere to be seen. He took a detour via the station but both platforms were deserted. The next train to London wasn't for another hour.

He resumed his journey towards Snetsham, branching off into a shortcut over a scrubby common which he guessed, since it was daylight, she would have taken had she been coming the other way. The path lay over a grassy hillock topped by straggling birches, beneath which a bench commanded what the Council clearly considered one of Wemborne's finest views. A meadow, where cows grazed listlessly, was bordered by a stream, beyond which a line of sombre hills hid all but a glimpse of the sea. He sat down, resting his back against the inscription "Jade 4 Terry" scrawled with a marker pen and wondered what to do next. He could see clearly below him the orderly semi-circle of substantial houses comprising Dunstan Crescent, surrounded by spacious lawns and lofty trees and, in some cases, a swimming pool. In the sixty years since its construction, the crescent and its neighbouring streets and avenues had acquired a look almost of grandeur. This was no hideous executive housing tossed up on some former spinney, with barely room to park the Landcruiser and the BMW. This was where the old new money of

Wemborne lived. It looked so much more depressing in daylight than it had at night, modelled in *sfumato* tones by the streetlamps.

His gaze turned back to the cows, though his thoughts were miles away. The only hope of finding Nicola, he knew, was to go down there and brave her mother. What would she make of this scruffy, middle-aged man on her doorstep inquiring into her daughter's whereabouts? Whatever her feelings, she would no doubt make them plain.

Bracing himself, he rose from the seat and walked down the slope. An elderly lady, with a Yorkshire terrier on a lead, gave him directions to Mrs Pearson's house – number twenty-three – but when he found it, the tall, wrought-iron gates were locked. An intercom was embedded in one of the pillars. He pressed the button.

'Yes?' crackled a woman's voice after a few moments.

'I'm very sorry to bother you,' he said, wedging his mouth close to the grille. 'My name's Ted Haymer and I was wondering if I might speak to Nicola.'

'She isn't here.'

'Do you happen to know where I might find her?'

'I've no idea. On her way to London, I should imagine.'

Ted wondered if it might help if he made clear to this woman that he was not just some old rake with dubious designs on her daughter.

'The thing is, I'm a writer by profession and I'm also a friend of Ian's at The Queen's Head. Nicola very kindly agreed to read one of my manuscripts and give her opinion of it. I feel it would be very helpful to me, since she's young. A different perspective and ... so on.'

The machine did not respond.

'You wouldn't have a mobile number by any chance?'

After a pause, the voice said, 'Come in' and the gate buzzed and unlocked.

Ted entered and advanced across what seemed an acre of driveway, his tread deafening on the gravel. A brand-new silver Audi stood before the garage doors. As he was approaching the porch, the front door opened.

He could see at once where Nicola had got her looks. The woman who stood before him was tall and beautiful, with a perfectly cut bob of ash-blonde hair and, though wearing jeans and a jumper, looked smarter than Ted would have looked in black tie. If there had been a bust-up with her daughter only hours earlier, her face betrayed no sign of it – no sign, in fact, of anything.

'I can't keep track of her mobiles,' she said. 'She keeps losing them or having them stolen.'

'I see.'

Seeming to sense that the intruder was not going to give up, she finally said, 'I might have an email address.'

'That would be great.'

She disappeared, leaving him hovering on the doorstep. He leaned forward surreptitiously and peered into the house. The hall and stairs and the part of the drawing room visible through its open door betrayed exactly what Nicola had suggested – wall-to-wall carpeting in muted, perfectly-balanced shades, carefully positioned pictures and ornaments purchased solely for their effect. Nothing had been inherited from a loved one or bought on a whim or received as a gift or simply washed up as part of the flotsam and jetsam of life.

The woman reappeared holding a flowery notelet which she handed to him. He read the email address, written out in a very neat, schoolgirl hand in which the most expert graphologist would have been challenged to find any trace of character: thepearsonbitch@hotmail.com

'I'm afraid my daughter's rather young for her age,' she remarked with a hint of embarrassment.

'Well, this is marvellous. Thank you.'

'You're welcome,' said Angela Pearson as she shut the door.

Ted went straight home and composed the email, taking some trouble to make it sound as though he had tossed it off in a moment.

Hi Nicola
Sorry I missed you before you left. I hope everything's okay. Our conversation last night really cheered me up and, if you still want to read the novel, I'm sending it to you by attachment. But you may be too busy.

He wondered whether to mention her sudden departure and what might have caused it but decided against. He hardly knew her and, whatever had happened, it was none of his business. He concluded:

Take care, Nicola. And don't get discouraged. It's a tough road but you'll make it, I know you will.

Ted

He put his mobile number in a postscript, then deleted it. The last thing he wanted was to seem importunate. She had his email address. If she wanted to contact him, that would be enough.

He then attached *The Tyranny of Love* and launched it into cyberspace, hoping that, wherever she was on the planet, it would find her. But, in his heart of hearts, he doubted if she would ever read it or if he would ever see her again.

Chapter Three

THAT LITTLE TENT OF BLUE

The Dragon's Head occupied the first floor of a small office block off Seven Sisters Road, a short walk from Finsbury Park underground station. Dominic remembered vividly the bleak entrance hallway from the morning he came for his first interview – fifteen minutes early, his heart racing, nerves aquiver. It had been empty but for an abandoned filing cabinet stacked in a corner, alongside a desk and a cardboard box. They were still there – even the cardboard box. How full of hope and trepidation he had been that day he climbed those two flights of stairs to try to sell himself to his prospective employer. Now, at eight-thirty in the morning, he was climbing them again, not for an interview this time but for his first day in the job. His insides were churning but he was also savouring a sense of victory.

He entered the half-glass door and stood gazing around, wondering what to do next. When you're looking completely spare, standing just shy of six foot five only makes matters worse, as he had often been made painfully aware. A girl's voice asked, rather haughtily, 'Can I help you?'

This was Sonia. Dominic had encountered her at his interview and was a little dismayed that she did not remember him. He was moving towards her desk to explain himself when another voice intercepted him: 'Dominic! Hi! Welcome to the wonderful world of publishing.'

He turned to find Darren – plump, fresh-faced, late thirties – advancing towards him with palm outstretched. He was the editor who would be his immediate boss and Dominic was glad, since he had taken a liking to him at his interview.

'Alistair won't be along for a while and you'll meet the rest of the gang as they stagger in,' he said, leading him through the large, chaotic room full of desks, computers, books and stacks and stacks of files and papers. 'I'm afraid we haven't organised a desk for you yet but we'll get onto that ASAP.'

'Thanks.'

'Tell me, have you ever heard the term "slush pile"?'

Dominic smiled. Although only starting out on his writing career, he knew that vanishing into the bottomless vortex of the slush pile was the dread of all aspiring authors. 'Yes I have,' he replied.

'Well, I haven't got time for mine so I'm giving it to you. You can make it your private kingdom. I keep telling Alistair to stop accepting unsolicited manuscripts but he won't listen to me. "You never know what gems you might find in there," he says. So find us a gem, Dominic old son, and turn us all into millionaires.'

The slush pile in this case was a large cardboard box beside Darren's desk within which lay an assortment of manuscripts which – Dominic had to admit – did look pretty slushy. Some were in folders, some in A4 envelopes, some were loose-leaf and secured by giant plastic paper-clips or elastic bands. Beside the box stood another with 'Read' scrawled on one flap in black marker pen and the journey between the two was about six inches. 'I've filtered this lot out on the basis of synopses and cover letters,' he said, scooping an armful of typescripts from the top of his filing cabinet. 'We always ask for that.' He took the uppermost and lodged one buttock on the edge of his desk while Dominic positioned himself at his shoulder. 'Imagine you're a shopper in Waterstones. You're bored, you're knackered, your legs are aching and you've got to find something for the wife's birthday. You pick up a book because the cover catches your eye. The blurb on the back tells you it's the greatest thing since sliced bread but you ignore that. You open it and read the first paragraph. The question is, do you read the second or move on to something else? Take this one, for instance. "The house where I spent my childhood was by the sea." Okay. Sea's good. "The windows of the kitchen and living room looked out over the bay, but the little latticed window of my bedroom looked towards the path leading to the lighthouse." Okay, the lighthouse could be interesting. What happened there? you ask yourself. Did she get raped there? Did she have her first kiss there? Did she find a dead body there? But instead of holding your interest, she bangs on about the colours of the gorse-covered hills. So thank you, madam, you've cured my insomnia in a paragraph.'

'So that's a rejection, then?'

''Fraid so.'

'And supposing I am burning with curiosity?'

'Then read for as long as it holds your attention. If you get to the end of the sample and are feeling seriously onanistic then write "RFM" –"Request full manuscript" on the attached slip. But don't do it lightly – we don't want to give the poor bastards false hope and saddle ourselves with a load of work into the bargain. Otherwise put "SR" – "Standard rejection".'

'Right,' murmured Dominic, wondering what 'onanistic' meant.

'When it gets back to Debbie or Sonia, they'll send a pro-forma to the author giving them the good news. The manuscripts only get returned if they've enclosed an SAE, otherwise they go in the recycle bin. If they haven't been reclaimed after six months, they get pulped and go to make more paper on which more authors can write yet more books to be rejected. So basically we're a recycling centre – we recycle dreams. Hey, that's not bad.'

Dominic was feeling slightly seasick. Having slaved away on his own novel for eight long years, he felt nothing but sympathy for those poor authors whose beloved manuscripts lay slumped in that box like corpses after a battle.

'But don't you think a book sometimes ... takes a page or two to get going?' he ventured.

'Your shopper in Waterstones isn't going to give it a second chance, so why should you? He, or she, is your customer, Dominic – instant gratification required, boredom threshold nil. Any you're not sure about, just refer them to me or Alistair.'

He was called away to the phone. Dominic took the heap of manuscripts and retreated to a chair against the wall, dumping them beside him on the floor. He took the uppermost and held it as reverently as if it had been an unknown work by Jane Austen, unearthed in an attic in Godmersham. To him, it was no less precious. For, however poor the book, it would always have another significance, unknown to the author: it was the first manuscript which he, Dominic Seeley, would read as a professional editor.

He removed the massive elastic band and the pages sprang out of his hand, flying everywhere. He glanced anxiously around and spotted a girl watching him from her desk. He smiled sheepishly and she smiled back, very sweetly, as if to say, 'Don't worry'. The next ten minutes were spent crouched on the floor, gathering up the pages and getting them back in numerical order.

Finally settled, he read the first paragraph then mentally stood back and considered his reaction. Was he burning with curiosity to read the second? Well, he wasn't exactly burning, but he was quite interested. So he read the second paragraph, then the third… and the fourth, and the fifth.

It was the autobiography of a woman whose husband had been posted as ambassador to all sorts of weird and wonderful parts of the world. Dominic was in the middle of a hilarious passage about a dog which had found its way into a reception at the embassy and eaten all the canapés, when he noticed an outstretched palm in front of his nose.

He looked up at a tall, gaunt man with striking features and a mop of curly, greying hair, then shot to his feet and shook the hand.

'Welcome to The Dragon's Head, Daniel. How are you settling in?'

'Oh fine, Mr. Milner. It's … Dominic, by the way.'

'Sorry. Dominic. And I'm Alistair from now on. We don't stand on ceremony around here.'

'Right.'

'I see Darren's offloaded his slush pile onto you.'

'Yes!' Dominic laughed.

'Well, you never know, you might find us a gem in there. God knows we need one. Sorry about the desk situation, by the way. We'll arrange one for you ASAP.'

'Thank you.'

'Right! Mustn't let the grass grow. Don't hesitate to ask if you have any problems.' And he swept off into his office and shut the door.

Dominic returned to his manuscript, having now reached page twenty-seven without coming to a decision. He had formed a picture in his mind of the author – petite, bustling, efficient. But he was also detecting another dimension – a pathos, a vulnerability. It was at about ten thirty that the thought suddenly struck him: this woman had devoted months – years, even – to writing this book; she had poured all her precious memories into it – her moments of joy, her moments of loneliness, her moments of triumph and of feeling unequal to the task expected of her. She had honed sentences, polished paragraphs, worked until one or two in the morning on those stubborn passages that refused to come right. Then, full of hope, she had sent a sample to The Dragon's Head, knowing that some faceless editor was going to make a decision which could change the course of her entire life. And that editor was him. He imagined her waiting for his response, her heartbeat quickening when she saw the packet addressed in her own hand lying on the doormat. Then she would tear it open and discover ... what? A standard format rejection letter full of insincere regrets and good wishes for her writing career. Only then did it occur to him what a weight of responsibility rested upon his shoulders. And he had been in the job just over two hours.

Around eleven, Darren brought him a cup of coffee. 'I didn't know whether you take sugar so I took a chance and bunged in two.'

'Thanks. That's perfect,' smiled Dominic, who didn't take sugar.

'How are you getting on with those scripts?'

'Um...'

'Not as easy as I made it sound, is it?'

'No, it isn't,' he laughed.

'Are you ready for some more?'

'Well, actually, I'm still on the first one. The trouble is it seems pretty good. And she once met the Dalai Lama. And Bill Clinton. I just can't decide.'

Darren held out his hand, eyeing his protégé sternly. Dominic put the manuscript into it. He spent three minutes glancing over the first page. 'Rejection,' he pronounced, handing it back.

Dominic said nothing.

'Look, mate, I know where you're coming from. I felt the same way myself when I started out in this business. But the fact is we get around three hundred unsolicited manuscripts a month – most of them aren't bad but we simply don't have time to read them all. You'll need to learn to be a bit ruthless. And to speed up.'

Riding home in the tube to the little room he had found in Walthamstow, Dominic reflected on his first day at The Dragon's Head. He hadn't made any disastrous cock-ups and all his colleagues seemed to like him (except Sonia, who, he'd quickly discovered, didn't like anyone except Alistair). Jim, Darren's fellow-editor, was helpful. Patrick, the marketing director, who always seemed to be in a hurry, was perfectly friendly whenever he paused for breath. Greg, who looked after IT and the company's website, was pleasant enough in a mumbly, geeky kind of a way. And Debbie – the girl who had smiled at him when he dropped those pages – she was sweet. He felt a little glow of warmth whenever he thought of her.

He tried to speed up his reading but found it difficult. As a rather solitary child who had grown into a solitary teenager, reading, to him, had always been a pleasure, an escape, something he liked to savour. Some offerings he could see at a glance were just plain bad, but so many seemed pretty good. 'If there are any you're not sure about, just refer them to me or Alistair,' Darren had said. But if he really did that, he would be referring almost everything to him or Alistair. So he reluctantly wrote 'SR' on slip after slip, every time feeling he was stabbing some fellow author in the back and terrified he was making a mistake. It was his recurring nightmare: another J.K. Rowling had popped up, a literary superstar who was earning millions, whose latest novel her fans camped outside Waterstones to grab the moment it appeared on the shelves; and Alistair was saying to Darren, 'Didn't we get a manuscript from her when she was unpublished?' And Darren was answering, 'Yes. I gave it to Dominic.'

On the Tuesday of the second week – after a flurry of rearrangement that put Sonia in a vile mood – he acquired his long-promised desk. Okay, it faced a wall rather than a window or the body of the office but, nonetheless, his heart soared at the sight of it. No longer would he have to perch on a plastic chair, like some anxious patient in a doctor's waiting room. He could swivel, he could expand, he had somewhere to put his coffee. The next morning, he brought in two little framed photographs from his room – one of his dog and one of his parents – and positioned them carefully, not so much to remind him of his loved ones as to consolidate his claim to the desk and deter anyone who might feel inclined to whip it away again.

*

One evening, about a week later, he and Darren happened to be leaving the building together and Darren said, 'Fancy a pint?'

They went to The Green Monkey – a poky Victorian watering hole where he was clearly a regular – its main attraction a cramped courtyard garden at the back where he could smoke. They took their drinks to the one free table squeezed in a corner and he offered Dominic a cigarette, which he accepted. He was not really a smoker but did not wish to seem uncompanionable.

Darren lit both cigarettes, took a deep drag then contemplated his colleague benignly. 'So how's it going, do you reckon?'

'Fantastic. I'm really enjoying the job. Especially now I've got my desk.'

'That's great,' Darren smiled, tapping some ash sharply into the ash-tray. 'Look, Dominic, a word to the wise, mate. Keep an eye on the appointments columns. I am.'

Dominic stared at him in confusion. 'Why?'

He shot glances to left and right, as though the little courtyard were full of prying ears and eyes. 'I shouldn't be telling you this, and for Christ sake don't go repeating it to anyone, but the place is on its uppers. Alistair's crazy about literature, as we all know, and he's got integrity in spades but the company's in debt up to the eyeballs. I'm not saying we're going to the wall tomorrow but if we don't get a major commercial success in the very near future, we'll be fucked.'

Dominic murmured, 'I see.'

'Best case scenario – people start getting laid off. And you know how it works – last in, first out.'

'Me, in other words.'

'It's nothing personal. And if it's any comfort, it won't stop with you, though how we can run the place on fewer staff I don't know – we're all going flat out as it is. The other possibility is that we get *rescued* – in inverted commas – by one of the giants and become an imprint but I reckon Alistair would rather die than let that happen. Anyway, sorry to piss on your parade, old son.'

'No, no,' said Dominic, still stunned. 'I'm glad you told me.'

It was only as he rode home on the tube that evening that he realised how much he had come to value his job at The Dragon's Head.

II

Two months later, Darren suddenly fell ill, throwing the office into turmoil. Everyone had to adjust their own job description to cover for him and Dominic would often find himself talking on the phone to some major agent or author because Alistair, Jim and Patrick were busy on other lines. He was also dealing with agented manuscripts, which he found easier since they had already passed through one screening process. He still had his dreaded slush pile, of course, though he felt he was becoming more adept at separating the wheat from the chaff.

'How are you coping with Darren away?' asked his boss.

'All right, thank you, Alistair.'

He seemed in a jovial mood that morning, which emboldened Dominic to ask his opinion of the sample he was working on. 'I was going to reject it but … I don't know … I think it may have something.'

Alistair cast an eye over the first page. His face formed into a frown. 'This is awful. Why are you wasting my time on this? Rejection,' he said, thrusting it back.

His reaction angered Dominic. 'It's just that it … rather reminded me of Robbe-Grillet, who's a hero of mine.'

'Who?'

'Robbe-Grillet, the French *chosiste*.'

'Dominic, this woman has spent the entire first page of her novel describing a garden gate. One lives in hope that it's the gate of the main protagonist but in my opinion it's an exceptionally boring gate, even by the standard of gates generally. Now *please*. We're under a lot of pressure here, so get a grip and develop some critical faculties.' He moved swiftly on, his thoughts already focused elsewhere.

Dominic felt his insides coiling with fury and humiliation. Robbe-Grillet, for Christ's sake? The entire office must have heard their exchange and be having a good laugh at his expense, especially Sonia – possibly even Debbie. He seethed with fury all the way home and shut himself in his room to avoid having to be civil to the lodgers who shared the kitchen. He could barely bring himself to get up in the morning and seethed all the way in to work. And, for want of anyone else to take his fury out on, he took it out on the poor old unsolicited authors. Fuck it! If everyone wanted him to read at the speed of light and leave all discrimination at the door then that's what he'd do – it hardly mattered since he'd soon be on the dole anyway. Darren had said you could tell if an author could write from the first paragraph. Dominic decided you could tell from the first sentence. From the first word. Manuscript after manuscript received the two letters of condemnation – 'SR'.

With the office under so much pressure, his new approach won him the approval of everyone, even Sonia. 'We've made an editor of you at last,' smiled Jim, and then – to his amazement – Alistair sort of apologised. 'Don't take any notice of me,' he said. 'I'm an awkward old cuss.' Darren tottered back to work – minus his gall bladder – and was delighted at how his protégé had shaped up in his absence. Dominic's wounded pride was appeased, his pleasure tainted only by a recurrent pain, like a dull toothache, whenever he thought of all those rejected authors.

Nonetheless, he found himself wondering if the moment was ripe to execute the plan which had been his reason for seeking a job in publishing – to show his own work to someone with influence and get his career off the ground. 'It's all about who you know in this life,' his father had often remarked. 'It's not about what you know, it's who you know.' Well, he knew Alistair and that would surely give him the edge on all those other faceless authors whose efforts he rejected every day. He reckoned a good time to catch him would be late on Friday afternoon when he was always in a good mood. With any luck, he might start reading it over the weekend.

On Thursday evening, he brought down two massive folders from their stowage on top of the wardrobe in his room – Part One and Part Two of *That Little Tent of Blue* – the title taken from the line '*That little tent of blue which prisoners called the sky*' from *The Ballad of Reading Gaol*. He sat down on his bed, hoisted Part One onto his lap, caressed it lovingly, then opened it at random and started to read. Throughout most of his teens, this novel had been his escape route, sometimes his tormentor, always his companion. He had started it in his fifteenth year as little more than a series of *pensées*, employing a technique so free it was almost stream of consciousness. Later, under the influence of the many authors he admired – Joyce, Lawrence and Salinger in particular – it had transformed itself into a work of fiction. Its youthful hero had suffered all the traumas of his own young life – his profound sense of the futility of all existence, of the infinite void which is the universe, of the absence of any God other than those men fashion, for whatever reason, in their own hearts. He had spoken fearlessly of the curse of his artistic gift (his hero was also a budding author) and the isolation from his fellow man to which it condemned him. He spoke of pain, of loneliness, of being out of touch with his true self, of feeling like a stranger in his own skin. He had once shown it to a girl he loved called Marianne in the hope that it might encourage her to sleep with him, and she had pronounced (after reading seven pages) that it was 'quite good but could do with a bit of humour'. That had been the end of that brief affair and the one time he had contemplated suicide. But he had kept on going, and now, as he fondled page four hundred and forty-seven, he felt that finally, maybe, the baby he had born so long in his creative womb might surface into the light of day.

Around teatime on Friday afternoon, he knocked on Alistair's office door, having noticed his mood warming up in anticipation of a weekend's golf. His boss called out 'Come!' – his customary way of summoning lesser mortals into the inner sanctum. Dominic entered, explaining falteringly that the manuscript he held in his hands was his own novel (even though, strictly speaking, it was only half of it) and he wondered if he might possibly see his way to having a look at it some time.

Alistair reached up from his desk with an avuncular smile and took it from him. 'So this is the *magnum opus*?' he said, giving the beautifully printed, comb-bound manuscript a friendly pat.

'I'm afraid so.'

'I like the title. Good old Oscar.'

'Thank you.'

'Well, leave it with me, old man. I promise I'll give it my full undivided attention.'

He told himself not to get his hopes up. But he couldn't help it. Throughout that weekend, he constantly caught himself thinking, 'Maybe he's reading it at this very moment. Maybe he's ensconced in his armchair, drinking it in.' His thoughts raced forward to Monday morning, he imagined the scene: Alistair calling him into his office, his words: 'Dominic, I'm bowled over! This is one of the most intense and passionate pieces of writing I've ever read in my life. It brought tears to my eyes.' He even dared wonder if his novel might prove to be the 'major commercial success' that would save the company from ruin.

Monday morning came and nothing happened. From time to time during the day, as Alistair swept through the office, Dominic would glance up from his desk and catch his eye, smiling, and he would smile back, rather distantly. By Wednesday, he was becoming increasingly mystified, not to say a little annoyed, by the constant smiles and asked, 'Dominic, is everything all right?'

'Yes, yes, fine, thank you, Alistair. I just wondered … whether you'd had a chance to look at my manuscript yet.'

'Oh yes. No, I'm sorry, I should have said. All hell broke loose at home last weekend. Family, you know. But I will read it this weekend, I promise.'

Overhearing the conversation, Darren cast his colleague a weary, knowing smile which was nonetheless tinged with compassion. He had once written a novel himself.

Dominic did not spend that weekend in the agony of anticipation that he had spent the last. More a state of cautious optimism. Alistair was a busy man. He might find the time to read it, he might not. It was nothing personal.

Another Monday morning came. Nothing happened. But then, just after lunch, Alistair asked him into his office. He obeyed, his heart pounding. It was only a few short steps and yet, to him, it was like crossing into another dimension. Alistair's office, to Dominic, was like a chapel, a place imbued with a quasi-religious aura – the aura of hope.

'Shut the door, old man.'

He did so, then turned to face his boss, who was already seated. He noticed his manuscript on the desk. He took the seat opposite him.

'Well, I had a look at your novel over the weekend and I must say I was amazed. An incredible amount of work has gone into it.'

'Yes.'

'I can't pretend I've read it all, but I've read enough to see that you definitely have the potential to become a writer.'

'Thank you.'

'And I don't see any reason why you shouldn't publish.'

'You mean ... publish this novel?'

Alistair hesitated. 'Well, maybe not *this* novel, but I don't think the experience of writing it will have been wasted at all. It reminds me of a novel I once wrote when I was your age and living in Morocco.' He stretched back in his chair and interlocked his fingers behind his head, a distant, wistful smile transforming his face. 'I was going through my Jack Kerouac phase – I think everyone does, don't you? I felt I needed to get a lot of stuff out of my system before settling down to a career as a writer. Not that I ever did settle down to a career as a writer. I didn't really have the application, somehow.'

Dominic, his facial muscles bolted into a fascinated smile, was inwardly seething. He didn't want to talk about Alistair; he wanted to talk about himself. His mouth already sour with the taste of disappointment, he said, 'Do you think you could give me some pointers on how to make my work more publishable?'

Ten minutes later, he carried *That Little Tent of Blue* – which suddenly weighed a ton – back to his desk. He knew emotion would come in its time, but at that moment he felt only stunned, as though he had been struck a glancing blow by an express train. Darren cast him the look of a kindly elder brother. 'If you want to pop out for a fag or something ...'

'No, I'm fine. Thanks.'

'Well, if it's any comfort, I know what you're going through, mate. I've been there myself.'

It wasn't any comfort. Dominic snatched a manuscript from the pile on his desk and started to read, though he could barely focus on the words. He dragged the back of his hand across his face, sniffing strenuously. 'What the *fuck* is this?'

Darren looked up in surprise. Without waiting for a reply, Dominic scrawled 'SR' on the slip then added, after a moment's hesitation, 'This is the biggest load of shit I've ever read in my life, ARSEHOLE!!!' Not that Sonia would include that comment in the rejection letter, sadly.

On the way home, he stopped at the Spar on the corner near his room and bought a packet of cigarettes and a bottle of whisky. They would be his companions through what would be a long, dark night of the soul. Far into the small hours he sat in his little armchair, smoking, drinking and thinking, in front of his one bar electric fire. What was the point? What the *fuck* was the point? If the work into which, over eight long years, he had poured so much love, so much passion, so much agonising honesty was not going to make the grade – even when he was on the inside of the publishing business – what hope was there for his writing career?

Then, for the first time since he was thirteen years old, he burst into tears.

Chapter Four

THE FAMOUS MR HAVERS

Anne and Ted had just settled down to supper on trays in front of *Eastenders* when the telephone rang.

'Perfect timing,' sighed Anne.

'Just leave it.'

'No, I'd better get it. It might be one of the children.'

She went out into the hall to answer it and returned a few moments later. 'It's for you. Someone called Nicola.'

His reflex reaction was a studied look of bewilderment. 'Nicola? I don't know anyone called Nicola.'

'Well, she seems to know you.'

He set aside his tray and went out to where the receiver lay waiting for him on the hall table. He closed the door. He took a deep breath. It was five months since he had sent her his novel, five months in which he had sought her address every day in his inbox. It had never occurred to him that she would phone. He grabbed the receiver.

'Nicola! Hello! You got my email?'

'Yeah, hi Ted. Sorry I didn't get back sooner – life's been totally crazy. But I've finally got around to reading your novel. I think it's amazing!'

'*Really?*'

'Yeah, I couldn't believe a guy your age could get right inside the head of a teenage girl like that. And it's so *funny*.'

'Well, I'm … overwhelmed.'

'That guy who wrote you that letter, I don't know what his problem was but he was talking out of his arse. For Christ sake, just keep at it. It's brilliant. Although the title's pants.'

'Oh. I thought *The Tyranny of Love* was quite a good title.'

'Yeah, for Mills and Boon, maybe. This book needs something modern. Edgy. Maybe a single word …'

'Yes but the whole point of *Tyranny* is that it resounds throughout the book. It's about the emotion of love itself being tyrannical – when it subjugates people, when it makes them vulnerable.'

'Yeah, yeah, I get all that. I just don't like it.'

He smiled, finding her honesty refreshing. 'Nicola, I've had a thought. Why don't you do some work on it? Edit it. I'm sure, with your background, you could bring something fresh to it ...'

'My background?'

'Well ... you're young, kind of irreverent. Like Kim in the novel ...'

'A total fuck-up, you mean?'

'I wouldn't go so far as to say that.' There was a pause. 'Of course, I'd pay you,' he added hastily. 'Not much, I'm afraid, but something.'

'I'd love to, especially if you pay me. Not that it needs any work – maybe the odd tweak here and there.'

'Are you sure you're not just being kind?'

'*Kind*? Give me a break. I told you I'm a bitch and I meant it.'

He smiled as he recalled their first inauspicious meeting. 'So, how's it going?'

'Okay. I've got this job in a bistro. I'm being even sweeter to the customers than I was at The Queen's.'

'Any progress on the acting front?'

'Nah, just a couple of auditions but nothing yet. I did get a commercial for disposable nappies where I had to pretend to be this baby's mummy and kiss its tummy and shit. The fucking thing wouldn't stop crying and the real mother was going mental in case I dropped it or something.'

'Well, it's a start. Have you got somewhere to live?'

'No, I'm crashing with friends. Look, I've got to go, I'm out of call time. I'll email, yeah?'

'Nicola...' But the line was dead.

He thoughtfully replaced the receiver then, after a moment's hesitation, re-entered the living room. Anne was engrossed in a violent row about the fate of 'The Vic' – the Mitchell family pub.

'I hope your supper's not cold,' she remarked distantly.

'It doesn't matter.'

'So who was that?"

'Oh, just a girl who worked briefly at the pub. Quite bright, actually – an Edinburgh graduate. She wants to be an actress. I got talking to her a while back and she expressed an interest in reading *Tyranny*. I'd forgotten all about it.'

They carried on watching television in silence but later, during the weather forecast, she said, 'That girl who phoned earlier. It wasn't Nicola Pearson, was it? She was at Edinburgh. And she wanted to be an actress.'

Ted turned and stared at her. 'I'm not sure what her surname is. How do you know her, anyway?'

'I don't, but I met her mother once at a dinner party at Cynthia's. Rather an odd woman. I didn't care for her, to be honest. Terribly pretty and not a hair out of place but sort of ... *cold* somehow. I think she'd been an actress or dancer herself before she got married. From what I gathered from Cynthia, Nicola was the daughter from hell – sex, drugs, you name it. And she had mental problems.'

'What kind of mental problems?'

'I don't know. Her mother was rather cagey about her. A bit of an embarrassment. The son, on the other hand, she couldn't stop talking about.'

'It doesn't sound like the same girl.'

Later, after Anne had gone to bed, Ted started re-reading *The Tyranny of Love*. He read far into the night and continued reading for the whole of the following day. He and Anne had an early supper that evening and, after watching some television, he excused himself and returned to his study to carry on reading. He finished at about midnight and stared into space for twenty minutes, thinking.

Lying awake beside his soundly sleeping wife, he felt exhausted and depressed. He had hoped that re-reading the novel through Nicola's eyes, riding on the wave of her youthful enthusiasm, might reveal it in a different light. But the sneaking reservations he had always had about it were stronger still, the cracks in its structure ever more glaring. He had been crazy to even think of submitting it in that state and he knew that *The Tyranny of Love* (or whatever 'edgy' title she wanted to give it) would never see the light of day. He had moved on, he was writing better stuff and could not see himself returning to it. All that passion. All that work. For nothing.

*

Two days later, he found an email from her in his mailbox. It said, simply, '*Call me. N xx*' then gave a mobile number. He did so late that morning, while Anne was at work.

'I've been thinking about what you said the other night. About me doing a bit of editing on your novel. I'd quite like to have a go at that, if you're still up for it.'

His heart sank. How to break it to her that he had decided to abandon *Tyranny*?

'Well, yes, that would be great, Nicola. And, like I said, I'd pay you. Have you got somewhere you can work?'

'No, that's the problem. I'm still crashing with friends.'

'Is everything okay? You sound a bit down.'

'Yeah, I'm okay. It's a pain, though – I'm losing all my girlfriends because their boyfriends keep trying to hit on me. It's not like I'm giving them any encouragement.'

'You need a place of your own.'

'Tell me about it.'

'So how's the job going?' he asked after a pause.

'It's not.'

He hesitated, seeing the situation at the pub replaying itself. 'Dare I ask what happened?'

'I just dropped this fucking chip – sorry, *pomme frite* – on the table-cloth then picked it up and put it back on the customer's plate. The bitch complained and I got the sack. I mean, for Christ's sake, it's not like I'd picked it up off the floor.'

'That does sound a bit harsh. They should have given you a warning.'

'Yeah, well, I've already had a couple of those. This prat Gary, the manager, took me on one side and told me I should smile more and pretend that serving food is all I could possibly want to be doing with my life. "You're an actress," he says, "you should be able to manage that." Bastard.'

'But you couldn't?'

'Damn right I couldn't! Acting's a serious business – it's not about being a performing monkey. It's bad enough getting the sack without him slagging off my profession.'

'Nicola, maybe ...'

'Maybe what?'

'Maybe you should try being a bit less ... confrontational. Play the game – try to have a sense of humour about it – and that way you'll get into a position where you can do stuff you do care about.'

'Christ, Ted, who's side are you on?'

'Sorry.' He was already regretting his words. 'I'm just repeating what I've heard people say about starting out in the acting profession.'

'I must be in the wrong profession then.'

'No, you're not.' He groped for some anodyne phrase to soothe or console, but found only platitudes. 'You've got to have faith in yourself is what I'm saying.'

'Yeah, yeah.'

'Well, I've got faith in you, if that means anything. One day I'm going to see you on stage, or on the screen, and you're going to bring tears to my eyes.'

'I wish you were up here, Ted.'

He felt suddenly out of his depth. As he fumbled for a reply, she added, 'So we could work together on the book. That would be good, wouldn't it?'

'It would. It would be great. Nicola, are you sure you're all right?'

'Yeah, I said I'm okay.'

'Have you ... got somewhere to sleep tonight?'

'For Christ's sake, I'm not on the streets. I'm just a bit short, that's all.'

Why couldn't she ask her mother for help? he wondered. All that wealth just sitting there, doing nothing. Then he remembered the icy condescension of that woman who had written out her email address. Help from her would come with strings attached.

He lowered his voice to a murmur even though he was alone in the house. 'I could send you the money up front. For the editing. How about a hundred at a rate of ten …'

'I'm not asking for money,' she cut him off curtly. 'But … yeah, okay. A hundred will be fine.'

He was touched by the note of relief which she was trying hard to disguise. Poor girl. He pictured her shivering on a bench somewhere.

'Give me an address and I'll send it straight away.'

That afternoon, he walked into Wemborne and withdrew two hundred pounds in cash from his own savings account – the dregs of his brother's legacy. He sent it by recorded delivery then walked swiftly home, wishing to forget what he had done as quickly as possible.

II

He heard nothing more from her, though the money was not returned. Then, one evening while he and Anne were watching *Gardener's World*, the phone rang. Anne went to answer it and was gone nearly half an hour.

'One of the children?' he asked when she returned.

'No, that was Marie.'

His heart sank. 'What did she want?'

'She wanted to ask a favour. I'm afraid I lied and told her you were out so you wouldn't be put on the spot.'

'That was very thoughtful of you. What's the favour?'

She perched back on her seat. 'It's quite a big one, even by her standards.'

'Well, come on then, tell me.'

She seemed awkward, as though she were asking the favour herself. He suspected she had promised Marie she would 'work on him'. 'She's going to Australia for two months and wondered if you'd be interested in babysitting Cordelia. Apparently Gladys has got too arthritic to go down there every day, what with the steps and everything. She's not expecting you to stay the full two months – just as long as you can manage. She thought you might be able to work in peace there, though why she imagines I don't leave you in peace here ...'

'Where's David, then?'

'In America, working.'

David was Marie's husband, who had also been his best friend at Oxford.

He thought for a while. 'Well, thanks for not committing me.'

'So you're going to say no, are you?'

'Of course I'm going to say no. I hate London, you know that.'

'Well, Richmond isn't exactly London. It's lovely out there.'

'It's all London to me. And the last thing I want is to spend two months babysitting that obnoxious cat.'

'She's not an obnoxious cat. She's a sweet little cat. And you've only got to feed her and stroke her once in a while.'

'The last time I stroked her, she scratched me,' he grunted.

'She doesn't like people touching her head. I think she's got a sensitive spot. Marie warned you about it, if you remember.'

They watched Monty Don enthusiastically firming in an *acer*.

'Anyone would think you wanted to get rid of me.'

'It's not that. I just think a change of scene would do you good. You don't have to go for the whole two months. You could just go for one. Or even a couple of weeks – just as long as you want. She said she'd be grateful for any time at all you could manage.'

He did not reply and nothing more was said on the matter. The following evening, however, while they were in the kitchen making supper together, he said, quite out the blue, 'I'd miss you. If I went to Marie's.'

'I'd miss you too. But I'd manage. I really think it'd do you good, Ted. You've been so depressed since you got that letter and you're just stuck here all the time with hardly any human contact except that bunch at the pub. And when you're depressed, everything around you becomes tainted with your depression, even me.'

'That's rubbish.'

'No it's not. I'm just talking about the benefits of a change of scene – there's no great mystery about it. It's why people go on holiday, after all. I just think you should go up there and see a bit of life, get a new perspective on things.'

Ted considered her words. 'And you're quite sure you'd be all right without me?'

'I'd be fine.'

III

The following Thursday week, Anne spent an hour ironing her husband's clothes in the conservatory, while listening to Radio Two. As he was moving around, getting his things together, he paused for a moment in the doorway and contemplated her back view as she worked – lifting his shirt and turning it over, spreading it out, her hands moving methodically, efficiently and quite independently of her brain, which seemed to be miles away. The radio was playing an old instrumental version of *All of Me* and she was swaying gently to the rhythm and singing along to the tune – *All of me, why not take all of me?* It was something he had not known her do in years.

She dropped him at the station on her way to work the next morning. Before he got out of the car, she said, 'Ted, I just want to say this now so there's no misunderstanding. I'm not going to phone you while you're in Richmond. Unless there's an emergency, of course. And I'm not expecting you to phone me.'

'Okay. If that's what you want.'

'It's not that I'm not interested in how you get on. I just don't want you to have to ask polite questions about how I am or pretend your writing's going well if it isn't. I want you to be spared all that, just for a week or two.'

'It's not a matter of asking polite questions. I worry about you.'

'I know, but you needn't. If you're depressed and want to talk about it, that's a different matter. I'm just explaining, so you're not hurt.'

'Okay. Thanks.' Then he took her in his arms. 'I hope you enjoy having the house to yourself.'

'Believe it or not, I will miss you.'

'Liar.'

*

It rained on the journey but by the time Ted reached Richmond the sun was shining. His first task was to call on Gladys, a neighbour whom Marie adored and whom she considered (by virtue of paying her a small retainer) her 'favourite member of staff'. He rang the bell, causing a cacophony of yapping and an elderly voice shouting, 'Be quiet, you little so and so!' Eventually, the door opened. Gladys was small, grey and stooped, but with a disarming smile.

'Ah! So you must be the famous Mr Havers. Marie's told me all about you.'

'Actually the name's Haymer,' Ted smiled. 'But I answer to Ted. I just need to pick up the keys.'

'Ah yes, the keys! The keys! The keys to the kingdom!'

They smiled at each other for a moment.

'So ... if I could possibly have the keys?'

'Of course! Silly me. I wonder where I put them?'

Gladys's obvious dottiness was a relief to Ted since he had feared that his stay might be closely monitored, with regular *sitreps* going back to Marie.

'Well, I hope you manage to do it all right in the flat, Mr Havers,' she exclaimed when she finally returned and handed him the keys. 'Your writing, I mean. So *clever.*'

Marie and David's split-level apartment comprised the upper half of a large Edwardian house off Richmond Hill. Ted dumped his bags and supplies in the hall then wandered into the living room. The place was just as he remembered it – sunny, south-facing and minimalist, the stately *armoire* and other lumps of French furniture – no doubt from Marie's family home in Provence – blending in, thanks to her flair for interior design. He had been there twice in the twenty years they had owned it, once after taking Jess to see *Les Misérables* for her eighteenth birthday treat and, years later, he and Anne had come for a weekend. Marie had taken them to a very odd play by Genet and they had tried out a newly-opened French restaurant where Marie, for no apparent reason, had taken a violent dislike to the waiter. It seemed strange to be alone here now, the place silent but for the murmur of traffic beyond the double glazing. He moved to the bay window and gazed out over gardens and woodland parted by a wide bow of the Thames – a view which, but for the tower blocks poking through the horizon and the airliners stacking for Heathrow, might have been painted by Constable. The leaves were yellow now in the afternoon sun and the sparrows and blue tits flitted among the branches just as they did at home.

He went through to the kitchen where he found a letter explaining Cordelia's complex feeding regime; then Cordelia herself – a petite, smoky-grey Burmese – was rubbing against his leg and purring passionately. He returned the greeting with a tentative stroke of her back then swiftly withdrew his hand. From the French windows some iron steps led down to a terrace and a little walled garden where Marie liked to recline in the summer, drinking Piña Coladas and managing her friends' lives using her cordless phone. He climbed the short staircase to the landing off which lay the bedrooms. It was hung with old photos, some dating from Oxford. There was even one of him and David – both looking slightly the worse for wear – taken during a picnic in Christchurch Meadow. Ted smiled, remembering the occasion vividly since an attractive law student named Anne had been there and he had tried to dazzle her with his knowledge of post-modernist poetry. David – two years his senior and about an inch taller – had his arm round his shoulder, like an older brother.

He commandeered the largest of the three bedrooms, which faced south, away from the road. There was a table which could be moved to the window and would be perfect for work. After unpacking, he went down and opened a bottle of Shiraz – having some difficulty with the vacuum-powered corkscrew – then sat in the garden for a while gazing at the pots of geraniums and listening to the aircraft descending overhead. Familiarising himself with the kitchen, he put on some ravioli and refilled his glass. His instinct was to phone Anne, just to say he'd arrived safely and that everything was okay, but he desisted. He ate his supper watching *Das Boot* – one of David's huge collection of DVDs – then fell so soundly asleep during the German classic that he lay awake half the night, staring at the ceiling and listening to the distant, unfamiliar drone of traffic. As a recluse and lover of solitude it often surprised him how easily he succumbed to loneliness. He told himself it was the strange surroundings and that everything would be fine once he got down to work. He fell asleep at dawn, rose late and made coffee but found it hard to focus on his writing.

He forgot to eat lunch and at three o'clock, suddenly ravenous, went down to the sun-drenched kitchen and laid into a cottage loaf he had bought on the journey. He heated some soup and forgot to eat it. He decided to go for a walk up to Richmond Park, which lay serenely under a silver-blue sky, and sat on a bench for an hour, watching the world around him – people walking their dogs, people pushing babies, people jogging, someone performing *tai chi*. The vast metropolis lay sprawled to the north-east in a violet haze, its incessant muffled roar punctuated now and then by the scream of a siren or a burst of mechanical hammering from a construction site. He thought of the millions of people out there, living their lives as best they could – coping with jobs, with relationships, with problems, each with their dream which was stubbornly refusing to come true. And he thought of Nicola somewhere among them, battling on with her life.

Back at the flat, he opened a bottle of Chardonnay, forgetting he had an already-open bottle of Shiraz. He was still having trouble with the corkscrew but mainly because his hands were shaking. He fed the cat and put on some macaroni, then went up to his desk where he sat at his laptop, gazing out at the evening sunlight burnishing the leaves. It was ridiculous. Nicola was out there somewhere – homeless, living off the goodwill of her friends and no doubt stretching those friendships to breaking point. And here he was with this huge apartment all to himself. It would be a crime, an act of inhumanity, not to invite her there. Then his nostrils twitched and he tore back down to the kitchen. 'Fuck!' he shouted, thrusting the congealed lump of pasta under the tap and wondering, in a cloud of steam, how he was ever going to restore Marie's saucepan to its former glory. He leant on the side of the sink and heaved a sigh. Then he fetched his address book, went out to the telephone in the hall and dialled her number.

She answered almost at once, although he could barely make her out.

'It's Ted!' he shouted. 'Ted! The famous author! How's it going?'

He thought he detected the word 'terrible' then the signal improved. '...You gave me all that money and I haven't done a stroke of work on your book. I just can't find anywhere quiet to concentrate.'

'Come here, then,' he said.

A moment's hesitation. 'Where's here?'

*

The doorbell rang around seven. Ted went to answer it and stared at the girl who stood before him. It was like looking at a stranger since she resembled in barely a single detail the girl he had met at the pub. Where she had then been plastered with makeup, she now wore none, and the hair which had fallen in straight black rods was shimmering red and cut in a bob to the base of her neck. She seemed smaller, almost waif-like, but when she smiled – her lips tightening and puckering in a charming way he had never noticed before – her delicate features formed themselves, for the first time, into those of an individual.

Unsure whether to shake her hand or peck her cheek, he did neither. 'It's ... great to see you again,' he said.

'It's great to see you.'

'I like the hair. What colour is that?'

'Nuclear red. It's good, but you have to do it loads of times to get it right.'

'It's very attractive.'

'Thank you.'

They surveyed each other in silence.

'So. Can I come in?'

'Sorry,' he laughed, moving aside and gathering up her suitcase, grip and laptop case.

'*Wow*, Ted,' she gasped, as she entered the living room. 'You've certainly fallen on your feet here, you clever sod. This'd cost like a zillion to rent.'

'And all I have to do is feed the cat and show it a bit of grudging affection. Do you fancy some tea or coffee? Or wine?'

'Wine, thanks,' she replied as she wandered off on a tour of inspection. 'White if you've got it.'

He fetched the Chardonnay from the fridge. 'Are you hungry?' he called out.

'Nah, I'm fine!' she called back from upstairs.

He took a gulp of Shiraz. "I've bagged the room at the front! It's away from the road and peaceful for work. You can have either of the other two.'

'Oh my *God*. There's a photo of you up here – when you were young! You weren't bad looking!'

'You don't have to sound so surprised!'

She reappeared in the kitchen a few minutes later and he handed her a glass, whereupon she sat down at the table and reached for her bag and – Ted guessed – her cigarettes. 'Nicola, I'm really sorry, I'm afraid you can't smoke in the flat. Marie's fanatical about it. You'll have to go outside on the terrace.'

'Oh. Right. Let's go outside on the terrace then.'

It was a warm, late summer evening. They settled in two garden armchairs, Nicola kicking off her red slip-on shoes, unfurling her slender legs in their skinny jeans and crossing her feet on the little wall surrounding the herb bed. He noticed her toenails were varnished the same colour as her hair. Cordelia jumped on her lap and made herself a nest, Nicola stroking her distractedly.

'I should watch her. She scratches,' he said, although she didn't seem inclined to scratch her.

She offered him a cigarette but he declined. She lit her own, tilting back her head and blowing the smoke straight upwards towards the sky in a way which reminded him of that first evening they met at the pub. 'This is nice,' she sighed.

'I was completely thrown when you vanished like that. I was

wandering round and round Wemborne with my manuscript in a shopping bag, feeling like an idiot.'

'Sorry about that. But it was all your fault.'

'*My* fault?'

'Yeah, that evening you walked me home it made me realise how much I'd missed the company of the human race. All of a sudden I couldn't stay in that dump a moment longer.'

'I never understood what you were doing there in the first place.'

'I'd been ill. When I came out of hospital, I had nowhere else to go.'

He sensed she did not want to enlarge on the subject, so he did not press it.

'I'm really sorry about the editing. Or lack of it.'

'Don't worry about it.'

'I have had this brilliant idea, though – about how I can earn that money and then some.'

'You don't have to earn it. But tell me anyway.'

She dragged deeply on her cigarette, as though as an overture to the disclosure of her plan, like the parting of the curtains before a play. 'Okay, here's the background. So I've had the sack from the bistro and I'm wandering down Charing Cross Road feeling like shit when I see all these people hanging round outside Foyles.' Her voice rose on the last syllable, as though seeking his affirmation. 'Then I notice this guy giving me the eyeball. He looked like some knackered old rock star and seemed vaguely familiar but I couldn't place him. So I ask him what's going on and it turns out it's the launch of Howard Mosberg's latest pile of poop about miserable old gits. He asked me if I'd read it, and I said, "Nah, not really my thing," and he laughed and said, "Nor mine, and I'm supposed to be the guest speaker at this bash. I'll just have to read the blurb on the back and bullshit."

'I found myself kind of warming to this guy. He didn't seem to give a shit about anything, even though everyone was fawning on him like he was Jesus or something. So when he asks if I want to come in and hear him bullshit, I think, sure, why not? I might get a free glass of bubbly if nothing else.'

'So who was this person?'

'I'm coming to that. So we all drift in together and, sure enough, I get my free glass of champagne – and some nibbles – which was great, since I was starving. Then comes the really amazing bit. He holds out his hand and says, "I'm Tom Newcomb, by the way. Who are you?" '

Ted stared at her. 'Tom Newcomb? You mean *the* Tom Newcomb?'

'Yeah, *the* Tom Newcomb. I couldn't believe it. I mean, the guy was a hero of mine when I was fifteen. I used to sit up till two in the morning glued to his tales of sex and drugs and murder in the back streets of Blackburn and 'Ooderzfield and Christ knows where. I even had a crush on him once – at least, a crush on that puppy-eyed, stubbly face on the back of the Penguin editions.'

'He was my English teacher when I was at secondary school,' Ted remarked coolly.

Her jaw dropped. 'You're *joking*. How old was he then?'

'I don't know. Early thirties, maybe. I was in my teens.'

'And what was he like? Was he gorgeous?'

'To be honest, I thought he was a bit of a prick.'

She was taken aback by his irreverence. 'Anyway, I told him I'd read all his books and he was amazed. "I thought I went out with miniskirts and social consciences," he said and I pointed out that miniskirts are back in – I'd got a couple at home to prove it. God, I was so crawly, Ted – you'd have despised me. He seemed to be loving it, though. Although his wife had gone a bit stiff.'

'She'd be used to it. So what else did you say to him?'

'I told him I was an actress but was having real trouble finding work. He said he knew a few people in the business and might be able to pull some strings. Then he gave me his card and told me to call him in a couple of weeks.'

'Good for you.' Ted grabbed the bottle and topped up both their glasses. 'You'll have to watch him, though. I've been told he can't keep his thing in his pants for five minutes.'

'I'm afraid he's going to be out of luck there,' she snorted. 'I don't sleep with geriatrics – even famous ones.'

'Right. So, come on. What's your plan?'

'Well, I got to thinking, there I was with this great writer eating out of my hand, and I could have used that contact to push the novel.'

He looked at her. 'You mean *my* novel?'

'No, I mean the neo-post-modernist novel in general. Of course *your* novel. I could get him to introduce me to an agent or publisher. You're a writer, not a salesman. But I could be. I could change my image – get a couple of Armani suits from TK Maxx, dye my hair some classy colour and get some streaks, bung on some killer heels. I reckon I could get you a book deal in a matter of weeks. Days, probably. It's all about packaging after all, isn't it?'

Ted laughed. 'Somehow I can't see you as a power-dressing mover-and-shaker, fluttering your eyelashes at a commissioning editor.'

'Ted, I'm an actress. I'm a blank canvas. I can be whatever you want me to be.'

He took a thoughtful sip of wine. 'It's strange. You say you're a blank canvas and yet to me you have the most distinct personality of anyone I know.'

'Yeah, yeah. Come on, I want to know what you think of my plan.'

'I think it's an excellent plan. And I really appreciate your enthusiasm – I'm sure you'd be great at promoting my book. The problem is, *Tyranny* isn't up to it. I read it again the other day – after I'd spoken to you – and I'm more convinced of that now than ever. It just isn't good enough.'

She sighed sharply. 'You're talking complete and utter crap, and if you don't stop being so fucking self-deprecating and grab this opportunity, I'll lose all respect for you.'

He responded with silence.

'And what about Julie, your adopted sister? Doesn't she deserve to have her story told?'

'I think she'd understand.'

'Yeah, well, she doesn't have much choice, does she?' she mumbled.

'Look, I really appreciate your faith in me,' he persevered, trying to be assertive, 'but I have to be true to myself. It's my novel and I'm the only one who can decide when it's ready to go out there.'

'Yeah, but you're not *being* true to yourself. You're wallowing in self-pity.'

He took refuge in the wine bottle, though when he raised it to refill their glasses, he found it was empty. ''Scuse me,' he said.

Standing up, he had to grab the back of her chair to steady himself. He stepped carefully up to the kitchen and returned a few minutes later with a fresh bottle, refilled both their glasses then sat down rather heavily.

'We'll discuss this again when you're not so pissed,' she grunted.

'You sound like my mother now.'

'Yeah, well.'

They were both silent, Nicola stroking Cordelia's coat somewhat manically. The night had folded around them, the sky outshone by the lights of the houses.

'You're disappointed in me.'

'Disappointed. Exasperated. That book could be a bestseller, I know it could! It's got that quality about it – it's truthful. Young people would get it. And it'd make an amazing film. Trust me, marketed the right way and with Tom Newcomb behind it, it could make us a fortune.'

Ted was gazing into the ruby depths of his wine. 'I'm touched you feel so strongly about it.'

'I do. Because I understand it. And I recognise it.'

He raised his head and faced her. 'What do you mean, you recognise it?'

Instead of replying, she lit another cigarette.

'Nicola?'

'Okay, when I was thirteen, I was going through this really shitty time and I just … made up this little fantasy to comfort myself, that I had a real mother out there who'd been forced to give me up for adoption because she was too young and too poor to take care of me. But later, she went in search of me and I was just waiting for the day she'd find me. I even had a name for her – Gina. Gina Carson.

I'd been reading about Kit Carson, the hero of the Old West, and I liked the name – it was tough. Edgy. Then my mother had to go and shatter even that little illusion by describing, in graphic detail, how giving birth to me had nearly killed her – like that was my fault as well. But Gina was so real … for a while … that I understand.'

Ted thought about her words. 'Like Kim's journey. Only in reverse.'

'Yeah, like Kim's journey. Except that Kim's mother let her down. Gina was never going to let me down.'

'By killing herself, you mean?'

'Suicide's the most selfish thing when someone loves you.'

They both lapsed into silence.

'Oh, fuck it,' she suddenly snapped, tossing the cat from her lap and standing up. 'I'm going to bed.'

*

Ted could not sleep that night. He lay on his back, gazing at the faint fan of light from the streetlamp across the ceiling, thinking about Nicola and about Julie and about Kim and about Gina, fact and fiction and fantasy interweaving inside his fevered brain. A wind was rustling the leaves and branches, and, as it rose and fell, it was hard to distinguish, at certain moments, from the murmur of the city. Then he caught snatches of something else, something he could not make out. At first it sounded like a voice, like someone calling from a vast distance, the wind carrying away parts of their sentences, making them incoherent. But then he realised that what he could hear was crying.

Now wide awake and stone-cold sober, he propped himself on one elbow and listened intently. He got up, put on his bathrobe and stepped out into the corridor, her muffled sobbing now clearly audible. He moved the few steps to her door – his bare feet making no sound on the carpet – raised a hand to knock, then dropped it to the handle, turned it slowly and pushed it open.

Chapter Five

FORWARD FIVE YEARS TO 2007

Dominic's mobile rang just after one in the morning, waking him from a deep sleep. A robotic hand reached out and groped round the surface of the bedside table, located it and dragged it to his ear.

'Hello?'

Katie had also been woken and was now looking anxiously at her boyfriend, fearing it might be an emergency.

'Yes ... yes,' he murmured, hauling himself into a sitting position. Suddenly he was wide awake. 'That's fantastic, Hank! I'll look forward to it. Thanks for letting me know.'

He ended the call, puffed out a breath and sank back among the pillows.

'*Well?*'

'I've got it. I've got the job.'

*

The Dragon's Head, despite Darren's gloomy prediction, had survived. Darren himself had moved on to become an agent with Coleridge Brown and Dominic had taken his position. A pale, nervy English graduate called Naomi was now his protégée as he had once been Darren's, and Dominic, remembering what it had been like, was especially kind to her. Sonia – feisty as ever – still ruled from her desk by the entrance and Alistair still spent most of the day shut up in his office. Dominic had made no further attempt to write a novel.

He spent the last afternoon of his employment clearing out his desk. It was a poignant task. Every object was pregnant with memories – book fair catalogues, publicity material for works whose birth he'd attended as midwife, a tray full of correspondence (mostly cleared), his chipped blue mug stuffed with biros, pens and pencils, the little china tray where resided a jumble of paperclips, pencil sharpeners, coins, an eraser, an ageing pot of Tippex, some elastic bands. He even found, buried in the bottom of his bottom drawer, an envelope containing a cover letter and some sample chapters of a novel. 'Oh my God,' he muttered, drawing them out and glancing at the title page, and the memory of the most inglorious moment of his career came flooding back.

He read the first page. He stretched back in his chair and read the second. He found himself chuckling. This was the first time he had actually read this manuscript since, back then, he had been too ashamed to open it. And there was no doubt about it, it was good – it was *bloody* good. As an older, wiser man he felt more acutely than ever his guilt at allowing this novel to be passed over. The only grain of comfort was that work of this quality would be bound to have found a home elsewhere, although he had to admit, in spite of being pretty *au fait* with the literary scene, that he had never seen a novel called *The Tyranny of Love* in print. As he read on, his shame intensified, but he still could not put it down. It was riveting. At the end of the chapter, he forced himself to stop and tossed the pages into the bin bag along with the envelope and cover letter as though they were contaminated. That was all in the past now. He had to move on.

At ten to five, he knocked on Alistair's door. He called out 'Come!' and Dominic entered his office for the last time.

'Well, Alistair, I'm off. I just wanted to say thank you. For everything. I've learnt everything I know about publishing from you.'

'I suppose that's a compliment,' he smiled, rising and coming around from behind his desk.

'And thanks for the recommendation. That was what clinched it for me.'

'I wouldn't have done it if I didn't think you were ready for it – and deserved it.'

He shook his hand then patted him warmly on the shoulder. 'Good luck, old fellow. I'm sorry to be losing you. Spare us a thought when you're out there living life in the fast lane. And what I said about your novel, all those years ago? Don't let it put you off your ambition to write.'

Dominic was surprised, and rather touched, that Alistair even remembered his novel. 'I won't,' he said.

He gave Naomi a farewell kiss on the check, then braced himself and gave Sonia one as well. To his relief she did not seem to object. 'Go on, piss off,' she said.

Before leaving the building, he paused in the bleak entrance hallway, remembering the very first day he had come there, more than five years earlier, for his interview. The abandoned desk and filing cabinet were still tucked in the corner against the wall, though someone had finally got around to removing the cardboard box.

As he walked through the crowded streets towards the underground, he thought of the person he had been then – at one moment gauche and anxious, at the next bubbling over with all the arrogance and optimism of youth. Then he remembered Alistair's parting words: 'Don't let what I said about your novel put you off your ambition to write.'

His route to the station led across a small public garden and he paused and sat down on a bench. The September sunshine felt warm on his face. He found he was in no hurry to return to the flat and another onslaught of frenetic excitement about their future in America. What had happened to his dream of becoming a writer? It seemed that in the process of growing up, of becoming less lonely and idealistic, more comfortable in his own skin and with the world around him, his dream had not so much been abandoned – it was nothing as dramatic as that – it had simply faded into the background. And now, here he was, heading off to the States to the job he was sure he wanted with the girl he loved. Yet, deep down, he sensed that nothing in life could be that simple, nothing could be that perfect. The smoothest of plans always snagged on the thorns of reality, yet it was that which gave life its texture and, ultimately, its meaning. And it was that which, some day, would make him sit down at his computer and write again.

II

Katie had dreamed of living in California ever since she was fourteen and, even though their departure was more than a month away, she had thrown herself wholeheartedly into the preparations. On the Monday evening after his departure from The Dragon's Head, Dominic was entering the flat with two bags of groceries when he noticed various brand-new items of clothing strewn over the chairs and sofa, including a rather dashing pair of royal blue and cream bathing shorts for him. Katie now supervised the purchase of his clothes – as well as the cutting of his hair – and he looked a lot more 'together' as a result.

'Been shopping?' he called out, rather pointlessly.

'Just a few basics,' she called back from the bedroom. 'We can't turn up in LA looking like a pair of scruffy old Brits, now can we?'

Three glossy paperbacks lay in a heap on the armchair. Dominic picked them up one by one and glanced at the titles. He loved the smell of brand new books.

'I bought those for the flight,' Katie remarked as she walked into the room.

'*Loss*,' he murmured, reading the title on one of the covers, 'by the lovely Nicola Carson.'

'I know, I can't stand her. *Bitch*. How dare anyone be a best-selling author and a film star *and* be beautiful.'

'Well, you're beautiful,' Dominic observed distantly.

'Yeah, and I reckon I could act as well as her, too, given the chance. Personally, I can't see what all the fuss is about.'

'Why did you buy her book then, if you loathe her so much?'

'Just grabbed it. It was on a three for two and I was over-parked.'

Dominic sat down on the sofa, casting a practised eye over the first page. He was curious to see if this book deserved all the hype it had received. As he read on, however, he frowned, his face forming into a grimace of disbelief. Katie looked at him in amazement. It was as though he literally could not believe his eyes.

'But ...'

'What?'

'This is that manuscript ...'

'*What*?'

'This book. I was reading it in manuscript form just a few days ago. At least, a sample. It's been sitting in my bottom drawer for the past five years. It's *identical* – word for word. This wasn't written by Nicola Carson. It wasn't even written by a woman – it was written by a man called Edward Haymer.'

'Well ... maybe she submitted it under a pseudonym.'

'Of course she didn't. Why would a gorgeous and highly marketable girl in her twenties pretend to be a man?'

'Maybe he was short of cash and sold her the manuscript.'

'Or maybe she stole it. Whatever happened, this novel's *plagiarised*. And it won the Connaught, for Christ's sake. You can't win a major literary prize with a book that's been written by someone else.'

Dominic gazed at the text in silence as the full implication of what he had discovered began to sink in.

'Nicola Carson was the youngest Connaught winner ever. And she never wrote another word. Instead she became one of the hottest stars on the planet – on the strength of this novel. A novel she didn't write. And I could be the only person in the entire world who knows it. Jesus, this is ... *unbelievable*.'

Katie was growing alarmed. She didn't want Dominic getting excited about anything but their departure for America.

'Well, the guy who wrote it must know.'

'He may not. It's under a different title. A lot of writers don't have time to read other authors' work – they're too busy with their own. And if he'd noticed, he would have protested when it first appeared. Oh shit, I've just thought of something. I threw that manuscript away – the only proof I had. I put the bags in the skip myself. And the rubbish got collected last Friday. *Shhhh-it*.'

'Well, that's that then,' Katie pronounced with satisfaction. 'End of story.'

'Maybe if I phoned the council I could find out where they've taken it.'

'Oh, come *on*. It'll be in some landfill in Essex by now. What are you going to do, search through every bag? It'd take you the rest of your life. If they haven't already buried it.'

'*Fuck.*'

Dominic was distracted for the rest of the evening. He barely spoke to Katie, who grew increasingly disgruntled as she wanted to curl up on the sofa with her boyfriend and a glass of Chardonnay and watch a DVD entitled *Practical Advice for Green Card Applicants*. In the hope of shaking him out of his new obsession, she proposed eating out. 'I can't be arsed to cook.'

He did not respond. She repeated her suggestion, more assertively.

'Sorry?'

'I said, let's eat out. I can't be bothered to cook.'

'Oh. Right,' he mumbled, not having heard a word.

'Dominic!'

'I need to track down this Edward Haymer. That's the only way to find out how this happened.'

Katie was losing patience. 'Dominic, we're emigrating in a month's time! We've got a million things to do before then! We haven't got time to go chasing around the countryside after unknown authors!'

'Look, sweetheart, I don't think you quite grasp what's happening here. This is *Nicola Carson* we're talking about – best-selling author and megastar Nicola Carson – with Oscars and BAFTAs and Golden Globes coming out of her ears. If she comes crashing down it could be the biggest thing since ... well, the biggest thing ever.'

'Oh, for Christ's sake, she's not *that* big. In a couple of years someone else will've come along and everyone will've forgotten about her.'

'All the more reason to strike while the iron's hot. Imagine the embarrassment to the Connaught people. And her publisher. They'll have to pulp every copy. It'll cost them millions. She'll be a laughing stock. And *I'll* be the one to make it happen.'

Katie was staring at him. 'This is revealing a side of your character that I'm not sure I like very much.'

'I thought you said you couldn't stand her.'

'I can't, but I'm not foaming at the mouth about it.'

'Okay, okay, I'm sorry. The fact is, I don't give a shit about Nicola Carson one way or the other – it's just my career I care about. This could be the break I've been waiting for all my life. I could write a piece for one of the national dailies and get interviewed on telly – "The man who exposed Nicola Carson" – then follow it up with a book and make my name as an author. *Jesus,* talk about a USP.'

'I thought the job in the States was the break you'd been waiting for all your life.'

'Babe, it's just a job. A more glamorous setting, a bit more money, but basically more of the same.'

'I'm sorry you feel that way,' she murmured, looking away and blinking.

Dominic turned her towards him and looked her in the eyes. 'Sweetheart, I'm sorry. I'm looking forward to going to the States. I'm looking forward to going to the States with *you.* But this story's dynamite.'

'You're talking like you're some sort of hack journalist,' she retorted, releasing herself. 'But you're not. You're a publisher.'

'I'm a writer, Katie. That's all I've ever wanted to be. That's the only reason I went into publishing. And I want to write serious novels, not moronic crap about celebrities. But you can't imagine how hard it is to break in nowadays – it's like acting or anything else. Once I've published, once I've got my name out there, I can write the sort of books I want to write. Just give me a couple of weeks. If the worst comes to the worst, we can say we've got family problems and ask them to keep the job on hold for a bit. I'm sure it can't make any difference.'

'Dominic, get real. They're six thousand miles away in a foreign country. If they think you're not committed to this job, they'll give it to someone else. Besides, we've already booked our flight. And I've arranged our leaving party. There's nothing sadder than having a leaving party and then not leaving.'

'Okay, okay. We'll go as planned. You get on with the preparations. Just give me a free hand for a fortnight. That's all I ask.'

'Anyway, you say you're at the centre of this, but you've got no proof, now that you've very cleverly thrown that manuscript away. And even that could have been forged.'

'Why would anyone want to forge something like that?'

'For the reasons you said. To bring her down. Create a scandal. People may love her but plenty of people loathe her too. They'd love nothing better than to see her wiped off the map.'

'I received that manuscript five *years* ago. No one had heard of her then.'

'But you can't *prove* you received it five years ago. You can't prove you received it at all. There's only your word it ever existed. And even if you still had it, what would it prove? You could take any one of those books I bought, type out the first fifty pages, change the title and the author's name and say "Hey, look everybody! This is a manuscript I received five years ago and just *happened* to shove in my bottom drawer instead of returning it to the author like I was meant to do. And it proves this book's plagiarised." You see how crazy it sounds?'

Dominic was silenced for a moment. 'Okay, maybe you're right. But I happen to know that manuscript *did* exist and that it wasn't forged. And I happen to know that her novel's a fake.'

Katie said nothing. She felt she had made her point.

'Look, I know it's going to be hard to prove. But I sort of ... feel I owe it to that Haymer guy to try.'

'Why?'

'Because there was a reason that manuscript was in my bottom drawer.'

'What reason?'

Dominic hesitated, reluctant to revisit the memory. 'I took the decision not to reject it. I didn't have the authority to accept it for publication, my job was just to separate the wheat from the chaff and pass anything promising on to Darren or Alistair. But I forgot. I stuck it in my drawer and just forgot about it. I was so *fucking* disorganised. Then, when I came across it, more than a year later, I was too embarrassed to say anything. That novel should have been published, Katie, and Edward Haymer should be an established novelist by now. And it's my fault he isn't.'

She considered his words. 'Well, you shouldn't feel badly about it. These things happen.'

'They shouldn't happen, not when a man's career's at stake. And I've never forgiven myself. I've pushed it to the back of my mind but I've never forgotten about it. It's only once in a lifetime that a real gem like that turns up – and if I'd been responsible for discovering Edward Haymer, my career in publishing wouldn't have been entirely wasted.'

'Everyone makes mistakes when they're starting out in a job. And he must have sent it to other publishers. Plenty of other editors must have rejected it too or he'd be famous, wouldn't he?'

'Yes but Alistair's one of a dying breed. He's still prepared to take a chance with a novel if it's really good, whoever the author. He isn't ruled by ad-men and accountants with profit margins and financial targets. He only cares about quality. And The Dragon's Head's been teetering on the brink of ruin as a result.'

Katie closed her eyes as she heaved a sigh, then opened them again. 'Look, just take your fortnight and do what you can in that time.'

'Really?'

'Yes, really. After all, if you expose Nicola Carson and turn this guy into a star, it won't do our reputations in the States any harm, will it?'

'Thanks hun,' he murmured, sliding his arms around her waist. 'Thanks for being so understanding. I love you.'

'I love you too.'

*

Dominic couldn't sleep. He had gone to bed with Katie as usual, had lain awake gazing at the ceiling and, as soon as she was slumbering soundly – no doubt dreaming of California – he got up and made for his laptop in the living room. He was in turmoil. At one moment he was giddy with excitement about the story he had unearthed, at the next he was recalling Katie's prophetic words. With or without the manuscript, how the hell *was* he going to prove what he knew to be true? He sighed with despair, feeling his scoop already slipping away from him.

No. He mustn't go there. He had to keep calm, think clearly, logically. He cast his mind back to the manuscript he had seen a few days earlier, straining to recall something –anything – about its author. He tried to picture the address on the envelope and on the cover letter. All he could remember was that it was in Sussex.

As his computer was loading, he contemplated the copy of *Loss* he held in his hands. He turned it over and reread the snippets on the back:

'This is the voice of the new millennium – fresh, youthful, sexy, terrifying.' *The Guardian.*

'Carson doesn't so much use language as take a Kalashnikov to it. The effect is horrifying at first, but when the tatters have floated back to earth, we are left with something almost unbearably beautiful.' *The Independent.*

'Read this novel if you dare – but don't expect your life to be the same again.' *The Observer.*

He scoured Google yet again. There were a number of references to a Nathaniel Haymer who had farmed in the Appalachian Mountains and sired seventeen children but there was no sign of an 'Edward' or even an 'Ed' or 'Ted' Haymer anywhere. The only reference to a Haymer in the UK was to an Anne Haymer, who was a partner in a small firm of solicitors in Eastbourne and was involved in the case of a young single mother who was being systematically beaten up by her boyfriend. At least Eastbourne was in Sussex. It was a long shot, but it was worth a try.

At nine the next morning – when Katie was at work – he made for the telephone. Bracing himself, he tried to summon up the character traits of an investigative journalist – pushiness, tenacity, unscrupulousness. He snatched up the receiver.

Anne Haymer was unavailable. Could he call back in an hour?

When he finally got to speak to her, he began, hesitantly, 'I'm really sorry to bother you, but I'm trying to track down someone called Edward Haymer. It's rather an unusual name. I wondered if you might possibly ...'

'Who am I speaking to?' she asked in a clipped tone.

Dominic panicked, realising he had rehearsed only questions, not answers. 'I'm in publishing and I've come across a piece of information which I think Mr. Haymer should know. It concerns a novel he once wrote called *The Tyranny of Love*.'

The line went silent and he sensed that the title had struck a chord.

'You say you're in publishing. Are you a publisher yourself?'

'Well no, not exactly. I work for a firm called The Dragon's Head – or, I did, until very recently.'

Another silence.

'My husband is the Edward Haymer you're looking for. But we're separated.'

'Oh, fantastic. I mean ... no, I'm sorry, I didn't mean ...'

'It's all right, I know what you meant. I mention it only because communication between us is sporadic and rather difficult, to say the least. I could give you his mobile number, I suppose, but his battery will probably be flat.'

'Maybe if I could have an address? I might go and talk to him in person. I quite fancy a trip out of London.'

'Well, I wish you luck. Have you got a pen?'

III

Despite her concession, Katie had not ceased to voice her opinion, at every opportunity, that the whole thing was insane. And, as the rhythmic swish and thud of the wipers lulled him deeper and deeper into thought, Dominic began to wonder, for the first time, if she was right. But then, Katie only knew half the truth.

He spotted the sign to Wemborne-on-Sea and his heartbeat quickened as he slid the car into the filter lane and reached for the instructions Anne Haymer had given him. They led him over miles of rolling farmland under a featureless sky, past camp sites and caravan parks and into a windswept hinterland of swamp and shingle, dotted by shabby farmsteads surrounded by rusty cars, a few sheep and shaggy ponies and tatty, stranded boats. Vast, angular slabs of concrete lay at random – some half-submerged in ponds and ditches – and mechanical shovels swung back and forth on the skyline, like dinosaurs engaged in some bizarre mating ritual.

Since Anne Haymer was a solicitor based in Eastbourne, Dominic had been surprised to learn that her husband lived in a caravan. He had assumed it would be quite a smart caravan, maybe with a name and some window boxes – even a quaint little garden enclosed by a quaint little fence. But as he advanced along the lane over Whitesands Marsh – as this wilderness was called – weaving around the worst of the puddles and potholes, he could see nothing remotely quaint anywhere. 'I believe he's somewhere near the pumping station,' she had said. Well, there was the pumping station but, as far as he could tell, that was all there was – apart from some very depressed-looking sheep. He pulled the car into a bay by a gateway, clambered out and gazed around. At least it had stopped raining, for the moment.

He cast his eyes back and forth over the landscape, finally spotting a shabby protuberance which could have been the corner of a caravan, poking out from behind a clump of bushes. Then he glanced down at the tan leather Clarks he had selected for the occasion – his smartest and most comfortable shoes – and there flashed through his mind some advice his father had once given him: 'Never go into the countryside without taking wellies, my son. Even in summer. You never know.' He wished now that he had heeded his Dad's advice but then he reminded himself of the importance of this mission, of how – if all went well – it would divest him of the burden he had carried all these years and open up new horizons both to him and to Edward Haymer. If he pulled this off, he could have as many pairs of shoes as Imelda Marcos and he knew that to be deterred by a bit of mud was absurd. So he dragged open the collapsing iron gate and picked his way as best he could along the soggy track.

The caravan was even worse than he had feared. No window-boxes, no picket fence, and it certainly didn't warrant a name. It was nothing more than a large pea-green box with one wide window at the front and two smaller ones at the side. Its paint was peeling and gleaming lichen lined the window-seals. He could barely imagine a tramp living in such a place, let alone a writer.

He braced himself and knocked. No reply. He knocked again, a little harder. Still no reply.

Turning, he surveyed the desolation all around him, its sombre horizons broken only by a line of pylons far in the distance. There was no sign of life anywhere – just a low, grey farmhouse standing among some trees about half a mile away – and the only sounds were the hiss of wind in the reeds and the intermittent cry of gulls.

He walked around to the front and peered through the window, using his hands as blinkers. His first impression was that the place was full of books – mostly old hardbacks which had long since lost their jackets – the sort of books his Grandma had owned by the truckload, which smell of mould and whose authors no one has ever heard of. They were crammed into shelves, piled on the sideboard, on the seats, even on the floor. A flimsy integral table between two bench seats seemed to serve as a desk, with an old portable typewriter marooned in a sea of paper and notebooks, along with a mug and an empty wineglass. Deeper in the gloom, he could just make out some sheet music spread on a music stand, but no discernible instrument to play it with.

Confident now that no one was home, he ventured around the back where the meagre accommodation had been extended into a kind of encampment. A crude brick barbecue stood before a picnic table and a tatty canvas chair. A red gas cylinder, plumbed into the caravan's innards, clearly provided the only power. A green, plastic box for garden tools, its lid padlocked, overlooked a vegetable patch. He noticed the rotting relics of leeks and cabbages among the weeds, but one small patch in the farthest corner looked clean and freshly dug, as though it were being prepared for sowing.

'You looking for Ted?'

Dominic nearly jumped out of his skin. Where the man had appeared from he had no idea, but there he was, about thirty yards away on the far side of a ditch, watching him – a squat figure clad from head to toe in waterproofs, a shotgun under his arm and a spaniel poised at his heel.

'Yes I am!' he called back, with some difficulty, since, as a town-dweller, he was not good at projecting his voice. 'Do you happen to know where I might find him?'

'He'll be at The Queen's!' the man called back with absolute certainty, 'The Queen's Head at Wemborne!' Then he gave him directions – proving that he was not too hostile after all, despite the twin barrels dangling from his arm.

'Could you give me some idea of what he looks like – so I can pick him out? I've never actually met him.'

'He's an ugly sod. Grey hair and a beard. You can't miss him.'

Dominic thanked him and squelched back to the car, grateful to be heading somewhere warm and dry, with alcohol.

Having repaired the worst of the damage to his shoes with a rag he kept for the windscreen, he set off and, ten minutes later, found The Queen's Head.

It was raining again and he sat in the car for a while, listening to the drone of the wind and watching the raindrops quivering on the windscreen. What would he be like, the man who lived in that caravan? For his brief visit to the place had affected him deeply – it had spoken so clearly of what could happen to an artist when deprived of success, of recognition, of hope. What had once been passion had hardened into obsession and finally despair, so that he barely noticed the world around him and the squalor into which his life had descended. Yet he was a writer, just as Dominic was, or wanted to be. Edward Haymer, once upon a time, must have been as he was now – a young man on the brink of his career. How many years of disappointment and rejection had led up to the day he had sent those sample chapters of his novel to The Dragon's Head, the one brave little independent publisher that might have been his salvation? The chapters which had landed on his desk?

Katie was right. He ought to start the car and head straight back to London this very minute, forget about Edward Haymer and focus on their future in the States. But he couldn't. After all these years he had to confront this man. He had to get this over with.

He left the car and hurried through the rain to the entrance, bowing his head under the lintel. Suddenly he was surrounded by warmth, chatter and the smell of beer and cooking. The barman greeted him cheerily and he decided to forgo his usual pint of Fosters and order a brandy instead. He couldn't afford it but he needed something to warm him up and to give him courage.

Installed in a corner from which he could survey most of the saloon and public bars, it occurred to him that, in other circumstances, this would be rather a pleasant place to spend time. It was simple, old-fashioned, unpretentious. There was no piped music, no Sky Sports on television, no bleeping gaming machines, not even a snooker table. Beyond a wide arch a bunch of locals – all men – were clustered around the public bar – looking like locals clustered round bars throughout the world – but none of them conformed to the man on the marsh's description. Here, beneath the beamy ceiling of the saloon – from which hung a colourful assortment of hops and floats and fishing nets – a scattering of middle-aged couples were tucking contentedly into lemon sole or rhubarb crumble or were deep in discussion about the menu, warmed by a pile of glowing logs in the inglenook.

The inglenook formed a barrier between the bars, and it was in an alcove beside it that a man sat alone with his pint, some papers spread before him on the little table. He seemed oblivious to the noise and bustle around him and had the calm, proprietorial air of a regular installed in his favourite seat. Though scruffy, bearded and weather-beaten, with wavy, silvery hair, it was not just his outward appearance which suggested to Dominic that this man was Edward Haymer. It was a more intangible quality, an aura which seemed to say firmly to the world around him, 'Piss off. I'm a writer. And I want to be left in peace.'

He observed him for a while, growing ever more certain. Then he drained his brandy, stood up and crossed the room. Pausing a moment, he looked down at the object of his journey.

'Mr Haymer?'

The man raised his eyes from his papers, frowning as though it were an effort to focus on the newcomer. 'Yes.'

'My name's Dominic. Dominic Seeley. I work in publishing and I've come down from London to give you a piece of information which you may or may not already know.'

His announcement was greeted by a blank stare.

'I'm sorry, do you mind if I sit down?'

The almost imperceptible shrug seemed neither to grant nor withhold permission. Nonetheless, it was enough to embolden Dominic to lower his lengthy frame into the seat nearest the fire, its proximity to the table forcing him to sit sideways with his knees pressed together. Instantly, he felt too hot in his leather jacket but refrained from removing it, sensing this man might resent him getting too comfortable.

'So, what's this information which I may or may not already know?'

'It concerns an actress and writer named Nicola Carson. You may have heard of her.'

The eyes narrowed and the forehead gathered into furrows but he said nothing.

'Her novel *Loss* won the Connaught Prize in 2003,' Dominic persevered. 'There was some controversy over it.'

The man gazed at him for so long that Dominic wondered if he had somehow failed to understand him. Then he said, 'I may be a bit of a hermit, young man, but I don't live on Mars. Of course I've heard of Nicola Carson. What about her?'

'Well, I have reason to believe – and you may think I'm completely insane here – but I have reason to believe ... that she's a fraud.'

The steely blue eyes belied the air of vague indifference the man was assuming. 'What do you mean, a fraud?'

'That novel of hers – the one which launched her career. She didn't write it. It was written by someone else.'

Edward Haymer raised his eyebrows. 'Really? Well, that's an interesting theory. But why are you telling *me* all this?'

'Because that someone else was you.'

Life continued in the bar – chatter, laughter, the clink of knives and forks and glasses – but to Dominic it was as though the place had gone silent, as though it were being shown on a screen from which the sound had been cut.

'What are you talking about?'

'It was your novel, Mr Haymer – the one you sent some sample chapters of to The Dragon's Head more than five years ago, under the title *The Tyranny of Love*. She must have somehow got hold of the manuscript and published it under her own name. She changed the title, of course, but that's all she changed. But if you haven't seen it – which you clearly haven't – you wouldn't know that.'

The man stared at him for what must have been a full five seconds, eyes almost closed, the furrows in his forehead deepening. It was as though he were trying to perform some complex piece of mental arithmetic.

'Let me get this straight. You're telling me that some famous film star stole *my* manuscript and published it under her own name? And it became a bestseller?'

'Well, she wouldn't have been famous then. It was your novel that made her famous – or, at least, kick-started the process.'

The man was shaking his head, frowning. 'Are you *sure*?'

'Well, I'm almost one hundred per cent sure that the first three chapters of her novel are identical to the chapters you sent us. So I'm assuming the rest is identical too. But that's something you could easily verify. I've brought a copy ...'

'And how do you know all this?'

'I was an assistant editor at the time. Your manuscript passed through my hands.'

'You can remember a manuscript that passed through your hands *five years* ago?'

'Well, I have to be honest, there was a bit of a cock-up in the office and it was never returned to you.'

'I know. I remember.'

'Then … somebody found it. Recently. A colleague.'

'I see. So you're saying that *my novel* – which you rejected and subsequently lost – won a major literary prize?'

'Well, yes. The Connaught. It's …'

'I know what it is. What I want to know is, what the fuck's going on.'

'Well, I … I don't know. That's why I've come to see you.'

The man took a deep, trembling breath. Mystification was turning into anger.

'To be fair, Mr Haymer, it couldn't have been our fault. The plagiarism, I mean. All we had was a sample.'

'Yes, but, if it turned out to be such a great novel, why didn't you publish it in the first place?'

'I don't know.'

The older man shook his head slowly and closed his fingers around his glass, his gaze now transferred from Dominic to his drink. 'I never even liked that book,' he chuckled grimly. 'It was my first novel and I was convinced it was a masterpiece. But as time went by I became more and more doubtful about it. The style was too clever-clever, too self-conscious. And it had structural flaws. In the end I gave up submitting it.'

'Well, the public clearly didn't agree with you. It made her a fortune.'

'Yeah, but her film star looks would've had a lot to do with it. If I'd published it under my name with my ugly mug on the back, it would've been a different story.'

'It should have been published under your name, Mr Haymer.'

He took a thoughtful draught of beer. 'Yeah, well, you should've told that to your boss, shouldn't you?'

'My boss?'

'Alistair Milner. The bastard who wrote me that letter.'

'I … I did,' said Dominic, his voice quavering.

He looked up at him. 'And he ignored you?'

Dominic felt trapped, a feeling intensified by the confines of the tiny table and his proximity to the scalding chimney-breast. 'I was just an editorial assistant at the time. I'd only been in the job a few months.'

Edward Haymer drained his drink. 'So, what's he like? Milner.'

'He's a good bloke. Volatile. Eccentric. Passionate about publishing. Not always easy to work for but I grew very fond of him.'

His words were met with a cynical grunt.

'I'm so sorry your book wasn't accepted, Mr Haymer. It should've been. If there's … anything at all I can do …'

'You can start by getting me another drink.'

Dominic was only too glad to be able to unfurl himself and take a break from the heat and that penetrating stare. 'Sure,' he said, sliding out of his seat. 'Same again?'

'No, a brandy. And after what you've just told me, you'd better make it a double.'

On his way to the bar, Dominic sneaked a glance inside his wallet. Five minutes later he returned with the brandy and a coke for himself but, before sitting down, he whipped off the Armani jacket Katie had found on eBay as part of her campaign to turn him, as she put it, 'into a human being'. He was past caring what Edward Haymer thought.

'By the way,' he said, 'the barman told me to tell you there's another parcel for you.'

He suddenly looked awkward. 'Oh. Right. Thank you. I'm afraid I live in the middle of nowhere and use this place as a post office.'

Dominic wondered, fleetingly, whether he was in the habit of ordering something to wile away the lonely nights in his caravan – something which tended to arrive in unmarked parcels.

Haymer took a sip of brandy. 'So what are you planning to do with this information you've uncovered?'

'I want to put things right. I want the true authorship of that novel to be established and I want you to get the credit for it that you deserve.'

'Well, that's very big of you. But why?'

'*Why?*'

'Yes. Why? You don't know me. Why should you care?'

'Because I feel partly responsible for what happened ...'

'I thought you said it was nothing to do with you.'

'No, I mean ... on behalf of The Dragon's Head. And, to be honest, it would give me the greatest pleasure to get one over on someone like Nicola Carson. To me she represents everything that's wrong with publishing today.'

'What do you mean?'

'Well, she's eye candy, isn't she?'

'Which I'm not?'

It took him a moment to realise the man was actually making a joke. 'What I mean is, it's all about packaging, isn't it? Look at the rubbish they foist on you in bookshops nowadays – footballers, film stars, celebrity chefs. And they're not content with writing their boring autobiographies, they all want to write novels now for which they get six figure advances before their ghost-writer's even switched on their laptop. And even so-called "literary" writing's just the same old names churning out the same old same old. What the industry needs is a shower bath of fresh, original talent – like yours.'

This time Edward Haymer not only smiled, he laughed. Dominic felt he was finally breaking through the ice. Unless it was the brandy.

'I do agree with a lot of what you say. It used to make me angry too. Now I just don't care.'

'Well, I care.'

'You're still going to have to convince the rest of the world, though, which won't be easy. Film companies must invest millions in her and they're not going to stand politely by and watch you destroy her credibility.'

'No, but if I can prove she plagiarised your work, there won't be much they can do about it.'

'And how do you propose to do that?'

'I ... don't know." he responded lamely. 'I was hoping you might have some ideas.'

'Well, I'm sorry to disappoint you, but I don't even have the computer I wrote it on anymore.'

'You didn't back up the file somewhere else? On another computer, maybe, or a memory stick?'

'You probably think I'm very irresponsible and my wife would agree with you. But I'm a different generation to you. I was brought up with typewriters – good old-fashioned typewriters with ribbons in. To me a manuscript isn't a manuscript until you can hold it in your hands. I don't even have a computer anymore, since I don't have electricity.'

'Well, there is circumstantial evidence.'

'I don't think that'll cut much ice with those red hot lawyers she's going to throw at you,' he laughed.

'But that novel's a major piece of work. Surely no one can seriously believe it was written by a twenty-three-year-old girl – or however old she was at the time?'

'They believed it enough to give her a prize, according to you.'

'They had no reason not to believe it. But if you look at it again in the light of this allegation it becomes glaringly obvious. That book was written from first-hand experience – your first-hand experience.'

They sank back into hopeless silence.

'And you've no idea at all how she got her hands on your manuscript?'

He shook his head. 'Have you still got those sample chapters I sent you?'

'No, stupidly I threw them away. I didn't realise their significance until afterwards.'

'Just like I threw away that computer. If only we could see into the future, eh?'

The conversation lapsed again, but there was something else Dominic had to say to this man – something he still could not bring himself to say, even though relations between them seemed to have risen a few degrees above arctic.

'I understand your wife's a solicitor,' he said instead.

He looked up at him in astonishment. 'How the hell did you know that?'

He told him about the listing on Google and the phone call to her office. 'That's how I found you.'

'My God, you have been busy. And did you tell her about this?'

'No, I thought I should speak to you first. But her testimony would carry a lot of weight, surely?'

'My wife hates me. We're separated.'

'I'm sorry. But does she hate your writing as well?'

He gazed down at his brandy. 'I don't know. It's hard to say how she'd react to this news.'

'Are you going to tell her?'

'I doubt it. We don't communicate these days.'

'Do you mind if I tell her?'

'Yes I do,' he retorted, looking up at him. 'If anyone's going to tell her, it'll be me. In my own time.'

'Yes, yes, of course. I'm sorry. I didn't mean to ...'

'Have you got a number I can reach you on?'

He sensed this was his cue to leave. Edward Haymer had had enough of him. But he couldn't leave – not without saying what he had really come to say. The whole journey would have been wasted if he left now. He fished out his wallet, extracted a Dragon's Head business card and handed it to him. 'My mobile number's on there,' he said.

'Look, why are you really doing this? Are you a journalist?'

'No! No, I'm just a lowly editor in a publishing house. Or I was. I just want to see justice done.'

He was staring at Dominic again, as though deciding whether to buy his account of his motives. 'Well, that's up to you. As for me, I want nothing to do with it. I've decided. As I said, I didn't like that book and I'm quite happy with my life just the way it is. I'm working on stuff I'm satisfied with and one day – who knows? – someone might deign to publish it. I don't want to get caught up in some high-profile scandal that could backfire on me and cost me millions in damages. Mainly because I haven't got millions.'

'You mean, you're just going to let her get away with it?'

'I don't have any choice.'

'Well, I'm sorry,' said Dominic, 'but I don't think that's right. You wrote that book. When people praise it, they should be praising you.'

'I don't care about praise.'

Yeah *right,* he thought. You're a writer – you thirst for praise the way a dying man in the desert thirsts for water. 'I'd like to go on pursuing it, anyway. With your permission, of course.'

'You don't need my permission. You're free to do as you please.'

'Just the same, I'd rather do it with your blessing.'

He sighed with impatience, as though he'd reached the point where he'd say anything to get rid of him. 'Okay, you can have my blessing. But that's all you're having.'

Dominic's eyes lingered a moment on the man across the little table from him. 'Mr Haymer, there is something else I have to tell you ...'

'Not another earth-shattering revelation?'

He caught an expression on the bearded face which, inexplicably, looked close to hatred. All of a sudden, he needed the meeting to end too.

'No, it's nothing. Forget it. I have to go.' And the next moment he was on his feet, holding out his hand. Edward Haymer, looking rather surprised, shook it.

Outside in the chill, damp air, Dominic felt he was going to throw up. He grabbed the little wooden gate at the entrance to the car park, bent over and took a few deep breaths until he felt better. Then he straightened up and walked unsteadily back to his car.

*

'So did you find him?'

'Yes, I did.'

'And did he know?'

'No, he didn't. Or, at least, he said he didn't. But there was something very weird about his reaction. I expected him to be grateful but he was so *defensive.*'

'It must have come as quite a shock.'

'I suppose so.'

'And what happened to your shoes?'

He knew she would notice his shoes, the purchase of which she had also supervised. 'It's a long story,' he said.

IV

In the days following his trip to Wemborne, Dominic felt acutely frustrated, not knowing how to move things forward. He was determined not to waste what little time Katie had allotted him and so spent it going through *Loss* yet again, underlining sentences and passages and making notes in the margin. And the more he did so, the more he was convinced that no sane person could believe this novel had been written by someone born in 1979. A world had been created – the world of Wimpy Bars and bubble cars and the threat of nuclear war, the world which had ended long before she had drawn a breath. It could be argued (and no doubt would be, by Nicola Carson's lawyers) that these details could have been researched or obtained from an older relative but, having read hundreds of manuscripts, he could always pick up on received material. It never lay quite comfortably into the grain of the work, however good the writing. And there was something about the way this author wove a bleak and unique poetry from that forgotten age which convinced him that he (there was no question now that it was a 'he') had felt, not been told, what it had been like to live through those years.

On the evening of the third day, his mobile rang.

'Is that Mr. Seeley? Dominic?' said a male voice he didn't recognise.

'Speaking.'

'Yes. Hello. It's Ted. Ted Haymer. You came to see me the other day.'

Dominic's spirits instantly revived. 'Mr Haymer. Hi.'

'Yes. Hello. I just wanted to … well, to apologise really. I think I may have been a bit brusque with you when we met. It was just the shock of being told that extraordinary news. But it was good of you to come all the way down here to put me in the picture. And if you're still determined to pursue the matter … the thing is, neither I nor my family can be involved in a lawsuit. We can't be the plaintiffs is what I'm saying. As you know, my wife and I are separated but we have children and grandchildren we have to consider. We can't take the risk.'

'No. Okay. I understand.'

'I mean, if Nicola Carson decides to sue someone for defamation of character or whatever, then you and I have never met.'

'Right.'

'But unofficially, I'll give you whatever help I can. Though, like I said, I'm not sure it'll be much.'

'I'm glad you feel that way.'

'I still think it's going to be an uphill struggle, though.'

'It will be. But it'll be worth it.'

'I hope you're right.'

Dominic hesitated. 'So, about your wife. Even if you're not the plaintiff, she could still testify and she could prove a tremendous asset.'

The line went quiet for a while. 'I really don't want to involve her.'

Dominic sighed inwardly. 'Mr Haymer, I don't mean to be presumptuous. I don't know your wife, I've only spoken to her on the phone, but I'm guessing she's a highly intelligent woman.'

'She certainly is.'

'I can't imagine that she doesn't respect your writing, then.'

'To do her justice, she always has.'

'So her testimony would carry a lot of weight. It might even swing it.'

His words were met with silence.

'One thing I've learnt in publishing,' he battled on, 'is that it's a cut-throat business and becoming more so by the day. And there's a lot more to it than just good writing. If we won this case you'd become famous overnight – you wouldn't just be any old published author, you'd be the author whose work was plagiarised by Nicola Carson. You'd be riding on the back of her fame and it could turn out to be the biggest career opportunity you could have hoped for. So we need to give it everything we've got.'

Another silence.

'I can't be the one to tell her,' he said at last. 'Maybe, if you could tell her? If you wouldn't mind ...'

'Okay.'

'But I don't want her to feel coerced in any way. Just inform her of the facts, like you did me, and see how she reacts. I want her to be free to make her own decision as to whether she supports me or not. If she wants to have nothing to do with it, then leave it. Don't try to persuade her.'

'I'll phone her. See if I can arrange a meeting.'

*

Dominic's second conversation with Anne Haymer proved even more awkward than the first.

'I went to see your husband,' he said, after the initial exchange of pleasantries, 'and there's something very important I have to tell you concerning him.'

'Can't he tell me himself, whatever it is?'

'No, he ... he said he'd prefer it if I told you.'

A pause.

'Look, Mr Seeley, I'm finding this all very mysterious. What exactly is your connection with my husband?'

'I'd really much rather we discussed it face to face. You just name the place – I'll come to you. It really is very important, Mrs Haymer.'

Another pause.

'I don't like discussing private matters in my office. There's a café called Gooseberries a few doors down the road where I sometimes go for lunch. I could meet you there tomorrow, at eleven. I'll give you directions.'

*

Gooseberries – when he finally found it – was bland and functional, the sort of place which aspires to nothing more than making an adequate living serving shoppers and workers on their breaks. Dominic paused in the entrance to compose himself. Only four tables were occupied and it was easy to spot Anne Haymer since she was the only customer sitting alone. She looked up from her paper as he approached.

'Mrs Haymer? I'm so sorry I'm late. I got stuck in a traffic jam on the M25.'

'They happen,' she remarked with little sympathy as they shook hands.

'Can I get you anything?'

'No, I'm fine, thank you.'

Dominic was too overwrought to order anything for himself. He sat down opposite her and cast a few nervous glances around the room, smiling as his eyes alighted, briefly, on her face. She was much prettier than in the headshot on her firm's website, with her silver-blonde hair neatly cut and just a judicious touch of jewellery and makeup. He was not surprised that she and her husband had split up – he could not imagine how they had got together in the first place.

'I do appreciate your seeing me,' he began. 'I wasn't sure if you had any idea what it was about.'

'I have absolutely no idea what it's about. But I haven't got long, I'm afraid. I'm seeing a client in twenty minutes.'

'I'll get straight to the point then.'

So he did. And although he was imparting the same information as he had to her estranged husband, her reaction was entirely different. She didn't look mystified, she looked annoyed.

'There must be some mistake,' she said.

'There's no mistake, Mrs Haymer. You only have to read Nicola Carson's book and you'll see at once it's identical – assuming you've read your husband's manuscript ...'

'Of course I've read it.'

He ducked down, extracted Katie's copy of *Loss* from a carrier bag and held it out. Her cool, angry and defensive manner vanished at the sight of it. She glanced at him, then reached out and took it in fingers that he was sure were trembling.

As she read, her eyes widened, and he heard her whisper to herself, 'So Nicola Carson's Nicola Pearson? My *God* ...'

It was now Dominic's turn to be confused. 'I'm sorry, who's Nicola Pearson?'

She did not seem to hear. She was still staring at the text. Then she murmured, 'But Nicola Carson's American.'

'No, she isn't. That's a common mistake. She's acquired an

American twang because she's lived out there and starred in American films, but she's actually as English as you or I.'

There followed another silence, then it became clear from Anne Haymer's face that something had come into focus. 'I can't believe this ...'

'Mrs Haymer, do you know her?'

'Yes, I know her. Although I've never met her. But Ted must have known.'

'He didn't seem to. He seemed as stunned by this news as you.'

A silence.

'I remember thinking, when there was all that fuss about this book, that the subject-matter sounded similar to Ted's but I never gave it another thought.'

'Mrs Haymer, if you don't mind my asking, how do you know Nicola Carson ... or Nicola Pearson?'

She hesitated. 'Look, Mr Seeley ...'

'Dominic.'

'Okay. Dominic. Much as I appreciate your coming all this way to give me this information, I don't know you from Adam and we're getting into an area I'm not at all comfortable talking about.'

But she didn't need to. Dominic had already guessed. 'It's okay, I understand. But, without wishing to pry, is it possible to ask if your husband knew her personally?'

'Yes, he did. Before she was famous, of course.'

'And may I ask how that came about?'

She hesitated again, as though trying to decide how much information to divulge. She told him about knowing her mother slightly and about Ted meeting her at his local.

'You'd think a little town like Wemborne would want to claim her as its own – put the place on the map a bit.'

'She wasn't born and raised there – her mother moved there relatively recently. And she practically disowned her. Too wild and unpredictable. She didn't fit with the county image she was trying to create for herself.'

Dominic was staring at the copy of *Loss* which she had set down beside her coffee cup, though his thoughts were miles away. What he was seeing was a whole new horizon opening up in the Nicola Carson scandal.

'So they ... became friends?'

'Mr Seeley, with all due respect I don't want to say any more on the subject. Ted and I were breaking up at the time.'

'Okay. I'm sorry.'

After a pause, she asked. 'So how do you fit into all this?'

He roused himself from an alarming mental picture of the man he had met a few days earlier *in flagrante delicto* with the girl whose bottom the readers of *Nuts* magazine had recently voted the most perfect on the planet. He told her about the loss and rediscovery of her husband's sample chapters. It was all to do with a colleague who had now left The Dragon's Head.

'It sounds as though your office was a bit of a shambles,' she said.

'It was, I'm afraid,' he laughed.

'And now you're on a mission to put things right?'

'I just feel very strongly that your husband should get the credit he deserves for his novel, and I'd like to make that happen, if I can. And I'd really appreciate your help. I wasn't sure what you're position would be.'

'My position?'

'Well, I'm aware that you and your husband ... I'm sorry, I'm putting this badly ...'

Anne Haymer seemed to soften a little. 'Look, Mr Seeley, one thing I've never denied is that my husband's a good writer – more than a good writer. I spent over thirty years of my life supporting him – in every sense of the word. After all that, I'm damned if I'm going to stand by and let that ... that *girl* take all the credit for his work. Not to mention the financial rewards.' She stopped herself. Then she said, 'So what are you proposing to do?'

'I'm not sure. Could one get the press on side? Nicola Carson's already controversial – a lot of literary snobs feel that anyone whose face has appeared on the cover of *Vogue* has no business winning the Connaught. The very idea of any Connaught Prize-winning novel being plagiarised would be a sensation, but especially hers.'

'Well, red hot though the story might be, the press wouldn't touch it with a barge pole without some proof. You do have some proof?'

In the silence that followed, the squish of the coffee machine and murmur of voices seemed amplified. 'I'm afraid not,' he said, staring at a ring on the formica table-top. 'Like an idiot I threw those sample chapters away. And your husband said he's thrown away the computer he wrote the novel on.'

'I'm afraid he's right there. It was old and painfully slow and I finally persuaded him to upgrade. He'd have hard copies, of course, but there's no way of proving they're genuine.'

'Could he have backed those files up somewhere else?'

'You'd think so, but he was hopeless and, to be honest, rather perverse about IT – and about the threat of plagiarism. I had enough trouble getting him to put the copyright symbol on his work.'

'So, assuming we can find some proof, how should we proceed?'

'Through the courts. That's what they're there for. If she stole his novel and published it, it constitutes infringement of copyright and theft of his intellectual property. Not that it would ever be tried as a crime. We'd have to go by the civil route.'

'And if we can't find any proof?'

'Then we'd be scuppered. Unless we can build such a convincing body of circumstantial evidence that it would be decided on the balance of probabilities. But that could be difficult.'

'It sounds as though you know what you're talking about.'

'Actually, I know almost nothing about IP law. But I do know someone who specialises in it. I'll talk to him. The press are bound to pick up on it anyway – she being who she is.'

Anne Haymer's involvement was making the whole thing seem far more real and possible; and a high-profile court case with him as the star witness would be fantastic publicity for his book. Then he remembered Ted's words on the phone.

'When I spoke to your husband, he said he didn't want to get involved in a lawsuit. I think he was worried that, if she won, she could be awarded colossal damages and then turn round and sue *him* for defamation of character, or whatever.'

'She'd do that anyway if we start making unsubstantiated claims in the press. The bottom line has got to be proof. Maybe I should employ a detective to find some.'

Dominic was horrified at the idea. The last thing he wanted was some detective muscling in on his territory. 'Let's hang fire on that for the moment,' he said. 'I've got a few other possibilities I'm looking into.'

Anne glanced at her watch. 'I've got to go,' she said, standing up. 'I'm going to have to give this matter some serious thought. Can I contact you?'

'Sure. Here's my card.'

*

Dominic set off back to London in a state of shock. Edward Haymer had had an *affair* with Nicola Carson. At least it explained his bizarre reaction when he had broken the news to him. Except that he hadn't broken the news to him. He had known all along – he must have done. But if that were true, why hadn't he acted sooner? Maybe, in spite of everything, he was still in love with her.

He put his foot down to overtake a juggernaut. In a way, the story was getting better and better. They now had sex as well as plagiarism. Nicola Carson had stolen the manuscript from an older man with whom she was having an affair – an affair which (judging by the hatred in Anne Haymer's eyes at the mere mention of her name) had caused the break-up of their marriage. But, as the miles rolled by, his enthusiasm became tinged with misgiving. He had taken a liking to Anne Haymer despite her defensiveness – who wouldn't have been defensive? – and he would have to consider her feelings. She wouldn't want the grief and humiliation caused by the break-up of her marriage splashed all over the newspapers and the pages of a subsequent bestseller. He was starting to feel, also, that this new development somewhat diminished Edward Haymer's charm as the innocent victim. Some readers – especially women – might hold that he, a married man in his fifties, had got exactly what he deserved. Others – especially men – might think, 'I'd give up a dozen manuscripts for a night in the sack with Nicola Carson!' He smiled to himself as he left the A22 for the M25.

When he got back to the flat, Katie was out. He was puzzled at first, then remembered she had been invited for a drink by her boss, Trevor, who was apparently pulling out all the stops to persuade her to stay, including a pay rise and a ride in his brand new Porsche. He had to admit he was rather relieved.

He had just opened a can of lager when the phone rang.

'Dominic? It's Ted. Ted Haymer.'

'Hello, Mr Haymer. I've just come from seeing your wife.'

'I know. I spoke to her, briefly. It sounds as though you've won her over.'

'I didn't do much. She seemed to be on your side from the start.'

'No, it was your charm that did the trick. If I'd suggested it, we'd have ended up having a row. So thanks. I hope it wasn't too awkward for you.'

'Not at all. But I was wondering, Mr Haymer, if we could meet again. Maybe tomorrow?'

'I'll be in the pub around one. And for God's sake stop calling me Mr Haymer. It's Ted.'

When he had ended the call, Dominic slumped down in his armchair and lit a cigarette. At least Katie wasn't there to hassle him about his smoking, which had increased markedly since he had reinvented himself as an investigative journalist. He'd have to open all the windows before she got back to dispel the evidence.

He blew out a cloud of smoke in a sigh. The fortnight she had allowed him to solve this mystery was running out fast and the great adventure that lay before them was beginning to feel more and more like deportation. If only he had a bit more time.

V

Edward – 'it's Ted' – Haymer stood up and proffered his hand as Dominic approached and this time it was he who went to buy them both a pint.

'Anne and I are going to meet,' he announced as he was settling back into his seat. 'Apparently she knows some red hot solicitor who specialises in this sort of thing and who'll be able to find us a suitable barrister. I told her I thought it sounded a bit risky but she seems determined to go ahead. I'm amazed, though. And quite touched.'

Dominic was astonished by the transformation in this man's manner. No longer surly or defensive, he seemed to be throwing himself wholeheartedly into the enterprise.

'I think you're right, though,' he responded, after an initial sip of beer. 'Going through the courts would be suicide without that computer or some other proof. And, as you said yourself, she's got a lot of money and clout behind her.'

Ted looked at him in surprise. 'You've changed your tune a bit, haven't you?'

'Not really. But meeting your wife has made me more of a realist.'

'Well Anne, bless her heart, is one of the few lawyers left who believes in justice. Once she gets the bit between her teeth, there's no stopping her.'

'Maybe she has her own reasons for that.'

Ted had raised his pint half-way to his lips. He set it down again. 'So she told you. I wondered if she would.'

'You mean, about you knowing a girl called Nicola Pearson who turned into Nicola Carson?'

'And what else did she tell you?'

'Not much.'

'Well, whatever she does tell you, take it with a pinch of salt.'

Dominic met Ted's eye for a moment, then glanced down at the table-top. 'It's just that, when we met before, I got the distinct impression you'd only heard of Nicola Carson through the media and had no idea how she got her hands on your manuscript. But, in fact, it's pretty obvious how she got her hands on it.'

Ted said nothing at first. When he spoke, it was slowly, choosing each phrase carefully, the way someone crossing a stream pauses on each stepping-stone to choose the next. 'I didn't mention it before because those few short weeks I knew her were traumatic – since they were responsible for the break-up of my marriage. I wasn't about to share that with a total stranger who comes waltzing up to me in my local without a by-your-leave. And I'm under no obligation to share it with you now. Just because you've made a mission out of this doesn't give you the right to go prying into every corner of my private life.'

'No, no, of course not. It's just …'

'Just what?'

'It's just that I can't believe that when I told you Nicola Carson had stolen your novel, you didn't already know. I mean, you had a … she was a friend of yours. She then publishes a novel, she gets into films, she becomes famous. Curiosity alone must have made you want to pick it up in Waterstones and have a look at it.'

'I never read other people's novels. I'm too busy with my own work.'

'But she wasn't just "other people", was she?'

Ted was glaring at him. 'Look, I don't have to defend myself to you. I never asked you to get involved in this. In fact, I could have the landlord throw you out for harassing one of his most lucrative customers. But I'm too civilised for that, so I'm going tell you what you want to know on condition you never mention the subject again. The Nicola Pearson I knew wasn't Nicola Carson the star, she was a young, unknown actress struggling with the world and with self-doubt. So we had a lot in common, despite the age difference, and we became friends. But it was a friendship Anne couldn't accept. When Anne and I parted, I went to live in a caravan in the middle of nowhere with no television and no internet. I used to have a radio but the batteries died and I never bothered to replace them. I don't miss it. And I don't waste what little money I have on newspapers. My life's moved on. I spend my days reading, growing vegetables, gazing at the sea. I don't even write novels anymore, I write poetry – about nature, about the universe, about the human condition. So no, I didn't know Nicola had published a novel. And even if I had, I wouldn't have cared.'

Dominic felt somewhat chastised by Haymer's speech, though he still didn't believe him. How could it have escaped his notice that someone who had been, at the very least, a close friend had written a bestseller and become a star? He may have been living in a field but – as he himself had pointed out – he wasn't living on Mars. He went into shops, he went into the pub, he talked to people.

'It must be tough,' he said.

'What must be tough?'

'Learning that someone you were fond of has turned against you like this.'

'It is.'

Dominic said, after some hesitation, 'Mr Haymer – Ted – I'm sorry if I sounded judgemental. I didn't mean to. But I'm just wondering how this new development affects our case – if we go ahead. We know she had motive and now, it seems, she had opportunity – the perfect opportunity. That should significantly improve our chances.'

Ted was not meeting his eyes. 'Look, I still haven't made up my mind about this. I'm going to have to give it more thought. If all this stuff's going to be dredged up again ...'

Dominic watched him for a while then got to his feet and held out his hand. 'I'll leave you in peace then. You've got my number. Just let me know when you decide.'

*

'I've heard from Shelby.'

'*Who?*'

'Shelby. You know – the real estate guy. He's sent written confirmation of our rent and deposit and emailed me some more photos of the apartment. It looks even better than we thought. You can even see the ocean, apparently. I mean, it's not exactly an ocean view but you can just make it out between a wall and a palm tree.'

'The ocean?' Dominic frowned. 'You mean the sea?'

'No, I mean the ocean. The Pacific Ocean ... *der*.'

'Okay. Sorry.'

'Do you want to see them?'

'Not right now. Maybe later.'

She stared at him, crestfallen. 'What's the matter now?'

'I just wasted an entire afternoon listening to a load of bullshit from Haymer. He insists he didn't know but I'm sure he's lying. And he also insists they were only friends but I know he's lying about that too.'

'Maybe he feels embarrassed.'

'Embarrassed?'

'Yeah, if she was just using him. Maybe he feels humiliated.'

He considered her words. 'I suppose so. Perhaps I'm being too judgemental. It's just so hard to make any headway with someone who lies all the time.'

'Everyone lies all the time. It's called life. Anyone who says that love makes the world go round is talking out of their arse. It's lying that makes the world go round.'

'Hey, that's not bad!' he laughed. 'I might even use it in the book. Come on then, let's have a look at these photos of yours.'

VI

Tidying the caravan, which was overladen with stuff and in which every movement was confined and constricted, was as exhausting as tidying a house. When he had more or less completed the task, Ted made himself a cup of tea and sat down for a rest.

Ever since his phone call from her, his thoughts had dwelt entirely upon Anne. If she came that afternoon it would be the first time they had been alone together since the day he parted from her in the car to take the train to Richmond. He had been back to the house to collect his stuff but she had made sure she was out.

*

She parked by the pumping station, put on her Wellington boots and trudged along the muddy path. The air was chilly, and grey, ragged clouds blew above the sea wall and along the faint horizon of violet hills. Ted had seen her coming and the caravan door opened before she knocked.

He stared at her for a moment. 'Hi.'

'Hello.'

'You're ... looking well.'

'I'd say the same about you, but I'd be lying.'

'Thanks. I've had a lot of pain in my back and shoulder. Too much digging, the doctor reckons.'

'Digging?'

'I've made myself a little veggie patch out the back but it's virgin ground and I'm having a real battle with the couch grass. I'll show you, if you like.'

'I hardly recognised you with that beard.'

'Just can't be arsed to shave in these conditions. Come in.'

She clambered into the confines of his home and looked around in dismay at the pathetic living space – made all the more so by his obvious attempt to tidy up for her. 'Well, this is ... cosy.'

'Yes, it was really squalid when I moved in, but I've cleaned it up and acquired a heater and a few home comforts. And Frank's laid on a proper water supply.'

'Frank?'

'Frank Brewer – the farmer who owns the land. He's a regular at the pub.'

'Oh yes, I remember. I see you're still collecting old books.'

'They're my companions. They remind me of a time when publishing was something special. Would you like some tea?'

'No thanks. Look, I can't discuss things in this environment. We'll have to go somewhere else.'

'Oh. Okay. Where would you like to go? The Queen's?'

'No, it's too public. Let's drive somewhere. We can talk in the car.'

They could have talked in the car where it stood but she wanted to get away from that desolate marsh, which she found deeply depressing. They drove in silence towards Wemborne, soon reaching the municipal playing fields bordered by a wide, potholed car park which was empty at that hour. She pulled in, parked facing the deserted football pitch and switched off the engine.

They sat without speaking, neither able to broach the subject which had brought them together after nearly five years, the subject of which neither wanted to be reminded. Finally she said, 'Pretty amazing news.'

'Yes.'

'There's something that mystifies me, though. I had no idea Nicola Carson was Nicola Pearson. But you did. Surely curiosity must have made you want to read her novel.'

Ted thought for a while before replying. 'That Dominic guy asked me the same question, and I ... Yes, I did know Nicola had published a novel, of course I did. But I didn't want to read it. I was so ashamed of what happened and the effect it had on our lives and I just wanted to forget her, to put her behind me. I knew reading it would bring it all back.'

Anne was gazing straight ahead, her eyes focused in the distance where a gaggle of children were playing on swings and a climbing frame. 'If I support you in this, you have to understand that it's got nothing whatsoever to do with ... our relationship. All this latest information proves is that she's a dishonest, scheming little minx, which I always suspected anyway.'

She expected him to come to Nicola's defence but he said nothing.

'You probably think that after more than four years I might have forgiven you or be moving towards some sort of reconciliation. But I can't. I've tried but I can't. They say that time heals all but it doesn't. The wound is still as raw as it was the day I found out. And that young man's bombshell has brought it all back.'

'I'm sorry.'

She thought of all the times she had almost called him. Once she had even lifted the receiver and dialled his number, then put it down again. 'If it had been a one-off, a moment of weakness with some girl from the pub while I was away, I might have forgiven you. But it was so ... calculated. The way you pretended to be reluctant to go to Richmond. And it went on for six *weeks* ... and would have kept on going if I hadn't ...'

Her shoulders suddenly hunched and she covered her face with her hands. Ted, dismayed, raised a hand to her shoulder. 'Anne ...'

She shook him away.

'If I do decide to support you,' she went on defiantly, 'it's because I care about your writing – and because I care about justice. And the truth.'

'That's more than I could've hoped for.'

She dried her eyes briskly with a handkerchief and resumed staring into space. In the middle of the field, a teenage girl in a blue anorak was throwing a stick for what looked like a red setter. They watched them in silence.

'Anyway, the solicitor I mentioned on the phone. His name's Bill Peach and he's a partner in a firm in Tunbridge Wells. I could have a chat with him.'

'How much are you going to tell him?'

'I don't think we need go into details at this stage. It'll be enough to say that she was a friend whom you met in the pub and that you emailed her your novel to get her opinion of it – all of which is true, isn't it?'

'It is.'

'So, shall I go ahead and do that, then?'

'I suppose there's no harm in hearing what he has to say.'

After a moment's hesitation, she reached forward and started the engine.

'You could drop me at the pub if you wouldn't mind. I need a drink. Would you … care to join me?'

'No. I have to get back.'

When they reached their destination, Ted lingered a moment in the car. 'I'm surprised you haven't taken this opportunity to sell the house. I know you wanted to.'

'This isn't the time for yet more upheaval.'

'I've heard a rumour, through the grapevine, that Linda's living with you.'

'She's not living with me, she's staying with me. The poor girl's been in a terrible state since her divorce and I'm just allowing her some breathing space.'

'I see.'

'Is that a problem?'

'No, no, of course not. The house is in your name. It's up to you what you do with it.'

There was a silence.

'Anyway, thanks again,' he said, reaching for the handle. 'I really appreciate your doing this. And ... it was good seeing you again.'

'It was good seeing you.'

*

Lying in bed, listening to the wind moaning over the marshes, Ted thought about the evening it had all started to unravel, the evening that David, *en route* from Seattle to Stuttgart, had turned up unannounced at the flat 'just to check he had everything he needed' and found Nicola – warm and fresh from the shower – sprawled on the couch in one of Marie's bathrobes. Not that it was David who had dropped them in it – that had been Gladys, who had proved a lot less dotty than she had at first appeared.

'I have to say you've won my admiration, old buddy,' he had remarked as they walked together back to his rented Mercedes. 'She's *fabulous.*'

'She is.'

They had walked a few paces in silence.

'Look, David, I hate involving you in this, but it's possible Marie might talk to Gladys and Gladys might mention Nicola and Marie might mention her to Anne. When I was chatting to her over the fence, I told her she was a family friend who was staying with me. I thought it might pre-empt problems if I explained her presence up front. So if Marie mentions it to you, you might, well ... corroborate my story.'

'I'm assuming Anne doesn't know?'

'Know what?'

'That you're having an affair, of course.'

'No, no she doesn't. I mean, I'm not having an affair. Not really. We're just ... she's just a girl I met down in Wemborne who came to London to try to make her way as an actress. But she's got no money and can't afford a place, so I thought you wouldn't mind if she dossed down here for a while. But I should've told you and I should've been open with Anne from the start.'

David had put an arm around his shoulder. 'Ted, how many years have we known each other? Trust me, I understand these little necessities better than anyone. You just have to be careful, that's all. We'd hate for anything to happen between you and Anne – you're two of our oldest and dearest friends. So don't worry, your secret's safe with me.'

'It's not a secret. You make it sound so …'

'Ted, lighten up, amigo. You and I both know we love our wives. You just, like I said … have to be careful.'

Alone in the darkness, Ted thought about David's words. In his shoes, he wouldn't have believed him either.

VII

Katie was out having yet another drink with one of her many friends and Dominic was enjoying a little peace online. He had Googled Nicola Carson yet again to see if there was anything fresh and was rather ashamed to find that what had begun as in-depth research had descended into an in-depth examination of her modelling a Calvin Klein bikini. In one shot she was seated on a rug with her legs tucked underneath her, her arms wrapped around her breasts in lieu of the bra and was staring straight at the lens – at him – with a look at once beseeching and faintly accusing which he found disturbing. He minimalised the photo, telling himself firmly to concentrate on the job in hand, then ploughed on through the entries. Many concerned her latest film – a blockbuster set in the super-rich fast lane entitled *The Beautiful and Blessed* ('blessed' to rhyme with 'best') and Nicola, as leading actress, was up for both BAFTA and Oscar nominations. She was trending yet again on Twitter and he found two postings on Facebook from people who claimed to have known her in her former incarnation as Nicola Pearson. One was clearly bogus but the other … He sat bolt upright and stared at the screen, murmuring, 'My *God*.'

He glanced at his watch and decided ten past ten was not too late to call Anne. They now spoke regularly on the phone.

'I've found a comment posted by a girl who knew her before she was famous. She was being treated for schizophrenia – the girl, I mean – so she wouldn't make a very reliable witness but she claims Nicola was a fellow patient at a clinic near Horsham. She'd just left uni and was having a breakdown at the very time she was supposed to have been writing *Loss*. She'd tried to kill herself – and it wasn't some half-hearted cry for help, either. She nearly succeeded.'

'Her mother kept that very close to her chest,' said Anne. 'Still, being suicidal doesn't stop you being a writer. Some people might even consider it a qualification.'

'Yes, but it's the logistics. There was a window of less than a year between her leaving uni and getting her book accepted for publication, and if she spent a large part of that having a breakdown, when the hell did she find the time to write a four hundred and seventy page novel?'

'She'll probably make out she wrote it on her good days in wild bursts of creativity. Or earlier, at university.'

'She did a lot of acting at uni, though. And she got a two/one so she must have done some work. Could she really have found time to write a book like that?'

'It's unlikely, I grant you, but I don't think that argument alone is going to swing it in court. But it certainly contributes to the overall picture.'

Dominic sighed. 'I suppose the clinic would never disclose the information about her attempted suicide anyway – patient confidentiality and all that.'

'No, but the court could subpoena her medical records if they're relevant to the case.'

Dominic, as he spoke, was still staring at the photo of the topless Nicola which had re-maximised itself. 'I've looked at loads of interviews and she becomes evasive whenever anyone mentions the novel. She always makes light of it and tries to turn the conversation back to her acting. And she lies all the time. Pretending to be

American, for instance. It's as though she's trying to distance herself from the English writer and create a new persona as an American superstar.'

'Acquiring an accent's not a crime, Dominic.'

'No, I suppose not.' He knew he was clutching at straws. 'Anne,' he went on, after a pause, 'you mentioned that you knew her mother.'

'I wouldn't say I knew her. I met her once – at a dinner party.'

'But you reckoned they didn't get on? She always tried to disown her, I think you said.'

'No, Dominic,' she said decisively, sensing where he was going. 'When it comes to the crunch, she might take her side. And besides, I'm a mother myself. I'm not going to sink so low as to persuade someone to testify against their own daughter.'

'No. No, you're right.'

VIII

'I've had a conversation with Bill Peach – the solicitor I mentioned.'

'And?'

'It's too complicated to tell you over the phone. I was thinking, I've got to see a client in Tunbridge Wells tomorrow but I'll be finished by one. And since you can get a direct train up from Wemborne, I thought maybe we could meet.'

'Are you inviting me to lunch?' he laughed.

'Let's just call it a working lunch.'

The place where they ended up was old-fashioned and unremarkable but at least had the advantage of being quiet. They found a table by a sunny window protected from the main body of the restaurant by a barricade of potted pelargoniums.

After the waitress had brought their drinks and taken their order, Anne said, hesitantly, 'I'm afraid Bill wasn't very encouraging.'

'How not very encouraging?'

'To put it bluntly, he advised us not to proceed.'

Ted stared at her. 'You could've told me that on the phone.'

'I know.'

'But you thought you'd buy me lunch to soften the blow?'

She glanced away, out of the window, at the shoppers walking up and down the Pantiles. 'You looked as though you could do with a proper meal.'

'That's thoughtful of you,' he smiled.

'I'm not giving up though,' she added, turning back.

After a pause, he asked, 'So your friend doesn't think we've got a case?'

'It's not that he doesn't think we've got a case. It's just that something like this could drag on for months – years, even – and cost us a fortune. And given that she's worth in the region of fifty million – something he gleaned from his sixteen-year-old son who's besotted with her – she's most likely to come out on top in the end, especially as her entire credibility's at stake. The problem is that all the evidence is circumstantial.'

'It's pretty compelling though.'

'From our perspective, maybe, but then we're the ones who know the truth. Looked at objectively, there are all kinds of problems.'

'Such as?'

'The fact that the novel was published more than four years ago, for a start.'

'Didn't you tell him we'd only just found out?'

'I did, but I could tell he thought it was pretty strange you never made the connection, given that you knew her.'

'But didn't you explain that I live like a hermit?'

'Yes, I did. But then there's the fact that *Tyranny* was never published – it's just a manuscript. Publication dates a book, doesn't it? In all the plagiarism cases he could think of, the material was stolen from an already-published work. The judge just had to look at both books and could see that the later work had been plagiarised from the earlier. Simple.'

'Not necessarily. A manuscript can exist long before it's published – or it may never get published. It's still the author's intellectual property.'

They paused as the waitress laid knives and forks and placed a basket of wholemeal rolls between them.

'He agreed that was true, legally,' Anne went on as soon as she had gone. 'He was just talking about the practicalities of building a case. What he was really saying is that basing everything on circumstantial evidence and the balance of probabilities isn't enough. If we're going to make this happen we've *got* to find some solid forensic evidence. If we had that, the facts would speak for themselves and all the other stuff would be irrelevant.'

Ted thought for a long time. 'The only possible forensic evidence is the email I sent her to which I attached the Word file, if that could ever be traced. I know it was sent on March 5th 2002 because it was the day after my birthday. But, even then, just emailing someone a typescript doesn't prove you wrote it. Anyone could have written it. Or I could have had it on my computer because she'd emailed it to me to get *my* opinion. Mind you, I do remember writing, "I'm sending you *my* novel ..." because I thought for a while about how to word it. Why else would I have said that?'

'You didn't email it to anyone else?'

He shook his head. 'You know I don't like showing my work to people until I'm satisfied with it. And if I ever showed it to anyone, it would've been in hard copy.'

'If only we'd kept that bloody computer. It had everything – outlines, rewrites, God knows how many drafts going all the way back to the planning stage – and all on a hard drive buried under twenty feet of soil.'

'You can't look into the future. As far as we were concerned it was just an old computer on its last legs. I'd saved everything as hard copy.'

She reached for a roll and ripped it in half. 'I'm going to get a detective. There's a firm we've used who specialise in IT. It might be possible to retrieve something somehow.'

'I don't like the idea. It'll cost a fortune and I don't want a third party poking their nose into our business.'

'If we go ahead with this,' she answered, slapping butter onto her roll, 'the whole world's going to be poking its nose into our business, so we'd better get used to it. And we can't afford to hide anything.'

'You mean about me allegedly having an affair with her?'

She paused in her buttering and stared at him. 'Allegedly?'

'I thought we decided that wasn't relevant,' he responded, avoiding her gaze.

'I never said that. I just said I wasn't going to tell Bill everything in our initial conversation. But it is relevant, isn't it? Highly relevant. It's the kind of environment in which you could have exchanged a lot more than ... And I know from experience that if you go into a legal battle from a position of complete openness, it gives you strength. If you're hiding something, you're fighting with one hand tied behind your back. Quite apart from the moral aspect.'

'So you'd be prepared to make my relationship with Nicola public?'

'I'd be prepared to make the fact that you were living together public. We could get David to testify she was there. Possibly even Gladys, if she's up to it.'

'And when her lawyers ask if we were having an affair? A twenty-three-year-old girl and a fifty-five year old man who gets dumped and wants revenge?'

'If you denied having an affair with her, I'd back you up.'

Ted's eyes narrowed. 'You'd do that?'

'It's circumstantial again, isn't it?'

'And if I denied it now?'

She held his gaze for a moment. 'Let's concentrate on the case.'

'Oh fuck it, let's forget the whole thing,' he said, taking a slurp of lager. 'I'm feeling less and less happy about it by the minute. And I'm too old for sleepless nights.'

'We can't just do *nothing*.'

'We've got no choice. And even if we did win, by some miracle, her fans aren't going to thank me for making her look a fool. People worship her, don't they? – like your friend's son. That's not what I want.'

'Even if it meant getting *Tyranny* published in your own name and under its proper title? And the rest of your novels. Isn't that what you want?'

'Not like that.'

'It looks as though she's won then,' Anne sighed angrily.

At that moment their food arrived, though neither had much appetite for the delicious-smelling dishes which were being placed before them.

'Do you think she had it planned from the start?' she asked when they were alone again.

'I don't know.'

'Dominic said that when he broke the news to you, you weren't as shocked as he expected, which surprised me.'

'I wasn't about to show my true feelings in front of him.'

'What were your true feelings?'

He gazed at his glass, turning it slowly between his fingertips. 'I don't know ... amazement ... confusion ...'

'And anger?'

'Yes, of course anger. And a sense of betrayal. I kidded myself that we were on the same side.'

Anne observed him for a moment. 'Poor Ted.'

'What do you mean, "poor Ted"?'

'Well, it must have been humiliating for you.'

'Because she was obviously using me? Making a fool of me? The – how did you put it? – middle-aged failed writer with the waning libido?'

'I was angry when I said that. And hurt.'

'Which is why I don't want to drag it up again. If nothing else, living alone with nothing has taught me a lot about life and about myself, and it's brought me a degree of inner peace I've never known before.'

'It sounds as though our splitting up was the best thing that ever happened to you,' she laughed bitterly.

'I didn't mean that.'

'Yes you did.'

He was silenced a moment.

'I didn't, honestly. It's just that I've had an awful lot of time to think and I realise the discontent I felt before had nothing to do with you – it was inside myself. You were the one bright spot – you and the children. I know I should have made more effort to make you aware of that. And another thing I realise is that getting my second-rate novels published isn't the most important thing in the world. There are millions of novels out there, most of them much better than mine. Whether or not I get published isn't going to make a scrap of difference to anyone.'

'Oh for God's sake, Ted, don't start going all self-pitying on me. For a start, your novels aren't second rate. Secondly, you do care about getting published, so don't pretend you don't. And thirdly, important or not, I don't feel like just standing by and letting her get away with it.'

He smiled slightly at her passion. It was one of the things he loved about her. 'I'm glad you still care,' he said.

'I've always cared about your writing. And, contrary to what you might think, it's not about getting back at Nicola Pearson or Nicola Carson or whatever she calls herself. Although I can't pretend that seeing that smug little smirk wiped off her vacuous face wouldn't be a nice bonus.'

Later, as they were strolling back to the car, Ted froze in his tracks. 'My God, I've just had a thought. I *did* email my novel to someone – or, at least, a sample. It's a long shot – a very long shot – but there may be some proof after all.'

Anne had turned to face him and was waiting for him to elaborate.

'You remember my telling you that Tom Newcomb was my English teacher at school?'

'Yes.'

'I sent him a sample of *Tyranny* on the strength of that, after I had my first round of rejections – since he used to tell me I showed promise. It was ostensibly to get his opinion but, of course, I was hoping he might put his weight behind getting it published. It was a measure of my desperation at the time.'

'You never told me about that.'

'To be honest, I was a bit embarrassed. I felt like a sycophantic teenager. I was waiting for a response before telling you.'

'What was the response?'

'There wasn't one. The bastard never replied. But he must have received the email – and the attachment – and it's just possible he may still have it. And it would have a date on it.'

'When was this?'

'I'm not sure, but it was before I sent the novel to Nicola.'

Anne stood motionless on the pavement, considering his words. 'You're right, it is a long shot. A very long shot.'

'It's worth a try, though, isn't it? What else have we got?'

'I suppose so. Emails can hang around in people's mailboxes for years and even if they open new accounts, they often forget to close the old ones. I've no idea how we'd get him on side, though. Maybe we could use Dominic, since he's got contacts in publishing.'

'There is another connection with Tom Newcomb. Nicola knew him. In fact, I suspect he helped her get *Loss* published.'

'He'd take her side, then, surely?'

'Not necessarily.'

They walked on, both considering this latest possibility. As they turned the corner into the car park, the din of traffic fell away. 'I just want to be clear about something,' he said. 'Since we're no longer together and the house is in your name and we have no joint assets, you wouldn't be liable in any way if we were to lose?'

'Not if you're the sole plaintiff, no.'

She unlocked her car and opened the door. He noticed the faded sprig of heather, which a gypsy in Granada had bullied him into buying for her, still twisted behind the rear view mirror.

'I bought you a present,' she said, reaching over to the passenger seat for a small, brightly-coloured box which she handed to him. 'It's a new mobile – the latest model. It takes no time at all to charge up and holds the charge much longer than your old one. Maybe you could charge it at the pub? It's all set up and I've put fifty pounds' call time on it, so there's no excuse for being incommunicado. The guarantee's in the box.'

'That's very kind of you.'

'Self-interest, mainly. Supposing something happened to one of the children? And I thought if we went ahead with this case we'd need to keep in touch. Anyway, you ought to have a proper phone, stuck out there on your own.'

'In case I have a heart attack or something?' he laughed.

'Well, you are in your sixties. And I've got some tablets for your back. They're not drugs – they're herbal. Linda swears by them.'

'You really are being very thoughtful.'

'Anyway, I'd better get going before the traffic builds up. You've got your return ticket?'

'Yes.'

She contemplated him for a moment. 'I hate to think of you going back to that place. Do you really have to live there? It reflects badly on me, apart from anything else.'

'Why should it reflect badly on you?'

'Because the woman always gets blamed for everything. Didn't you know?'

He smiled. 'Honestly, you don't have to worry about me. I'm fine. I'd far rather live surrounded by fields and sheep than by barking dogs and squabbling neighbours. Frank only charges me a tenner a week to cover the water so I have a bit left over for life's little luxuries – like the pub.'

'I just don't know how you manage.'

'Well, I do. So don't worry. And thanks for lunch.'

They faced each other for a moment, unsure how to part. It seemed absurd to shake hands after thirty-six years of marriage and raising three children together, yet it was hard to kiss. Finally they jerked in each other's direction like two large, ungainly birds performing a mating ritual, smiled with embarrassment and then Ted clasped her elbow and landed a peck on her cheek. It was the one which had been facing the window in the restaurant and was still warm.

IX

'Dominic? It's Ted.'

He was surprised to receive the call, given the awkwardness of their previous encounter. He wondered if he was going to apologise for his manner that afternoon, but the meeting was never mentioned. Nonetheless, his tone seemed conciliatory.

'There's something I'd like to look into,' he said, 'and I wondered if I could ask your help with it, since you have contacts in publishing. But only if you have time, of course. I know how busy you are, with your imminent departure.'

'What did you have in mind?'

Ted outlined his plan regarding Tom Newcomb.

'Well, I'd be happy to meet him, if it can be arranged,' he responded. 'But surely it'd be better coming from you – since you have a connection with him.'

'No, I'd far rather you did it. You're part of his world and he might feel there's something in it for him.'

Dominic suspected, yet again, that there were things Ted wasn't telling him. 'Okay,' he said.

'Your best course of action would be to go through his agent, who's a woman called Miranda Cole – so I discovered from *Writers and Artists*.'

'She's Nicola Carson's agent too.'

'Oh, really? Well, you'll have to tread carefully, then.'

*

'I'm going into town this afternoon.'

'I'll come with you.'

'Okay. But there is one thing I have to do alone.'

'It isn't to do with Ted bloody Haymer, is it?' Katie asked suspiciously, 'because you've had your fortnight.'

'This is the last thing – the very last thing, I promise. I just told Ted I'd pop into this agent and try and set up a meeting with some author who might support him. I'm just doing it as a favour to him, since I'm in London.'

'Why can't he do it himself? There is this amazing invention called the telephone.'

'It might take some persuasion and he thought it would be better handled face to face, by someone in the business. But once that's over, that'll be it, I promise. I'll focus all my attention on America and never mention Ted Haymer ever again.'

'You'd better not.'

*

Miranda Cole was a one-man band, operating from a plush first floor office in Farringdon Street. Dominic apologised to her receptionist for calling without an appointment but wondered if he might impose on Miss Cole for just five little minutes. It was very important.

The receptionist called her boss on the internal phone, explaining his connection with The Dragon's Head, then told him she could see him, but literally for five minutes. He was shown into an adjoining office where a small, gaunt woman with a boy's haircut and silver hoop ear rings stopped typing at a computer, stood up and shook his hand.

'I've met your boss a few times,' she said as they both sat down, 'and I certainly know him by reputation.'

'Yes, he's a great person to work for.'

'So, how can I help?'

Dominic hesitated. 'I'm just checking out some facts for an autobiography we're handling and I was wondering ... it's a big ask, I know, but ... I was wondering if it might be possible to speak to one of your authors. Tom Newcomb, to be precise.'

She looked surprised by the request. 'These facts don't compromise him in any way, I hope?'

'Oh no, absolutely not. He's not even mentioned. He just knew some of the people who are.'

'Whose autobiography is it?'

'Imelda Poppy's.'

They were the first words that came into his head. Imelda was his mother's name, Poppy his dog's. He was amazed by how good he'd become at lying.

'I've never heard of her.'

'Well, she's not very well known but she knew a lot of people who were and I think she's cashing in on that.'

'*Knew* in the biblical sense?' she laughed.

'In some cases, yes. But she's not as discreet as she might be. That's why we're having to check everything very thoroughly'

She shrugged slightly. 'Well, I can ask him. He's quite elderly now and lives a rather alternative lifestyle, but he might be willing to see you if you don't mind going to Gloucestershire.'

'Anywhere. I'm sorry if it sounds pushy but might it be possible to make it sooner rather than later? The thing is, I'm starting a new job in the States in a fortnight's time.'

It just came out.

'Oh. So you're leaving The Dragon's Head?' she asked, surprised.

'Well … yes. Yes, I am. And I'd love to get this wrapped up before I go.'

She observed him for a moment then snatched up her telephone and punched in a number she seemed to know by heart. 'Jo-Jo? It's Miranda.' She exchanged a few pleasantries with 'Jo-Jo' – whoever she might be – then passed on his request. She cupped her hand over the mouthpiece. 'Two o'clock tomorrow?'

'Perfect.'

When she had ended the call, he thanked her profusely. It seemed that the meeting had come to a natural conclusion but he hesitated.

'Miss Cole, I hope you don't mind my asking but aren't you Nicola Carson's agent as well?'

She looked at him warily, clearly wondering if he had another agenda. 'I still handle the rights on *Loss* but I have no involvement in her film work. Why do you ask?'

'Well, I have to admit I've always had a soft spot for her.'

'You and most of the male population of planet Earth.'

'I suppose so,' he smiled. 'And I just wondered, I mean, I've heard so many conflicting stories about her and I just wondered what she's really like … in person? You always do wonder that about celebrities, don't you?'

'You're not a moonlighting journalist, are you?'

'No. No way. Nothing like that.'

'Okay. I must say you don't look like one. So, what's Nicola

Carson like? To be honest, she was the biggest disappointment of my career.'

'Really? I've never heard her called that before.'

'I'm speaking from the literary point of view. I took her on when she was unpublished in the expectation that she had a brilliant career ahead of her and it never happened – as I'm sure you're aware. Okay, she's been pumped up into a huge star and made pots of money but to me she's wasted her talent. I don't normally make errors of judgement like that but I certainly did in her case. Still, she's only twenty-eight – there's still time. Maybe she'll get bored with the high life and go back to writing.'

'Or maybe she's not so much wasting her talent as pointing it in another direction?' he ventured.

'Princess Zara of the Planet Zog? I *ask* you.'

'Well, that was just a money-spinner, but she's done some good stuff as well. She was brilliant in *All about Me*.'

'You're probably right. I'm afraid I'm biased, being a boring old bookworm.'

'So what's she actually like in the flesh?'

She shifted her gaze to the leaves beyond the window, though she did not seem to be focusing on anything in particular. Then she murmured, as though talking to herself, 'She was special – not just on the outside but inside as well. People couldn't see it because she had so much attitude. She didn't take any crap from anyone. But under the surface there was such ... vulnerability. I knew she'd had a hard time. And I often wondered if *Loss* was rooted in her own past and if it was that which made it so moving, so authentic. But she seldom talked about it.'

Silence fell in the room. The cars and pedestrians going up and down Farringdon Street seemed to belong in a different world. Dominic asked, 'And what did you think of her novel? Did you think it was a very mature piece of work for a girl of her age?'

'It was. But then she'd had to grow up fast.'

He knew he was walking a tightrope. He had wondered vaguely if he might recruit this Miranda Cole to their cause as well as Tom

Newcomb, but he knew now that that was not going to happen.

'Anyway!' She suddenly stood up and extended her hand. 'Good luck with Tom. Get Sasha to give you his number and directions on your way out. You'll need them.'

*

'I've got to go out,' he said the next morning. 'Just for a few hours.'

'Where *this* time?'

'I have to say goodbye to a great-aunt up in Gloucestershire. She's in a retirement home up there.'

'You've never said anything about a great-aunt in Gloucestershire.'

'Well, I've never had reason to. But I'm very fond of the old girl and she's ninety-eight and may kick the bucket any time. I'd suggest you come with me ...'

'God, no thank you. I'm allergic to old folk's homes. And I've got stuff I need to do here.'

'I'll be back as soon as possible, I promise.'

*

Tom Newcomb's country retreat turned out to be a vast, ramshackle farmhouse in creamy Cotswold stone. Dominic was relieved. The spectacle of the former hard man of social realism living in a beamy cottage with roses winding over the porch would have been too much to take but, even so, the rural world in which he had buried himself was a far, far cry from the slums and tenements of northern England which had made him famous. Dominic had learned from Wikipedia that he was something of an authority on herbs.

Opening the front gate, he stared up at the towering, tatty gables in trepidation. He had no idea how this man was going to react to his request, nor even how best to broach it. He doubted very much if he would remember the teenage Ted.

A hen wandered across his path as he approached the porch, which was like that of a country church. He tugged on a dangling iron ring which he assumed was a bell, though there was no discernible sound within and no response. He plucked up his courage and tried the door, which was unlocked. Peering into the gloomy interior of the house, he listened intently for signs of life but all he could hear was the deep tick-tock of an invisible clock. He called out, timidly, 'Hell-o-o!'

A little voice behind him echoed, 'Hell-o-o.'

He spun round to find a tiny, blonde shrimp of a girl, with eyes like saucers, staring up at him. She must have been about seven and, despite the season, was wearing only jeans and a jumper, with red wellingtons and a red woollen hat perched on her head.

'Who are you?' she inquired.

'I'm Dominic.'

'You're very high. Can you see all the way to the sea?'

'Well yes, I can, almost. I've come to see Mr Newcomb.'

'I'll take you to him,' she said, holding out her hand.

Reaching down, Dominic took the tiny hand and she led him around the side of the house, through a gap in a hedge and across a soggy, unkempt lawn where they were joined by a rumbustious little boy, slightly older than the girl.

'Who are you?' he demanded.

'This is *Dominic*, silly. He's come to see Tom.'

Dominic spotted a tall, elderly man with a walking stick in a gateway ahead. He wore jeans and a collarless shirt under a corduroy jacket and was heavily lined with a thatch of silver hair.

'This is Dominic,' explained the girl as they approached.

'Pleased to meet you,' he said as they shook hands. 'Bracken, my love, would you go and ask Jo-Jo if she could bring our guest a nice glass of parsnip wine? Let's go and sit in the herb garden.'

The place he led him to, sheltered behind a greenhouse with a view over lawns and a wooded valley beyond, proved to be a sun trap. They settled in two wicker garden armchairs.

'It's a beautiful place you have here,' Dominic remarked.

Tom Newcomb considered his pleasantry at length. 'Yes but the rains have been terrible this winter. If it keeps it up, the spring sowing could be delayed for weeks.' He sounded more like a character from Thomas Hardy than the sixties *enfant terrible* from Salford. Beyond the lawn, a gang of children were playing hide and seek among some bushes.

'My grandkids,' he explained. 'I've got twelve in all – the fruits of three marriages and one or two others who slipped through the net, I'm afraid.' He spoke in a sonorous, 'poetry-reading' voice but with a Yorkshire accent still discernible beneath.

'That's … impressive. Do they all live with you?'

'Good God no. Just Ty and his sister Bracken – the ones you met – live with us as our own. Their mother ran off with her Ayurvedic masseur. Tell me, Dominic, do you eat meat?'

He was a little fazed by the question, wondering if it was a roundabout way of being invited to dinner. 'Yes. Yes I do,' he replied.

'Well don't. It's a disgusting habit. Did you know that reliable statistics have proved that vegetarians are eighty-seven per cent more regular than carnivores?'

'No, I didn't.'

'I won't have the kids eating meat when they're here. Just fresh vegetables, fruit, pulses, and my own homemade bread. It means they fart all the time but at least their farts aren't completely rank, which is a sign of a healthy digestive system, don't you think? It's hardly surprising that human excrement smells so disgusting when it's mainly rotting meat that's been sitting around in our guts for days on end.'

The great writer lapsed into silence for a while, no doubt savouring the joys of regularity.

'So, Miranda tells me you're researching a book. What is it? A novel?'

'No, it's a biography.' Dominic sensed that – now that the ice had been broken – the only way was to jump in with both feet. 'Mr Newcomb, I have a very large and rather bizarre favour to ask you.'

'Oh? That sounds intriguing.'

'I understand you were once an English teacher.'

He looked mystified and a little wary. 'Many years ago.'

'And when you were an English teacher … you had a pupil called Edward Haymer.'

'Did I?'

'Yes, he remembers you fondly,' Dominic lied.

'Well, I wish I could say the same about him. I'm afraid all my ex-pupils have merged into one amorphous, acned blur. To be honest, I never enjoyed teaching – I just did it to earn a crust and the holidays gave me a chance to write. I got out the moment I published my first novel. What about him, anyway?'

Dominic explained his mission. Was there any chance at all that he might still have Ted's email to which the sample chapter of *The Tyranny of Love* had been attached?

He hooted with laughter. 'None at all, I'm afraid. I had a highly efficient secretary who spent half her life replying to those letters and emails – of which there were thousands, I might add – then cleaning out my mailbox.'

'Oh.' The man's response had been so unequivocal that Dominic felt desolate. Another precious day wasted. He wondered whether to mention that his highly efficient secretary had neglected to send a reply to Ted but decided that might be imprudent.

'And there's no possibility,' he persevered, 'that she might have downloaded the attachment, at least?'

'If she'd downloaded every attachment she received, her hard drive would've exploded. No, I'm sorry, that attachment would've gone the way of the email. You probably think me callous but I do care about helping young writers. It's just that there aren't enough hours in the day.'

Not between brewing parsnip wine and regular shitting, Dominic thought to himself. 'No. I suppose not,' he said.

'Why do you need this stuff, anyway?' he asked brusquely.

'This biography I'm working on – it's about a current female celebrity and its USP is a startling and highly sensitive revelation we're planning to make about her …'

'USP,' he laughed. 'How I love that acronym. It says everything about our so-called contemporary culture, doesn't it? Historians of the future aren't going to call this the Cyber Age or the Digital Age, they're going to call it the Age of the Unique Selling Point. So who is this celebrity?'

'Nicola Carson.'

The whole of Gloucestershire seemed suddenly frost-bound.

'So what's this Heasmer's connection with Nicola Carson?' he grunted.

'Her one and only novel, *Loss*, wasn't written by her, it was written by him – Edward Haymer – in fact, it was *The Tyranny of Love*, a sample of which he sent you. They had a brief relationship and she used it as an opportunity to download the file onto her computer. I know this for a fact, though sadly I have no proof. That email would've provided proof.'

'Well, you don't need proof because I knew that.'

Dominic could not believe what he was hearing. 'You *knew*?'

'I did.'

'But … how?'

'Because she told me.'

Dominic grimaced in utter consternation. 'She *admitted* she stole Ted's typescript?'

'She didn't mention him by name.'

'But, what happened exactly? If you don't mind my asking.'

The old writer took a moment to collect his memories. 'The whole thing smelt fishy to me from the start. When I met her at Harold Mosberg's launch, she told me she was an actress but was having trouble finding work. I know people in the business, so I said I'd sound out some contacts for her. Then, a month or so later, she phones me up saying she's written a novel and could I put her in touch with an agent? And I remember thinking, why didn't she mention that at the start? I'm a writer, we were at a launch – it would have been the perfect opportunity. I could have introduced her to Miranda then and there.'

'May I ask if you read the novel?'

'I did. And it was good. Bloody good. Which was why I didn't believe she'd written it. Okay, she was a bright enough lass – bags of talent, I'm sure – but when I read her manuscript and thought about her, the two just didn't go together. There was a depth and a breadth and an authenticity about that novel … And she wasn't long out of college, was she? When was she supposed to have written it, in playschool?'

'So what did you do?'

'I challenged her. I'm from Yorkshire, lad, I don't mince my words. I said, "Come on, Nicola, you didn't really write this, did you?"'

'And how did she react?'

'She admitted it. She told me she'd got it off this reclusive old bloke she knew who was a struggling writer type and she was hoping it might boost her career. She begged me not to tell anyone. And she can be very persuasive, can Nicola.'

'You say she got it off him?'

'I wasn't quite clear whether she'd nicked it or whether he'd given it to her, but I assumed she'd nicked it since no writer just gives up a manuscript they'd probably worked on for years. But she said it didn't matter because he was dissatisfied with it and had decided to stop submitting it and move on. But I was still unhappy about it.'

'Mr Newcomb, I hope you don't mind my asking, but … did you feel tempted to tell the truth, in spite of her asking you not to? Did you feel the truth needed to be told?'

'I did. But I introduced her to Miranda before she told me. They got on like a house on fire, those two – well, it was a bit more than that – on Miranda's side, anyway. She knew Nicola was dynamite and she'd managed to screw a hefty advance out of Jonathan Hale. It's the stuff that agents' dreams are made of and I didn't want to piss on their parade – especially as Miranda had done a great job of reviving my own flagging career. I did mention my doubts to her but she brushed them aside, saying all young authors are influenced – that's how they find their voice. If I'd told her what Nicola had told me, she probably wouldn't have believed me and Nicola would've denied it.' He paused, his eyes fixed on the grass a few yards in front of him. 'I agreed – for Miranda's sake – to say a few words at her launch but I drew the line at writing a review. Just the same, I can't say I felt proud of turning a blind eye. Then I said to myself, "I've told Miranda what I think, she's her agent, and if she's okay with it then it's out of my hands."'

Dominic was thinking on his feet. 'Mr Newcomb,' he said, bracing himself, 'would you be prepared to tell what you've just told me to a court of law?'

He turned and stared at him. 'A *court*? I thought you were researching a book.'

'I am. But I'm also helping Ted and Anne Haymer build a case against Nicola Carson for theft of Ted's intellectual property. That's what my book's going to be about.'

'*Jesus.*'

'It would make such a difference to both their lives if you could help us out with this.'

At that moment Bracken hove into view, walking very slowly with a look of intense concentration in an effort not to spill the glass of cloudy lemony liquid she was carrying. She looked relieved when Dominic took it from her with profuse thanks.

'Hope you enjoy it!' said Tom Newcomb. 'I made it myself.'

He took a tentative sip. 'Mm! Lovely,' he pronounced as he set it down again.

'So what were we talking about? Ah yes. Your court case. So where's this going to happen?'

'Probably at the High Court in London.'

'Would we get lunch?'

'We?'

'Jo-Jo, myself and the kids. She could take them to the Natural History Museum. It'd be a bit of an outing for us. We haven't been to London in ages.'

'Well, your expenses would be reimbursed, naturally. And you wouldn't feel ... awkward?'

'Awkward?'

'Saying now what you could have said then?'

'No, because things have changed, haven't they, since my ex-pupil came crawling out of the woodwork?'

'And what about Miranda Cole?'

'There's no love lost between Miranda and Nicola these days. That woman moved mountains to build her career and all she's done is fuck in front of a camera for five years. Which is probably what she's best suited to.'

Despite his excitement, there was something in this man's tone that made Dominic uneasy. 'Well, to be fair, she's a good actress. She's the favourite to win a BAFTA – possibly even an Oscar – for her latest film.'

'Listen, everyone knows that Nicola Carson is a foul-mouthed, egocentric little madam who's somehow got it into her head that she's Marilyn Monroe. Film stars don't go on like that nowadays – like some medieval queen with their entourage. They push their babies round Sainsbury's and wait with the other mums outside the school gates. Even the blokes.'

Dominic was surprised by the sudden hostility. Would there follow yet more spicy revelations about Nicola's associations with men more than twice her age? He sensed he needed to tread carefully.

'Mr Newcomb, it's almost certain you'll be cross-examined. About your connection with her.'

'They can cross-examine me all they want. I'll just tell the truth – the truth, the whole truth and nothing but the truth.' Then the old man turned his attention to his pack of cavorting grandchildren and the frost vanished as suddenly as it had come. 'So, you're planning to write a bestseller on the back of this scandal and make your name as a writer?' he chuckled.

Dominic was a little shocked to hear his motives mirrored back at him quite so starkly. 'That's my plan. Yes.'

'Well, I don't blame you. We all have to grab our opportunities where we can in this grubby little world of ours. You'll have to be quick off the mark, though. Every Tom, Dick and Harry will be writing books on the subject once this comes to court. Although not this Tom, you'll be glad to hear.'

Dominic laughed, rather uneasily. 'Yes, but I'm a friend of the Haymers and it was I who saw the original manuscript.'

'Try telling that to the competition.'

His words sent a chill down Dominic's spine, despite the unseasonal sunshine. All of a sudden he wanted to get out of the place, to be on his own to think.

'Well, I won't take up any more of your valuable time,' he said, rousing himself and holding out his hand. 'Thanks a million for all your help. And for the parsnip wine. I'll be in touch as soon as we have a date for the hearing.'

Tom Newcomb looked a little surprised. 'Why don't you stay to supper? We're having cabbage.'

'That's really kind of you, but I ought to get back to London before the rush hour.'

*

A few yards from the house, he pulled into a lay-by and tried to get Ted on his mobile. By a miracle he succeeded, although the signal was very poor.

'No luck with the email, I'm afraid!' he shouted. 'But I've got something else. Tom Newcomb – the great Tom Newcomb – has agreed to testify in court that Nicola *told* him she pinched your novel!'

There followed such a long silence that Dominic wondered if he had lost the signal.

'He actually said that?'

'He actually said it.'

'He used the word "pinched"?'

'What he said was that she "got it off you" but we both know what that means!'

Another silence. 'Well, that's amazing, Dominic. Well done.'

Ted's lacklustre reaction infuriated him, especially after all the trouble he'd been to. Fucking typical.

'Of course it's still not actual proof,' he said. 'It's still his word against hers. But what a word! And we've still got all our circumstantial evidence to back it up. But I have to ask you, how did you know he loathed her so much?'

'I guessed.'

*

Katie slowly replaced the receiver then sat hunched on the sofa, gazing into space. Her gaze moved around the flat – the flat which they had found together, furnished together, which had been their home for more than three years. His laptop lay open on his desk, his Happy Pig mug beside it, drained to a dreg of coffee. She hated his Happy Pig mug with a passionate intensity but had allowed him to keep it since he seemed to love it so much and had had it all through university. She reached out and picked it up, turned it in her hand and stared down at the happy pig grinning up at her.

*

Driving back to London, Dominic found his elation at the coup he had just pulled off weighed down by unwelcome, depressing thoughts – thoughts incurred by Tom Newcomb's parting words. Writing a book took time and his special relationship with Ted and his manuscript didn't mean other writers were going to stand politely by while he honed and polished his work to perfection. How was he ever going to find the time to write it anyway, if he was settling into life and a demanding job in America? And as soon as someone else – possibly someone with a name – had brought out a book on the subject, there would be little chance for his own, however unique his Unique Selling Point. He had heard tales of publishers locking writers in hotel rooms with nothing but a box of Pot Noodles and a fridge full of Red Bull until they had finished their commissioned work on some red-hot topic of the moment. He longed to make some advances to publishers and agents, but he could not risk giving the game away; he must keep his powder dry. Nonetheless, he had to start mustering all the notes and material he had accumulated on the subject into some sort of first draft straight away. That very evening.

*

Using his shiny new mobile, Ted got onto Anne.

'She *told* him?' she responded in amazement. 'Why would she do that?'

'Because she knew he knew. And she also knew he fancied the pants off her. So she reckoned it'd be safer to have the camel inside the tent pissing out than outside pissing in.'

'This is amazing, Ted. Okay, it's a shame about the email but I never really held out much hope of that. But this is almost as good, in its way.'

'I've made a decision, Anne. I want you to get onto Peach and tell him we're going ahead. That's our novel – *we're* the ones who put all that time and sweat and effort into it – you and I and Julie – not her – and I'm sick and tired of taking this lying down. If nothing else, I owe it to Julie not to have her steal it from us. And when I win, I'm going to send a copy of the judgement to Alistair Milner along with precise instructions as to where he can shove it. And if I lose, they can award her all the damages they want, it won't do them any good, since I haven't got anything. They can even send me to prison. I'm too old and ugly to care about bending over in the shower. And don't worry about Peach, by the way. I've got money for that.'

The ether between them fell silent. "What are you talking about? You told me you had nothing.'

'I've got a little … put by. For emergencies.'

'From where?'

'Just bits and bobs I've saved up from here and there. But don't worry, it's in cash. Untraceable.'

'Ted, are you drunk?'

'Of course I am. It's the only way I can keep going.'

*

Dominic was parked in a service station, gazing at the bare masts of poplar and willow rising against a grimy sky. 'Katie … darling, about this America plan. I'm not sure …' He sighed, shaking his head in despair. If he couldn't say it in his imagination, how was he ever going to say it in reality?

He recalled their first meeting. She had been struggling with a mountain of shopping – mostly cases of beer – getting it from the check-out at Asda to her little Ford Ka, and she had gratefully accepted his offer of help. He had asked if the beer was for her personal use and she had laughed and told him she and her house-mates were having a party. 'Why not come along?' she'd suggested.

'It's the least I can do after all your humping. Bring your girlfriend.'

'I might do that,' he had replied, 'although I don't actually have a girlfriend at the moment.'

'Oh. Right.' She had eyed him swiftly up and down. 'Just bring yourself then.'

He had been determined not to arrive on time – that was so uncool – and the music and dancing and drinking had been well under way when he found the address in Wimbledon she had given him. She had screamed 'Hi!' when she spotted him above the sea of heads and they had got acquainted by yelling at each other over Shakira singing *La Pared*. He managed to convey to her that he worked in publishing and wanted to be a writer. She managed to convey to him that she considered the most important aspect of a novel to be a good plot. She was a huge fan of John Grisham and Dan Browne and wasn't above a bit of chick-lit – but only on holiday. 'I'm really fascinated by writing which suggests the symbolic meaning beneath the surface of everyday things!' he had shouted as he waved his arms and hips vaguely in time to the music and she had pointed an ear in his direction and shouted, 'Sorry?'

Parked in the service station with the dusk closing around him, he recalled every detail of that evening, and of their first date and their first night together – the faintly musky scent of her skin, her disarming giggle, the curves and hollows of her body, the extraordinarily soft and light texture of her hair. For months he had lived mostly at her place instead of his depressing little room in Walthamstow and finally, by mutual consent prompted by her house-mates' annoyance at his protracted use of the bathroom, they had looked for a place together. When they found the flat in Stratford, she had remarked, laughingly, that she had come down in the world. A talent of Katie's was for taking the maximum pleasure in the surfaces of life, and he had learned from her how to relax and be carried like a seed on the gentle currents of his happiness, not to be ruled by the past and the future and the compulsion to over-analyse things. He thought of their outings to pubs, to the cinema, to concerts, to the seaside, of their holidays in Ibiza and Tunisia, of that ridiculous camping trip to Cornwall (funds had been low that summer) before which she had spent three hundred pounds on equipment, thus defeating the object entirely. 'Getting back to nature's all very well,' she had said, 'but I'm damned if I'm going to be uncomfortable.'

It had been on that trip, as they lay in each other's arms watching the morning sunlight glow through the orange fabric of the tent, that she had said for the first time, 'Do you fancy going to America?'

'We can't afford it, can we?' he had responded, surprised.

'I don't mean now. In the future. I'd like to move out to California.'

'You mean *emigrate*?'

'Yeah. Why not?'

He had considered the prospect at length. 'Why California?'

'I don't know,' she had murmured dreamily. 'It just seems so... *nice* out there.'

The neon windows of the Welcome Break had darkened the sky and bestowed a false gaiety on the scene. The motorway to London was now an unbroken stream of headlights and tail-lights. Dominic heaved a sigh and reached for the ignition key.

An hour and fifteen minutes later, as he left the M25 and headed homeward through the northern suburbs, his heart felt like a lump of lead in the pit of his rib cage. He reminded himself that he was only going to ask for – no, insist on – a delay, but since their flight was mere days away and they would almost certainly lose their entire fare, it would, to Katie, be tantamount to calling it off. By the time he was edging his car into the gap between the garages and the bottle bank, he felt nauseous and his heart was pounding as he trudged up the double flight of bleak, familiar stairs. He reached their landing and stood a moment before the blank, brown door of their home – flat number 27 – then turned the key and entered, croaking the words, 'I'm back!' The absence of a response granted momentary relief but with an undercurrent of frustration – he wanted to get this over with.

It was not long before he saw what had happened. All his clothes – both clean and dirty – had been dumped in a heap on the living-room floor and all her clothes – in fact, all her possessions – had gone. His Happy Pig mug lay in fragments on the floor, having been flung in fury against the wall. Then he noticed a sheet of paper propped against the kettle in the kitchen. On it was written, in a large and – for Katie – unusually untidy scrawl:

I hope you enjoyed seeing your "great aunt". I'm going on my own. Goodbye Dominic

Chapter Six

THE MAGIC SHOES

In their house in Wemborne, Anne and Linda made tea and settled in armchairs in front of the television. In his converted barn near Goudhurst, William Peach poured himself a whisky and a G&T for his wife, Fiona, then settled beside her in front of the television. In their farmhouse in Gloucestershire, Tom Newcomb poured some parsnip wine, pushed two sheepdogs and a lurcher off the sofa then settled down with Bracken, Ty and Jo-Jo in front of the television. In their house in Kew, Miranda Cole and her partner, Dr Jenny Blades, opened a bottle of Pinot and settled down in front of the television. In his flat in Stratford, Dominic opened a can of lager and stretched out on the sofa in front of the television. Throughout Britain and beyond, people were making something to eat or drink then settling down to the evening's best alternative to darts or Celebrity Wife Swap – the BAFTAs. Ted settled down with a beer and looked at the stars.

No one was going to make a fortune backing Nicola Carson for Best Actress in a Leading Role. Her latest film *The Beautiful and Blessed* – a brash and vicious tale of life in the fast lane, which apparently held some profound message about the vanity of all human endeavour – had been number one at the box office for weeks and been nominated for three awards. Over the past four years, Nicola had won one BAFTA and had one nomination, and if her winning streak continued in America, it would be her second Oscar. A film in which she had starred had won Best Movie Oscar and another, the Palme d'Or at Cannes. She was still the golden girl. One bitter rival – Rachel Springer – had been overheard to remark that Nicola only had to fart and she'd be given an award for it.

The lesser categories had all been handed out and ageing Hollywood stalwart, Bill Ackworth, was introduced by the host for the evening, Russell Floss, to present the award for Best Actress in a Leading Role. The nominees were announced, clips of their films were shown on a gigantic screen above his head to rapturous applause. Then deathly hush as Bill opened the envelope, drew out the card bearing the winner's name and scrutinised it through a dramatic pause. 'And the BAFTA goes to ... Nicola Carson.'

Screams. Applause. Sporting smiles on the faces of the other nominees and their coteries (in case they happened to be on camera) but what filled the Royal Albert Hall at that moment was an almost palpable sense of inevitability. The object of their adulation – who had been positioned five rows back beside the aisle – seemed rather indifferent to her triumph but at least she didn't clap her palms to her cheeks in feigned astonishment. Rising along with her cohort – director, producers, writer, leading man – they all hugged and kissed as though they had been parted for thirty years by the Berlin Wall. Then she set off alone on the perilous journey up to the stage. The first impression was breath-taking – the exquisitely delicate frame, the glistening, raven-black hair cut in a curved-in bob to the base of the neck, the restrained make-up which was her trade-mark, tiny gold ear rings just pendant, the stunningly simple ash-green Armani gown, designed to offset the red carpet in the publicity shots. Yet none of these design masterpieces could disguise the fact that the Nicola Carson who ascended the stage was a far, far cry from the Nicola Carson of four years earlier, the startling new talent of *All about Me*. One could almost hear, mingled with the applause, a collective gasp of amazement. She looked drawn, underweight and ill. Bill Ackworth kissed her on both cheeks, handed her the famous bronze mask then withdrew to where Floss was standing, applauding. There followed a deathly hush.

'Thank you,' she whispered, almost inaudibly. Then she cleared her throat and repeated, 'Thank you. I'm grateful to BAFTA for giving me this award, and I want to thank Alan Layne, the director, Miguel Hernandez, my leading man, the screenwriter, producers...' her voice trailed away, seeming to lose all conviction. '... and I'm ... I'm sorry I let everybody down. My performance in that film was rubbish, and I mean *rubbish*.'

The audience glanced at one another, laughing uneasily.

'I'd use a different word if this weren't the BAFTA Awards Ceremony – one that would be far more appropriate. It's been rubbish in my last three films. I mean … hasn't anyone *noticed*? I've lost it …' She shook her head slowly, despairingly. 'I've just *lost* it. This award should have gone to Rachel. She was far, far better in *Torrent* than I was in *The Beautiful and Blessed*.'

Her magnanimous words invoked a wave of rather uncertain applause while camera five swung onto Rachel Springer, who was firing glistening smiles in all directions, beseeching everyone to agree with what her rival had said.

'But thank you anyway.'

It was with fresh applause and some relief that the audience watched her receive kisses on both cheeks from Bill, then waited for her to pick up the mask in preparation for the journey out through the wings. But she did not pick it up – instead her hands shot over her face and her shoulders heaved. They stared in disbelief, compelled to look yet hardly bearing to look at the waif-like figure whose utter loneliness was spot-lit in that vast wasteland of a stage. She looked like a little girl all done up for a party who had been accidentally elbowed in the face by an over-boisterous boy.

Silence fell over the auditorium. The old hands had seen some prize-winning performances in their time, but never anything like this. For five full seconds the only sound in the whole of the Royal Albert Hall was Nicola's amplified sobbing which was being beamed out into space and back into homes all over Britain, America, Canada and God knows where besides – five seconds that could have been an hour. Her anguish was a physical pain shared by a hundred million people. This was not histrionics. These were real tears.

Bill Ackworth appeared paralysed but then – ever the professional – he sprang forward and took her in a fatherly hug, while Floss looked on helplessly, no doubt trying to think up some snide witticism to get things back on track when this was over. Moved by the touching father-daughter embrace, someone started clapping, then two or three others joined in. The infection spread, the applause swelling and growing, powered by relief that the terrible moment seemed to have passed. Then someone got to their feet. Then another. Then another. And suddenly the entire auditorium was standing. Applauding hands were raised in the air. They whistled. They cheered. The looks of alarm on the faces of the director and producers turned to relief as they glanced around, then to satisfaction and finally elation. Rachel Springer mumbled, 'Oh … *please.*'

A limousine was waiting to whisk her away to the official post-awards bash at Grosvenor House. Flashbulbs exploded like fireworks the moment she emerged from the entrance arm-in-arm with Miguel Hernandez, her leading man and allegedly current 'squeeze'. 'God, Nicola, I *loved* your speech!' wept one female fan from the crowd who had watched everything on live stream. 'It was so *honest.* And you weren't rubbish, you were *brilliant.*'

*

Anne and William Peach, in their respective living rooms, had watched the ceremony with mixed feelings. At first they had thought her clearly unbalanced performance was going to do wonders for their cause; now they were not so sure. Dominic was even less sure. Only Ted, relieving himself under a moonlit sky, remained in ignorance of what had happened. He found out the next morning when he walked to the recycling centre with a bag full of empty bottles. Every single newspaper on the stand outside the corner shop – even the *Financial Times* – bore a front-page photograph of Nicola in tears. He departed from a lifelong habit and bought one.

*

Her refusal to give any interviews and her absence from all pre- and post-awards parties had her more talked about than all the lesser stars who relentlessly thrust themselves into the limelight. The major TV channels always reserved a few slots for the BAFTA winners on the day after the ceremony and were at a loss to know how to fill them. They solved the problem by digging up some old footage and interviews she had given in happier times. The media sought to explain her breakdown by publicly psychoanalysing her:

'What we are witnessing is a superb young actress who is bent on denigrating her own achievement,' proclaimed one eminent, grizzled psychologist in an interview with Jimmy Flaxman on *Newsbeat*. 'It's the Faustian conception.'

'But Faust sold his soul to the devil, didn't he?' grunted Flaxman.

'I believe she's convinced that's what she's done.'

'In what way?'

'Who can say? Who are we to understand the complexities and contradictions of genius?'

'You really think Nicola Carson's a genius?' sneered Flaxman. 'She's just a film star, isn't she?'

'No. She's an artist.'

A media psychologist on a competing channel was less reverent: 'It's a clear case of public professional suicide,' he said. 'And, like all suicide attempts, it's attention-seeking.'

*

Anne had been trying to reach Ted all day, but he seemed to be permanently on voicemail. Exasperated, she phoned Dominic.

'What did you think?'

'I have to say, I felt quite sorry for her.'

Anne sighed. 'I think that was what you were supposed to feel. Anyway, I've spoken to Bill and he seems to think it's strengthened our case.'

'I wish I agreed with him.'

'But, the way that girl's been behaving, and that fiasco last night, it's obvious she's cracking up. That should play right into our hands, shouldn't it?'

'Anne, I don't know much about the law but I do know a bit about celebrity. She turned up among all those glitterati looking like death and she still had the entire place wrapped round her little finger. Maybe it *was* all done for effect, I don't know, but her performance was pretty much what the public have come to expect from her – the volatile young talent teetering constantly on the edge. She's got the whole world talking about her now and she's won sympathy even from people who didn't like her before.'

'Is that really how you read it?'

'I'm afraid so. The next thing we'll hear is that she's in rehab.'

The desolate prospect drove them both into silence for a while.

'Oh, by the way, I'm so sorry to hear about your America thing falling through. I hope it wasn't to do with us and all our dramas.'

Dominic grimaced at the receiver. 'How did you know about that?'

'Ted told me. He phoned you up to find out how you were getting on with Tom Newcomb and when he couldn't get you on your mobile, he tried your landline and spoke to your girlfriend.'

After a pause, he murmured, 'Oh. I see.'

*

Ted sat in his caravan, gazing out over the marshes. He had been transfixed for more than an hour, thinking. A copy of *The Times*, with its huge front page photograph of Nicola in the throes of her now world-famous crying fit, lay on his lap. Critics were suggesting her performance had been calculated to curry sympathy, to affirm people's love and admiration while she was going through a crisis of confidence. That was rubbish. She didn't need to pull a stunt like that to affirm admiration and she never would anyway. He looked at the photograph again, focusing on the eyes – on the blackened, grainy hollows that were her eyes. He had seen that look before – the night he first met her and she had tried, unsuccessfully, to hide it under a ton of mascara. He remembered how she had burst into tears then as well, on their walk home under the stars, and how he had put his arms around her to comfort her. He wished he could comfort her now.

II

Dominic's prediction proved correct. Rumours were spreading that Nicola Carson was a patient at Malvern Hall – a private psychiatric and rehabilitation clinic near Bromley – though what she was being treated for, no one seemed entirely sure. Was it drug addiction?

Schizophrenia? Bipolar disorder? The tabloid press – their hawk eyes riveted to her ever since the BAFTAs – also got wind of the impending lawsuit. The tsunami of interest generated by this bombshell would have barely washed over a toddler's toes, since everyone assumed it was a joke. Nonetheless, as with all jokes in the highly conductive world of Wapping and Fleet Street, it went the rounds of the watering holes: some old nutter living on a windswept marsh in Sussex was cashing in on Nicola's determination to self-destruct by claiming *he* was the author of her prize-winning novel *Loss* and was taking her to court to prove it. It was all fantasy, of course, but it would have made a lovely story when there was nothing else going on in the world except the usual famines, wars and environmental disasters of which their readers were heartily sick. But none of their litigation-fearing editors would run with it since there was not a shred of proof.

*

In a pause between meetings, Anne was thinking yet again about Nicola's behaviour at the BAFTAs and wondering whether to add it to the list which lay before her on her desk and which formed the first page of the folder of notes, correspondence and other material she had compiled over the previous months. So far it said:

1) *Testimony from Tom Newcomb – renowned and respected author*
2) *Testimony from me – solicitor*
3) *Testimony from Dominic – former editor*
4) *Testimony from David – corporate lawyer*
5) *Time with Ted in Richmond – opportunity*
6) *Time frame*
7) *N C's time in clinic following attempted suicide*

She raised her eyes and gazed through the window for a while. Then she scrubbed out the final item.

III

On the morning of February 27th, a letter was delivered to Malvern Hall by special messenger, his instructions being to hand it to the recipient in person and obtain a signature. Dr Lennox, Nicola's psychiatrist and the director of the hospital, was called out of a counselling session. As soon as the messenger had gone, she tore open the envelope and gazed at its contents in bewilderment.

'What the fuck is this?'

Dr Lennox took the document from her and examined it, his face forming into a frown. 'It's a writ of summons, Nicola. We need to talk to your solicitor.'

She looked at once defiant and terrified. 'Is this that fucking Horizon Pictures again?'

'No, it's a private individual – someone called Edward Haymer. It seems he's bringing a civil action against you for theft of his intellectual property. But you mustn't worry. It's just some opportunist trying to cash in on your situation.'

She stared at him for five full seconds, shaking her head slowly in disbelief. Then she dissolved into tears.

Later that day, Dr Lennox murmured to Maisy, the nurse who had been assigned to their famous patient, 'Watch her. Watch her like a hawk.'

*

Nicola had a pair of magic shoes. She had bought them in San Francisco. They were red and she loved them and took them everywhere with her because, being magic, they gave her the power to escape whenever she felt trapped or in danger. Not that she had ever used that power – yet.

They had been ordinary shoes when she bought them (insofar as Ralph Lauren can ever be ordinary) but they'd been turned into magic shoes by this really clever guy called Jez – a friend of Hal's – who made unusual props for films. Jez was sweet and funny and tubby and a genius – though he did have some personal hygiene issues. He had been with Hal since the early days when everything had been done with models instead of CGI. Jez hated CGI. He was a craftsman. Okay, he had flunked chemistry in college but had gone on to do some amazing things with latex and silica and polymers and all kinds of rubbery substances, finding new ways to mould and model them and give them strength and suppleness and versatility. All the stuff in Hal's 'B movie' period – monsters from peoples' nightmares, horrible facial disfigurements, even the odd alien – had been cooked up by Jez and his assistant Bud in their amazing workshop, which was like some mad scientist's laboratory. He just couldn't stop making things. When he wasn't making things for films he'd make them for his friends – and that was how he came to make Nicola's magic shoes – although, strictly speaking, only one of them was magic – the left one. The plan had been to provide a covert conveyance for her little 'pick-me-up' over the many borders she had to cross in the course of her work. But she had found another, more important use for it.

It was the afternoon of the day of the summons. All of a sudden everyone wanted to see her in court. The company producing the film she'd dropped out of were suing her for breach of contract, or something. They were losing a fortune, they claimed. More fool them for throwing a fortune at her in the first place. She'd never asked for it. It was her agent who handled all that. She was just one little actress and a lousy one at that. There were loads of others they could have used. Thousands of others. Millions of others. All better than her. And now there was Ted. She had always known he would re-emerge from the shadows, sooner or later. She had never imagined it would be like this.

Maisy knocked on the door and entered without waiting for a response. Come on, she was late for group therapy. Round as a football in her white uniform, Maisy seemed to glide noiselessly like this great, grinning ghost. She was always grinning. She never stopped fucking grinning. She said she wasn't going to group therapy – she was too depressed. She wanted a bath. Maisy told her she couldn't have a bath. She could have a shower.

'I want a bath!'

'I'm afraid you can't, honey. Not today.'

'Why not?'

'Because there's a problem with the plumbing.'

'Yeah *right*. So how come the shower's working then?'

She knew she was on suicide watch. People could drown themselves in a bath. Although it was bloody difficult. She'd tried it once, just out of interest. The mind may want out but the body fights back. It spasms and chokes and gasps for breath.

Maisy sighed. 'Okay, here's the deal. If you want a bath, I sit in with you. If you want to be on your own, it's a shower.'

'I'll have a shower.'

Maisy would at least allow her the dignity of undressing in private and that was when she would transfer her precious cargo to the deep pocket of her bathrobe – a bathrobe with no belt with which she could strangle herself but with a razor-sharp blade in the pocket.

Alone in her room, she dropped the blade on the floor then hastily picked it up and gazed at it, transfixed for a moment by the clarity of its cutting edge, by the glint as it caught the light. There were blades and there were blades – some would do the job cleanly and efficiently, others would just make a mess; some were too small to hold in your trembling fingers (your fingers always trembled), others were the wrong shape. She had selected this one carefully and it was perfect. Ideally it should be supported by a handle but that would be impossible in these circumstances. And these were the circumstances in which it had to happen.

She was clutching her robe around her and smiling sweetly when Maisy was allowed in. She entered her *en suite* shower-room and closed the door, knowing that Maisy would settle down in the armchair with her book. A light came on and there was the low hum of an extractor fan. It was a windowless room with no lock on the door but there was no reason why Maisy should disturb her as long as she could hear her splashing merrily away. She took the blade out of her pocket, removed the 'suicide friendly' plastic dispenser from the soap dish and put the blade in its place. Then she took off the bathrobe and laid it over the stool.

She turned on the single shower tap. Hot and cold water came gushing out already mixed and the heat was regulated so patients couldn't scald themselves. They thought of everything, the clever bastards. But in a few moments the room was pleasantly warm and hazy.

She stepped into the shower, raised her face and swept back her hair, her eyes closed, her features screwed up in the spray, allowing the water to splash all over her cheeks and eyelids and forehead, to trickle down into the roots of her hair and over her shoulders. Echoes of sensations travelled up to her brain but she barely felt them, observing them as though from a distance. She lowered her eyes to the landscape of her body down which the rivulets of water were finding their way around every curve and swelling, through every valley and crevice – smooth, pale skin and purple, puckered skin and fine, downy hair and coarse, curly hair – and she thought of all the times in her life that that landscape had been kissed, had been caressed, had been violated. Why, she wondered vaguely, did they call it 'making love'? It had nothing to do with love. She had lost count of the men she had been with but not one of them had made her feel loved. Except one.

She was suddenly bored with delaying. It was time to go. She knew the pain would be horrific but she was not afraid of pain – not that kind of pain, anyway. That kind of pain was just a surge of electrical impulses carrying warning signals to the brain. You had to externalise it, to distance yourself from it, as though you were already out of your body. Besides, if she did it properly, the pain would only last a second and she'd be over the threshold, she'd be home and dry, she'd be safe at last where no one could get to her – not Ted, not Horizon Pictures, nobody. Suddenly, bizarrely, she thought of her father – how he had held her in his arms, how he had kissed her and said, 'I have to go, my darling. It's very important to me that you understand that.' It's important to *you* that I understand that! I'm seven years old, for fuck's sake! She observed dispassionately the purple tracks leading down the underside of her arm to the nest of veins under the ball of her thumb then everything was blurred. Fuck! She was crying! That was no good! That would ruin everything! She groped for the towel and dragged it across her face. Then she reached out and picked up the blade.

There came a knock at the door. 'Everything okay, honey?'

She hastily replaced the blade in the soap dish and slapped the dispenser over it. Christ, this was all going wrong! She was trembling like a leaf.

'Yes, of course everything's okay!' she yelled. 'Fuck off and leave me in peace!'

She had to act fast. Time was running out. She grabbed the blade, which was slimy from the soap, dropped it, picked it up then wiped it clean on the towel. She put it down again then took her flannel and wrapped it round her arm, just below the elbow, yanking it as tight as it would go and then, with great difficulty, tying it in a knot with her right hand, the other end gripped between her teeth. It wasn't much use as a tourniquet but it was better than nothing. Then she took a deep breath, clenched her eyes shut and gouged downwards into her flesh.

Why Maisy came in at that moment she would never know. Some instinct born of long experience telling her all was not well, something in the way she had smiled at her as she entered the shower room, something in her tone of desperation mingled with the joy of near triumph when she had yelled that everything was okay? In a split second her hand had grabbed her wrist, squeezing it with phenomenal strength, immobilising it in mid-air.

'Let me *go*,' she screamed, mustering all her own strength, which was considerable, to release her hand. But Maisy's grip could have been powered by hydraulics and was holding her arm rigid while she screamed 'Let me go!' over and over again and tried to pummel her thigh with her other fist. But Maisy, uniform drenched in blood and water, hair plastered over her head, was delicately prizing open her fingers and removing the blade with her other hand. Nicola, forced to her knees, was still screaming 'Let me go!' when the danger passed. Maisy did so, letting her slump down into a pool of her own blood, still crying – no longer in fury but in pleading, sobbing desperation, 'Let me go! Let me go! Just let me *go*.'

Then everything went black.

*

Dr Lennox was deeply shaken. It was his worst nightmare – or rather, his second worst nightmare. His worst nightmare would have been if she had succeeded. To have someone kill themselves on his watch was tragedy enough but Nicola Carson! All eyes were already riveted to her, following the BAFTAs, and the consequences for Malvern Hall and for his career did not bear thinking about. And he still couldn't figure out how she had got that blade into her bathroom. Patients in the Observation Unit were required to sign a document stating that, should it prove necessary, they would allow their personal possessions to be searched for illegal substances or the means by which they might harm themselves. The expensive but slender possessions Nicola had brought with her had passed with flying colours.

Miraculously, she had not penetrated an artery, only veins. The situation had been handled in-house, therefore – there had been no need to rush her into A&E. She would stay in the Observation Unit and be kept under close medical and psychiatric scrutiny.

He spoke to each member of staff individually but made the same speech – a very awkward one, since the subtext was that it would be prudent not to breathe a word about what had happened to anyone. It was not in his nature to make such a speech but he had no choice. Nonetheless, he was a committed professional and his first concern was the mental and physical wellbeing of his patient. How to protect her from these vultures who wanted to devour her in court? The production company was not such a problem – production companies only cared about money and would probably settle out of court for some colossal sum – a colossal sum being the one thing that was not a problem for Nicola. The other suit would be harder to deal with. It was being brought by some individual who believed he had right on his side and was interested only in proving it. Then, late in the afternoon of the day following the incident in the shower, a solicitor phoned asking to speak to Nicola. What he had to say was a gift from Heaven.

*

Anne's mobile rang as she was on her way from her office to her car. It was Bill Peach.

'I assume you know,' he said.

'Know what?'

'About your husband withdrawing the suit.'

She froze in her tracks, her face forming into a grimace of incomprehension. 'But he *can't* do that.'

'Of course he can.'

'But ... *why?*'

'I don't know. He just said he'd changed his mind and asked me to make up my account.'

Anne was shaking her head in consternation. 'Bill, just keep everything on hold for the moment. I'm going to talk to him.'

Luckily she had no appointments that afternoon and went to confront him face to face, taking her Wellingtons since they forecast rain. It started to fall just as she was entering Wemborne. The field across which she trudged was already a quagmire.

She hammered on his door. The grubby lace curtains twitched and, a moment later, it opened.

'What the hell are you playing at?'

'I'm sorry?'

'Don't go all vague on me. You know what I'm talking about.'

He sighed. 'You'd better come in.'

Frowning, she clambered into the caravan. At least she was now prepared for what met her eyes and her nostrils.

'Would you like some tea?'

'No, I wouldn't like any sodding *tea*. I'd like an explanation."

'I've changed my mind, that's all.'

'So I gathered, but why, for God's sake? And why didn't you talk to me first?'

'Because I knew how you'd react. We're not going to win. I know we're not. I was lying awake last night, thinking about it, and it all became glaringly obvious. We're going to lose and it's going to ruin me. It's just too big a risk.'

'I thought you didn't care about that. "Why should I care about ruin when I've lived on nothing all these years anyway? They can take my typewriter and my clarinet" – wasn't that what you said? Come on, Ted, where's that glorious fatalism when we need it?'

'I got cold feet, that's all.'

'But we've come so far! I always wanted to pursue this, as you know, but the lawyer in me had doubts. It was you who changed my mind. It was you who had the idea of getting Tom Newcomb on side ...'

'Tom Newcomb's lying,' he said.

'What?'

'He's lying. I know he is.'

'Why should he be?'

'Vindictiveness. He's born a grudge against Nicola all these years and this is his chance to get back at her.'

'What on earth are you talking about?'

'Look, Tom Newcomb may be a famous writer but he's also a serial womaniser and he always thought he was God's gift – he probably still does. He didn't take Nicola under his wing out of the goodness of his heart or because he cared about helping young writers, he did it because he wanted to sleep with her. I don't know the precise details – whether she politely refused or whether she mortally wounded his male pride in some way – but I'm assuming it's the latter, knowing her. And her smart-arse lawyers are going to expose him in an instant.'

'Of course they'll try to because that's what they're paid to do. But he's still a respected literary figure and his testimony has the ring of authority about it, whatever his motives. And the circumstantial evidence backs it up.'

'He's a respected literary figure but his personal life's an emotional bombsite. Two divorces. God knows how many mistresses. They'll ask him why he didn't reveal Nicola's duplicity at the time and he won't have an answer – other than that he wanted to get inside her pants. And someone's who's smitten doesn't make a reliable witness.'

Anne heaved a sigh of exasperation, swept a heap of Ted's underwear onto the floor and rammed herself down in the seat. 'I don't *believe* this.'

'Look, why don't you have some tea?'

'If it'll shut you up on the subject.'

'I've got some fennel tea. It'll calm you down.'

'I don't *want* to calm down.'

'It's just that, if we have ordinary tea, the milk might be off.'

'I'll have it black.'

'I usually put a dash of whisky in it – keeps out the cold.'

'Oh, for God's sake, Ted, just make the bloody tea. You can piss in it for all I care.'

He filled the battered kettle and struck a match and soon it was roaring away cheerfully.

'The thing is,' he went on, peering into his little cupboard in search of a mug that wasn't too chipped, 'I've been having a long, hard think and I've realised that what I said over lunch that day – about not caring whether I get published – isn't entirely true. But the fact is my novel has been published. Those are my words out there, not hers – they're my thoughts, my observations, my characters, my images – and, thanks to Nicola, millions of people are reading them – far more than if I'd published it myself. The only people I care about – you, the children, our close friends – already know I'm the real author. I've even won the Connaught Prize – indirectly – not that I give a damn about prizes except insofar as they make more people read the book. But it's the book that matters, not the name on the cover. Actually, thanks to Nicola, I've got everything I wanted.'

Anne grimaced. 'Everything you *wanted*? You wanted success. You wanted to be acknowledged as a serious writer. You wanted to communicate, to be remembered. And I wanted that too, which is why I supported you all those years and why I suggested you give up work to devote yourself to it. What's happened to you, Ted?'

'I've altered my priorities. Grown up, maybe. Like I said, living here on my own with nothing has put things in perspective. It's restored my sense of what's important in life.'

He was bouncing a tea bag in a cup of boiled water, into which he then tipped a slug of whisky before handing it to her.

She gazed at the black liquid for a while. 'It just seems such a bloody shame. What you say about Tom Newcomb may be true but it's only part of the picture. She played right into our hands by going on like that at the BAFTAs, whatever Dominic says. Something's cutting her up inside, I know it is. And more and more people are coming out of the woodwork saying that, now it's been brought to their attention, that doesn't look like the work of a twenty-three-year-old girl. We'd have won, Ted, I'm damn sure we would and you'd have finally got the credit you deserve.'

'I don't want the credit at the cost of destroying someone else. And as to being vindicated, I never will be. There'll never be absolute proof. Even if the court did decide in my favour, she'd still have her armies of loyal fans who'd always maintain she's the real author.'

'But she's committed a crime. She ought to be punished.'

'I think she's being punished by her own demons.'

Anne responded with a hopeless sigh and they both fell silent.

'And what about your other novels? Are you going to let her publish those too?'

'Of course not. But I will get them published, I promise. By the time-honoured method. I'm still determined on that.'

She snorted.

'Well, I'm touched by your faith in me.'

'Oh come on, Ted. You've spent your entire life trying to get your novels published by the time-honoured method. What makes you think anything's changed?'

'*I've* changed. I've always suffered from that negativity you talked about – an in-built conviction that I'm never going to succeed with my writing. And I've always been in awe of publishers even though I never stop running them down. But I don't feel that anymore. I've had some insight into how things work and I've realised that publishers are just people, working in an office and trying to make a living like everyone else. They're not Gods sitting on some Olympus holding our fate in their hands. So I'm going to take the bull by the horns and approach things in a positive way from now on. No more anger, no more righteous indignation, no more self-pity, just professionalism. It'll happen, you see. I don't need the backlash from some high-profile scandal.'

Anne was about to say something but she stopped herself. She knew it was pointless. When all was said and done, it was Ted's novel and Ted's decision and, whatever the rights and wrongs of the situation, they were no longer part of each other's lives. So she took a sip of her alcoholic tea – which was actually rather comforting – and sank into silence, listening to the patter of raindrops on the caravan roof.

'I never thought it'd end up like this,' she murmured.

'Like what?'

'When we first met at Oxford, I was convinced you were going to be a great writer. I imagined you getting your first novel published. The launch party. The glowing reviews. You being feted by all and sundry, me beaming with pride. I reckoned it'd be about two years after we graduated – poor, naïve little girl that I was.'

'I've always appreciated your faith in me. It's always given me strength. But I know you think I was never ambitious enough, that I never pushed myself forward enough.'

'I did at the time. But now, looking back, maybe it was just that you were an idealist, that you weren't prepared to make any compromises. I admire you for that. I just never realised how hard it was going to be. But now, here you are, winner of the Connaught Prize – by proxy at least. It's weird.'

'I'm sorry,' he said.

'What about?'

'Just that … things didn't work out differently.'

IV

Miranda Cole was surprised to see an email from Tom Newcomb in her mailbox. She opened it straight away.

Miranda

Long time no see – hope you're well. You may or may not know that I was recently asked to testify in court regarding the authorship of Nicola Carson's novel. I've now been informed that the whole thing's been dropped and I'm no longer needed and I must say I'm a bit pissed off. I was rather looking forward to it – Jo-Jo and I were bringing the kids down to London to visit the Natural History Museum. Did you know that Edwin Haymer – the alleged author – was once a pupil of mine? I remember him vividly because he showed so much promise. It's blatantly obvious to me that he was intimidated by some henchman of Nicola's into dropping the case. He was probably threatened, or his family threatened.

I had a feeling there was something fishy about that book the first time I read it – I mentioned it to you at the time, if you remember – but I never gave it another thought until this lad turned up on my doorstep asking me to testify. But it now seems plain as day that Haymer wrote it and that she pinched it from him and used it as a springboard to her glittering career. It all makes perfect sense, though I suppose it's too late to do anything about it now. I just thought I'd let you know my thoughts on the subject, since no one else seems to care anymore.

Jo-Jo sends her love. All the best,
Tom

*

Dominic heaved a sigh, having spent half an hour trawling through the appointments columns of the Guardian. For months he had been living his dream but reality could not be kept at bay any longer – his car tax expired at the end of the month, his television license was overdue, final demands were dropping like confetti through the letter-box. He could not believe he was back in this situation, back with the dreary round of filling out application forms, dredging up referees from his dim and distant past ('You may remember I was in your tutor group of 1998'), putting on a suit and tie and facing a squad of condescending arseholes, trying to convince them that the job they were offering was exactly what he'd always dreamed of, that he saw himself as an individualist and a team player, that he felt he had many unique talents to bring to the position and saw himself still loyally serving the company in ten, twenty, fifty, a hundred years' time, such would be his gratitude for being granted this glorious fucking opportunity. He folded the paper and slung it aside in disgust.

His gaze wandered around his flat – the flat which had become a tip since Katie no longer imposed her unique brand of order on it, the flat which he would probably have to abandon soon for something even smaller, cheaper and grottier. He thought again of California, of the California he had passed up, of golden sands and deep blue sea (or 'ocean' as Katie had liked to call it) and she in her black bikini, happy and suntanned, lying at his side. Oh Katie. Dearest Katie. He'd treated her like shit and now he was reaping the rewards.

No. He mustn't go there. He mustn't lose heart. Whatever had happened, however desperate the situation, he still had his scoop – *his* scoop – and he must hold on to it with all his might. He thought back to the evening he had first opened that copy of *Loss* and to all the horizons his discovery had opened before his eyes. Nicola Carson was still red hot property, even though she had dropped out of her latest film and hidden herself in rehab. And Ted had done him a favour with his inexplicable withdrawal of the lawsuit. The story would go cold and that would allow him a breathing space to muster his resources and get a clear, unobstructed run at his target. Ted and Anne Haymer, Tom Newcomb and William Peach were out of the picture. They were history. And if he did manage to prove that Nicola Carson was guilty after all, the glory would be his and his alone. But that was the operative word – *prove*. He had to find a way to prove, finally and irrefutably, what he knew to be true.

But how to do it? How the *hell* to do it?

Chapter Seven

2008

He sank back among the pillows, savouring the warmth of Nicola's nakedness coiled around his own. Gently he slid his arm round her waist and gathered her to his chest and she smiled up at him, caressed his cheek and kissed him gently on the lips.

The digital clock, glowing in the dark, said ten past one. Slowly, rhythmically, he stroked her shoulder and inwardly braced himself. The brainwave he had had that desperate day had born spectacular – if unexpected – fruit. He had found her in Malvern Hall, he had won her trust, she had come to his flat and finally to his bed. And now, though he wanted nothing less than to destroy the intimacy of this moment, he knew he could not carry on with this charade a moment longer – not now that things were the way they were between them. But then it was she who murmured, 'Dominic?'

'Mm?'

'There's something I have to tell you.'

He waited in silence.

'You remember when you asked me, yesterday, about my writing? About *Loss*?'

'Yes.'

'Well, whatever I said, I was lying. I never wrote *Loss*. In fact, there never was a novel called *Loss*. It was called *The Tyranny of Love* and it was written by someone called Edward Haymer.'

His fingertips froze on her skin.

'Did you hear what I just said?'

'Yes.'

'And what do you think?'

'I ... don't know what to think.' Then he added, 'So those rumours that were going around – after the BAFTAs. They were true.'

'Yes. They were true.'

They lay quietly in each other's arms, staring at the ceiling.

'Have you told anyone else?'

'No. Only you. I knew I was going to have to tell you sooner or later – if we were going to have a proper relationship. That's why I wanted to be sure you wouldn't let me down. But I have to tell the rest of the world. I can't go on living this lie.'

'You mean ... you want to confess to the entire world that you stole that manuscript?'

She jerked back in the crook of his arm, frowning. '*Stole* it? I never stole it.'

'You didn't?'

'No. Ted gave it to me.'

He stared down at her. 'You mean Ted – Edward Haymer – was *in* on it?'

'Yes. It was his idea.'

'Nicola, I'm not with you.'

'He knew he was never going to publish that novel himself and he didn't want to anyway. But he'd been working on another novel – a much better one, he said – and he desperately wanted to get his career off the ground – and mine too. I was young, pretty I guess, I had it all going for me. So the plan was that I'd pretend to be this totally cool young author and when I'd made a success of the book, we'd share the proceeds and I'd use my contacts to get his other book published.'

'But this Ted, he's some kind of weirdo who lives in a caravan miles from anywhere, isn't he? How did you even know someone like that?'

'He's not a weirdo, far from it. I met him at this pub where I worked and we became kind of soul-mates. United against the common enemy, I guess. He emailed me his novel to get my opinion and I thought it was brilliant. I'd moved to London by then but I was getting nowhere. I was skint, dossing with friends ...'

'So, how did it happen exactly?'

She was silent a while, remembering. Then she told him about their time together in Richmond. 'He didn't want to publish *Tyranny* under his own name. There was too much wrong with it, he said, though I thought he was talking crap. "But if you like it so much," he said, "why don't you publish it under your name?"'

'And how did you react?'

'I thought he was joking. When I realised he wasn't, I said "I can't do that! That's *your* novel. I can't take the credit for something I haven't done." But he pointed out that it was just going to sit in a bottom drawer for all eternity so somebody may as well get the credit for it.'

'*Jesus.*'

'It was even he who suggested I change my name. So I reinvented myself as Nicola Carson – cool, beautiful, super-talented Nicola Carson. I can't tell you how liberating it was to kill off Nicola Pearson. I wish I'd done it years before.'

'So he talked you round?'

'In the end. Like I said, I thought it was crazy at first but after I'd mulled it over for a while, it began to dawn on me, "Hey, this could actually work." And by a stroke of luck I'd met Tom Newcomb, the author.'

'He helped you launch it, didn't he?'

'Yeah, he was in his seventies by then but he still couldn't keep his hands off me, and I'm afraid I kind of led him on a bit. I showed him *my* – in inverted commas – novel and asked him if he could recommend an agent. That was how I met Miranda – Miranda Cole. And the rest, as they say, is history.'

Dominic sank into thought. And as he thought, the mists cleared. All of a sudden Ted's bizarre, defensive behaviour when he first met him at The Queen's Head was explained. He'd known about it all along, he'd had it planned all along, using his first novel which he'd decided was dispensable. 'I never even liked that book,' he remembered him saying. 'The style was too clever-clever, too self-conscious.' But when the novel proved a roaring success, he found he was not so idealistic after all and did want to take the credit for it. And it was he, Dominic, who had offered him that opportunity. That was why, when he first imparted his information, Ted had scrutinised him for hours without uttering a word. He had been weighing up in his mind something which had never occurred to him until that moment – the possibility of getting back at Nicola by claiming that she – as this stranger clearly assumed – had simply stolen his manuscript. If he believed it, why shouldn't everyone else believe it? She was already a star and the scandal would turn him into a star himself and establish his reputation overnight. And, of course, she couldn't say what had really happened without admitting she wasn't the author – something he had reckoned she would never ever do. But when the court case got going and the likes of Anne and Tom Newcomb started baying for Nicola's blood, he had lost his nerve. He knew she was volatile, unpredictable, emotionally unstable. Supposing she cracked under the pressure and *did* come out with what had really happened? His new-found fame would turn him into a laughing stock. And if the case had come to court, he would have committed perjury. That was why he had withdrawn the lawsuit at precisely the moment she had proved herself – at the BAFTAs – to be teetering on the brink of a breakdown.

'*Bastard*,' he murmured under his breath.

'He wasn't really. He was just Tom being Tom. And I did give him to believe ...'

'I'm not talking about Tom. I'm talking about Haymer.'

'I don't blame him either. I treated him like shit. I've never ever stopped feeling guilty about it.'

'In what way did you treat him like shit?'

'I betrayed our friendship. He was good to me, Ted. He believed in me when nobody else did. He could see that under that foul-mouthed, bolshy cow there was someone with a bit of talent who wanted to make something of her life.'

'How did you betray your friendship?'

'I forgot about him. Once I was out there in the fast lane, I completely forgot about him – the one person in the world who'd ever helped me. But I wasn't just being a self-centred little airhead – I wanted to forget him, I wanted to forget he was the person to whom I owed everything. I wanted to kid myself that *Loss* had nothing to do with my success, that it was all just down to my amazing acting talent. When it all went tits-up at Richmond, we agreed to keep contact to a minimum but I don't think he expected me to take it *that* literally. I never sent him his share of the advance or the royalties or the Connaught Prize money. And when my conscience got the better of me, I told Alison, my PA, to start sending him wads of cash in jiffy bags care of his local – money I never even noticed, I had so much by then. I made out to her that I was taking care of an old friend who wanted the money in cash to avoid tax.'

Dominic remembered the barman asking him to tell Ted that another of 'his parcels' had arrived – news that had clearly caused him embarrassment. Those unmarked jiffy bags had not contained erotica, as he had suspected, but something far more potent.

'Then she told me he'd been trying to contact me and wanted to see me.'

She paused for a while, still staring at the ceiling.

'I agreed at first, but then I bottled out. I just couldn't face him. I knew he was going to want me to pull strings to get his other novel published but fame had made me paranoid. I was terrified that if I started plugging this unknown author, someone might take another look at *Loss* and start putting two and two together.'

'So when was this?'

She thought about it. 'I don't know. Last October, I guess.'

Last October. And – he was willing to bet – sandwiched between his first visit to The Queen's Head and Ted phoning him to say he'd had a change of heart.

'Couldn't you have had a word in your agent's ear?'

'I didn't want to ask Miranda any favours.'

'Why not?'

She hesitated again. 'Miranda wasn't just my agent – she was more than that. Much more. She took me in when I got kicked out of Richmond and I lived with her while *Loss* was being launched. But she became possessive. If I went out for the evening with a mate, she'd want to know where I'd been – stuff like that. It got to the point where I couldn't hack it, so I left. She came after me to apologise and persuade me to come back and we had a row.'

'Right.'

'Anyway, I got Alison to phone Ted and tell him I was too busy to see him. He must have been furious – understandably – because he asked her to give me a message: tell her to take another look at the Hal Birling interview on the Left Bank Show.'

'What was that about?'

'They'd done a feature years before on Hal and his work. He was asked why he cast someone with no film experience in the lead of *All about Me* when there were so many great actresses around. He said it was the book. He knew I was a writer as well as an actor and when he read my novel, he knew I'd be perfect for Amy. "Actors only act," he said, "but she'd bring a dimension of honesty to the role, since those were her own experiences she was writing about." Ironic, eh? I was a mess at the time, anyway. I'd just broken up with Tony – Tony Basarro – who I was going to marry.'

'I remember reading about it.'

'So you'll also remember it was called off at the last minute.'

'Yeah, but I thought that was because …'

'Because I was seeing Miguel Hernandez? I was. But that wasn't why I broke up with Tony.'

'So why did you break up with him?'

'Oh come on, Dominic. How can you love someone, have kids with them, commit your whole life to them when that life just feels like one big lie? Can you imagine it? "Darling, Mummy didn't really write that famous book everyone talks about. She was just pretending. But we mustn't tell anyone – it can be our little secret, okay?" Or do I lie to my husband and kids as well, and spend my whole life in terror in case they find out? And yet I knew that if I told him the truth, he would always despise and distrust me, even if he stayed with me, which he probably wouldn't. And that wasn't the only relationship that ended that way.'

Tenderly he reached over and stroked a lock of hair from her face. He felt the wetness of tears. 'Hey …'

'It was all my fault. I've been a fool.'

'No, you haven't. You were a victim.'

'I was a fool. I wanted a short cut.'

He tightened his arm around her. Somewhere, out across the city, a siren was wailing – an ambulance racing to someone else's drama.

'So what happened?' he murmured, 'after Ted delivered his little barb?'

'I tried to ignore it. But I couldn't. It worked on me like a worm inside an apple. I'd always felt, in my heart of hearts, that there were loads of people who could've done Amy just as well as me – probably better. And I knew that was how it was always going to be. However far I went with my career, it was a career that never would've happened without *Loss*, and in years to come people would still look back and say it was the best thing I'd ever done. In fact, if it hadn't been for *Loss* I'd still be waiting tables and doing commercials for disposable nappies. There'd be no escape. And I'd never have the satisfaction of knowing that I'd achieved my success through my own talents, by my own determination. Acting was all I had, Dominic. It was the one pure and decent thing in my life, the one thing I trusted. And I felt it had been contaminated, like I'd somehow cheated.'

'That's bullshit! You were brilliant in *All about Me*. You won a BAFTA and an Oscar for your acting – your *acting* not your writing. That book was a lucky break, something to kick-start your career. Nearly all famous actors can trace their careers to some lucky break.'

'It wasn't a lucky break. It was a crime.'

'It wasn't a *crime*,' he snorted.

'Of course it was. We defrauded the publisher, Connaught International, the reading public ...'

'Nicola, you're just not getting it, are you? You say that book made you famous. It was you who made the book famous. I remember the publicity when *Loss* came out. Your face was all over the press, you were the darling of the reviewers, you had the crustiest old critics eating out of your hand. It was you they were raving about, not the book. You weren't cheating, you were doing what you do – acting. That was a role you pulled off and you pulled it off like a pro. Trust me, I'm a publisher. I know how these things work.'

'It's really sweet of you to say that. But you're talking crap and you know it.'

She sat up, hugging her knees, and stared towards the window where streetlight was filtering through the blinds, outlining the slender grace of her shoulders.

'I made a decision,' she said, 'just before you turned up at Malvern Hall. I was going to confess, come clean, get it off my chest whatever the consequences. Then you appeared, with your plan to write a book, and I thought … maybe that would be the way to do it. Leach it out little by little, explain the context, the mitigating circumstances because, the truth is, I didn't have the balls to stand up and announce it cold. But I need to do it, Dominic. And I need to put things right with Ted. I need to feel good about myself again, and maybe start over. And I can't wait for our book, not anymore. I need to do it now.' She turned and looked down at him, her eyes pleading. 'You'll help me, won't you?'

'Of course I'll help you. But you can't just come out and confess it cold. People need to know the context – about your childhood, about your father walking out on you, about your struggles, your breakdown. They need to know exactly what happened and then they'll understand.'

'But I can't say exactly what happened, can I?'

'Why not?'

'Because it'll expose Ted as a liar. People knew he was accusing me of stealing *Tyranny*. They may have thought it was nothing at the time, but they won't if I tell the truth. He'll be a joke. And that's the last thing I want.'

'It's no more than he deserves,' he mumbled.

'No it's not. He doesn't deserve that.'

'Nicola, this is a man who was prepared to lie in court to destroy you.'

'Can you blame him? Besides, it wasn't him who brought the lawsuit. His name may have been on the forms but his wife was behind it. She's a lawyer. And she hated me.'

'Because of Richmond?'

'Yeah. Because of Richmond.'

He lay in anguish in the dark. 'What actually happened in Richmond?'

'Something special.'

He laid his head back in the pillow and exhaled slowly. 'So what are you proposing we do?'

'We make out the truth is what you assumed – that I stole the manuscript.'

'No. No way.'

'It's the *only* way, Dominic. I'm finished. It's over for me. But if I can give Ted a chance to make it as an author, I'd feel my life hasn't been completely wasted.'

'Nicola, for Christ's sake! You're twenty-eight! You're a brilliant actress! You've got your whole life ahead of you!'

'Dominic, get real! The media loves nothing better than destroying celebrities – you know that – and they'll have a field day with this. They'll never let me recover from it.'

He relapsed into thought. 'There's got to be another way. Maybe I could try to get his novel published, if that's all he cares about. I've got contacts in the business ...'

'It's too late. Things have changed. *I've* changed. I've made up my mind what I'm going to do – I've just been waiting for someone I trust to help me do it. And now I've found you.'

He did not respond at once. 'What makes you so sure you can trust me?' he said.

'Because you said you'd never let me down.'

'Yeah, well, I'm not going to let you down. But I'm not going to assist in your professional suicide either.'

'All right then. Maybe I'll just find the courage to do it on my own.'

He heaved a sigh. 'Okay. Let's say I do agree to help you. What have you got planned for afterwards? After the press has torn you limb from limb and your publisher and the Connaught people have sued the pants off you and every stand-up comic in the land has made their audiences laugh their heads off at your expense? What are you going to do then? Assuming you're not in prison.'

'I'm going to kill myself.'

He was stunned into silence.

'Don't even joke about something like that.'

'Relax. I'm an actress. I'm going to pretend to kill myself. I'm going to fake my own death.'

'Don't joke about that either.'

'I'm not joking. I've got it all figured out. And it'll be easy since it's common knowledge I'm suicidal. They can tear Nicola to shreds all they want but she won't be around to give them the satisfaction. She'll have topped herself. And she'll have gone out in style. People in smart black coats and hats will have said all kinds of nice shit about her and she'll be peacefully stashed away in some country churchyard. I quite fancy Snotsham, actually – that'd be a laugh, wouldn't it? In the shade of some ancient yew with weeds growing out of me. My mother can come and arrange flowers on my grave – she'd be really good at that. She might even shed a tasteful little tear while secretly thinking how great it is not to have to be bothered with me anymore.'

'Nicola, for Christ's sake!'

'It'll just take a few hefty backhanders and luckily I've still got plenty of cash. Then I'll sneak off to New Zealand or somewhere – change my name, change my look, change my identity and start again from scratch. I'm good at that – changing my identity.'

Dominic was listening in rising alarm. He remembered what Dr Lennox had said about bipolar patients believing they could fly. He hadn't mentioned dying and being resurrected.

'You really think that's going to work? Everyone'll recognise you for a start.'

'No they won't. Hal once told me I've got one of those faces which can be made to look like anything I want – like one of those dummies in Harrods. And I can act a different person. I can *be* a different person. That's what I do.'

'That's rubbish! You're an individual. You're you. You're Nicola. And you're … special.'

She was quiet for a while. 'It'll work, Dominic. I know it will.'

'Look, this is crazy. We need to get back to reality. Tomorrow I'm going to get in my car, track down this Ted Haymer and tell him everything you've told me. I'm going to tell him how terrible you feel and how you want to make amends, and I'm going to tell him I'll move heaven and earth – on your behalf – to get his other novels into print. And I'm going to ask him to forgive you.'

'I've got to be the one to ask his forgiveness. To his face.'

'Okay, but I think I should go first, to prepare the ground. I'll explain why you're reluctant to see him, just as you were reluctant to see him when he contacted you. It may take him a while to come to terms with things but he will come to terms with them, I know he will. He's a decent bloke, deep down. He's just bitter. And then, when the time's right ...'

'How do you know he's a decent bloke deep down? You've never met him.'

He froze. 'Sorry?'

'I said, you've never met him.'

'No. No, I haven't. That's true. I'm just ... assuming he is. From what you've said.'

Nicola was silent. Dominic was holding his breath. 'Yeah, well, you're right, he is a decent bloke deep down, which is why I've got to make things right with him.'

He exhaled slowly. He was trembling, very slightly. 'And then ... when you explain about Ted – Edward Haymer, in your confession – you can say that he was understandably bitter but now you've made it up with him and he's getting his other novel published. Happy endings all round. Sort of.'

She considered his words. 'I don't know ...'

'I do. So come on, let's do it. Let's make the confession. I'll be behind you all the way.'

'Really?'

'Really. But how should we do it exactly? Make a statement to the press?'

'No. I've got a better idea.'

II

Later that morning, having passed under Eric Gill's lumbering frieze of Prospero and Ariel, they approached a vast reception desk with the letters 'BBC' emblazoned along its wall. One of the receptionists looked up and did a double take. Despite the tide of famous people ebbing and flowing past her station, the appearance of a Hollywood superstar didn't happen every day of the week.

'How can I help you, Miss Carson?' she smiled.

'I'd like to see the News Editor. It's very important.'

She looked a little nonplussed. 'Would that be the Director of News or the Head of Evening News?'

'I don't care. Whoever decides what goes in the news.'

'Just one moment.' She lifted a receiver, pressed a button and spoke to someone called Rebecca. 'She's sending down Mr Fanning who's our new Deputy Head of Evening News,' she announced when she'd ended the call. 'If you'd care to take a seat for just one moment?' She stood up and walked them the few yards to the cluster of sumptuous sofas as though there were a danger they might not find them on their own. She offered them refreshments but Nicola declined and the girl smiled and returned to her desk.

After a considerable wait, a bespectacled man in his fifties came striding towards them looking stressed and harassed, his expression seeming to say, 'What the hell's *this* about?'

'Miss Carson, it's a pleasure to meet you,' he said, shaking her hand briefly as she and Dominic stood up. 'I love your work and my daughter adored your novel.'

'Thank you. This is my boyfriend, Dominic.'

Dominic shook the man's hand rather dreamily, basking in the title which had just been bestowed upon him. They all sat down.

'I want to make a statement,' said Nicola. 'It should take three minutes air time tops and I want it to go out on the 6 o' clock news.'

The man she was addressing was actually not John Fanning, Deputy Head of Evening News but Alan Tilson, the new Deputy Director of News and Head of News Programmes, an old hand who had cut his teeth on Fleet Street before working as a foreign correspondent in Asia and the Middle East. Nicola's celebrity thus held no magic for him. Guessing the 'statement' had to do with her high-profile love life, he said, 'Miss Carson, with all due respect, do you think the evening news is the best medium for something like this? Maybe the newspapers ... or *Hello* magazine?'

Nicola stared at him then shot to her feet. 'Come on, Dominic, we're going to ITN.'

He raised a hand. 'I'm sorry. Forgive me. I'm having a very stressful day. Please, do sit down and tell me what's on your mind.'

Nicola, having simmered for a few seconds, resumed her seat. Dominic followed suit. 'My novel that your daughter adored so much. You can tell her I didn't write it. I stole it.'

The man's eyebrows rose. 'You *stole* it?'

'That's what I said.'

'From whom?'

'From the guy who wrote it. Edward Haymer. You won't have heard of him.'

'You mean, you just stole this person's manuscript?'

'Yes.'

'And he didn't object?'

'Yes, he did. He tried to sue me. But he couldn't prove it was his.'

The man became thoughtful. 'It won the Connaught Prize, didn't it?'

'Yes.'

'So you accepted the prize money fraudulently?'

'Yes. Along with a fifty grand advance, a couple of million in film rights and God knows how many more in royalties.'

He frowned. 'Miss Carson, are you sure about this?'

'Of course I'm sure. How could I have imagined not writing a novel?'

'No, I mean, are you sure about publicly admitting it? You have committed a crime, after all. Possibly more than one crime.'

'Yes. I want to admit it.'

He lapsed into thought again. 'We're going to have to run this by our legal department.'

'Why?'

'Because Connaught International could sue us. As could your publisher. Which is why it would be better coming from you. Who is your publisher, by the way?'

'Jonathan Hale.'

'Hmm ... an international corporation. We need to run this by our legal department. Definitely.'

'And how long will that take?'

'Not long. We can go ahead with the recording anyway. The question is whether we'll be able to use it.'

*

After leaving Broadcasting House, they had lunch in a French restaurant but Nicola was in a sombre mood. Dominic reached across the table and squeezed her hand. 'It'll be fine,' he said.

'I never realised telling the truth was so fucking complicated.'

'If only you had told the truth.'

'You know what I mean.'

After lunch they went back to the flat where she lay down on the bed. Dominic lay down behind her, threading his arms around her waist. 'So, I'm the official boyfriend, am I?'

'I couldn't be bothered explaining you.'

'*Explaining* me?'

'Yeah, that you're my chauffeur cum sex slave.'

'Right.'

She rolled onto her back and smiled up at him, caressed his cheek then folded her hand behind his head and drew him into a long, tender kiss.

*

The six o' clock news was announced by its rousing signature tune and ingenious graphics. There was a feature on the latest unemployment figures and another about an earthquake in Japan. There was a report from a correspondent about an explosion in Jerusalem, killing three civilians. Then, with an almost imperceptible modulation of tone to mark the transition from global news to a human interest story, the newscaster announced: 'The actress and author Nicola Carson, in a dramatic statement to the BBC earlier today, claimed that she did not write the best-selling novel *Loss* and that she stole the manuscript ...' She appeared in half-frame – head and shoulders, full to camera.

'God, I look like shit.'

'You look perfect. It wouldn't work if you looked your best.'

'I want to say,' said her image on the screen, 'that I'm making this statement entirely voluntarily, that I haven't been coerced or pressured by anyone in any way. I'm going away soon, but before I go I have something very important I want to say. My novel *Loss*, which won the Connaught Prize – I didn't write it. It was written by someone called Edward Haymer.'

She paused, the camera focused on her mercilessly. She rubbed her fingertips fiercely against the side of her nose.

'It happened like this. I met Ted down in Wemborne where I was working as a waitress in his local. I expressed an interest in his writing and asked to read it, so he emailed me his novel, which was called *The Tyranny of Love*. I thought it was superb.

'So why did I steal it and pass it off as my own? God knows. I was a total mess inside my head at the time – I was getting nowhere, flunking auditions, putting peoples' backs up. One night I got totally pi ... inebriated, and just changed the title and the author's name on the file and emailed it to the first agent I found on Google. When I sobered up the next morning, I couldn't believe what I'd done. I mean, if it ever got published, he or his family or friends would recognise it straight away, wouldn't they? But they didn't – not for ages. By the time Ted found out, I was famous and it was very hard for him to convince anyone of the truth.

'So you see, I'm a fraud. A total fraud. There's no way I could've written that book. I'm an actor, not a writer, and being the brilliant young author was just a role I cooked up for myself – a role I really enjoyed, at first. That's what acting's all about, isn't it? Pretence. Make believe. Deception. Lying. But the lying's gone on long enough.

And now, before I go, all I want to say is, I'm sorry. Sorry to everyone who supported me, who helped me, who employed me and who sat through my films. But, most of all, I want to say sorry to Ted. If you're out there, Ted, if you're watching this, I hope you'll finally get the credit you deserve, not to mention the Connaught Prize which is rightfully yours. And I hope you'll now get all your other novels published just like you've always wanted. And that's all I have to say. Just ... sorry again. And goodbye.'

'They used the whole thing,' cried Dominic as they cut back to the newsroom. 'They didn't edit a single word.'

'Shut up!'

There on the screen was Miranda Cole. She appeared to be standing in the street outside her office:

'It's nonsense,' she said into the microphone that was being held out to her, 'complete and utter rubbish. I worked hand-in-glove with Nicola on that book and there's no way it could've been written by someone else. She was right inside the spirit of the text. We discussed it endlessly. She did rewrites ...'

'So why is she saying it was plagiarised?' asked the reporter.

'I've no idea. I've absolutely no idea. But I'm not alone in being concerned about her mental state.'

'*What?*' yelled Nicola at the screen. 'Is she trying to say I'm crazy?'

'What do you suppose she meant by "I'm going away soon"?' asked the reporter.

'That's what I'm concerned about.'

'They have to put that in for balance,' said Dominic. 'Don't worry, it won't make any difference. You've made your confession, that's what matters. And everyone knows she's got a vested interest.'

He made supper that night but Nicola barely touched it. 'It's weird,' she said. 'I thought I'd feel different after I'd come clean. But I don't. I feel just the same. In fact, I don't feel anything.' She laid down her fork and, though it was still light, headed off to bed.

'Have you taken your medication?' he called after her.

'Yeah, yeah, I've taken my medication.' She paused in the doorway. 'We have done the right thing, haven't we?'

He was far from sure they had done the right thing. 'Yes, we have,' he said.

*

After she had gone, he slumped down on the sofa and fell into deep thought, finally giving in to exhaustion and drifting into a doze. Sometime later he was woken by voices down in the alleyway. He roused himself, crossed to the window and peered out. An explosion of camera bulbs blazed in his eyes.

He hurried to the bedroom and gently shook her shoulder. 'Nicola, wake up.'

'What is it?' she mumbled.

'There's a load of paparazzi outside with their cameras pointing at our windows.'

'Oh *shhhhit*. How did they find out where I was?'

'Someone in the building must have tipped them off.'

The doorbell rang. Dominic went through to the little entrance hall and peered through the peephole. The landing was crammed with reporters and photographers. He double-checked the lock and security chain then went round the flat drawing all the curtains. The doorbell kept ringing.

He went back to the living room and shut the door to try to banish it, with partial success. Nicola was now wide awake and sitting on the bed. 'We should've been more careful.'

The doorbell was now ringing continuously.

'Fuck!' he snapped, storming out into the hall and hammering on the door with his fist. 'Fuck off, you bastards!'

'Oi, Dominic, just tell 'er to give us a statement and a few shots and we'll leave you in peace! Fair's fair!'

He reached up and opened the fuse box, which was beside the meter just under the ceiling, and threw the mains switch. The doorbell died just as it was starting up again, along with the rest of the power in the flat. Though it was still just daylight, the whole place, with the curtains drawn, was plunged into gloom. He went back to Nicola.

'Maybe if I give them a statement, tell them you're ill.'

'They won't be happy with that. They'll keep this up forever, or until something better comes along – like World War Three. You don't know what they're like. We've got to get away from here, Dominic. I don't care where – just somewhere where we can be ourselves.'

He stared at her. 'You mean you … really want me to come with you?'

'Yeah, that's what I want. If that's what you want.'

III

Peering through the dawn mist, Frank Brewer wondered if he was hallucinating. He could have sworn he saw a young man with a load of gadgetry slung round his shoulders scuttling, bent double, between the bushes like a soldier taking out a military target. Then there was another. And another. And another. Bellowing 'Get off my land!' he raised his shotgun and discharged both barrels over their heads – the explosion cracking the air and sending them tearing back to their cars with cries of 'Jesus *Christ*.' and '*Fuck* me.'

Ted's head appeared in the caravan door. 'What the hell's going on, Frank?'

'Just shooting vermin!'

'Do you have to do it right on my doorstep? You scared the shit out of me!'

'It's you that's attracting them!'

'What, *pigeons*?'

'No, photographers! You're famous, mate! Didn't you know?'

It was true. Ever since Nicola's appearance (which was trending on Twitter and had notched up more than a million hits on You Tube), the search engines of the world had been trawling for information about the mysterious Edward Haymer from whom she had purportedly stolen her novel. The Queen's Head (which had quickly been identified as the 'local' she had referred to) was busier than Ian had ever seen it that lunchtime, despite his attempts to keep the press from harassing his regulars. He had expected Ted to stay away that day but he appeared right on cue for his midday sandwich and pint. His appearance caused a buzz like a stick being poked in a wasps' nest.

'I've had the BBC on the phone,' Ian murmured in his ear. 'They want to get your reaction to her statement but haven't got any contact details.'

'What did you tell them?'

'Mr Haymer, would you care to comment on ...'

'No he wouldn't!' Ian retorted to the journalist who had interrupted them. 'He hasn't had his lunch yet.' He turned back to Ted. 'I just said I thought it was unlikely you'd want to do it, since you're a bit of a loner.'

'Actually, I do want to.'

'Oh. Sorry.'

'It's okay. But I'd better see the darn thing first, if anyone's got a recording.'

'Of course. Oh, and Anne phoned. She's been frantically trying to reach you but couldn't get through. She wasn't sure if you'd heard the news ...'

'Thanks, Ian. I'm sorry about the kerfuffle.'

'Are you kidding? I'm making a fortune, thanks to you. No one puts it away like a Fleet Street hack.'

He was shunted into the private function room where Melanie, looking flabbergasted, brought him his lunch. 'I can't believe it. That stroppy cow who worked here all those years ago was Nicola Carson. Ian kept that jolly close to his chest.'

'She was Nicola Pearson then. Her mother made Ian swear not to mention the connection – didn't want to be hounded by reporters, so she said.'

Melanie shrugged. 'Well, it's a good job she's better at acting than she was at waitressing.'

The BBC outside broadcast truck was heading down the A21 as they spoke. The interview was scheduled for four o'clock in the saloon bar – when the place should be relatively quiet. But it wasn't quiet that afternoon, the onlookers having to be corralled to make way for the crew and equipment. Ted was positioned in front of the fireplace, a few feet from his precious inglenook. 'I'm going to put a plaque over that seat,' laughed Ian. 'Now that you're famous.'

The brindled correspondent was apparently well-known but Ted did not recognise him since he hadn't owned a television in years. A hand fell, a yellow light flashed to red and Ted's face was exposed to a million viewers. He braced himself. He mustn't dither. He must lie with absolute conviction.

'I understand you knew Nicola Carson. That you met her in this very pub, in fact.'

'I did.'

So far, so good.

'What's your reaction to her statement?'

'I ... find it incomprehensible. I can only guess that it's a response to the terrible pressure she's been under and another manifestation of her compulsion to denigrate and humiliate herself, in the same vein as her breakdown at the BAFTA ceremony ...'

This was okay, wasn't it?

'... It's common knowledge she's attempted suicide,' Ted went on, 'and I believe this is a form of professional suicide. I'm no psychologist but I'm sure there must be a name for it. I'm gratified by the way she spoke about me, though.'

'Yet, isn't it true that you publicly accused her of plagiarism and threatened to sue her for breach of copyright?'

Oh shit.

'Well, I ... I didn't *publicly* accuse her. A rumour got out ...'

'But a rumour based on fact?'

'Well, yes, but ... I was wrong, I admit that. I showed her a manuscript of mine many years ago and she borrowed some ideas from it for her own book, nothing more. On closer inspection, I realised that what I construed as plagiarism was just a rather overzealous response to my influence, for which I suppose I should be flattered. That's why I withdrew the suit.'

'Do you think your threat of litigation contributed to her breakdown?'

His heart was thumping. His armpits were soaking. Every face in the room was staring straight at him, as was most of the rest of the world.

'No. No, I don't think so. At least, I sincerely hope not.'

*

'What the *fuck* are you playing at?' Nicola screamed at the television.

'He's protecting you.'

'But I don't *want* him protecting me. Can't he understand that?'

The press had kept it up throughout the day, although the police, responding to a complaint, had at least removed them from inside the building. In the afternoon it had begun to rain heavily, forcing them into the shelter of an archway opposite, where they huddled disconsolately – chatting, smoking and drinking coffee from thermos flasks. Dominic's neighbour, Sandra – to whom he had confided their wish to escape – had joined them in the flat.

'I've got an idea. As soon as it's dark, I could get my boyfriend to pick us up in his old banger and drive us to Ashford where you could get the Eurostar to Paris and maybe fly from there. Less pressure than Gatwick or Heathrow. No one will expect Nicola to go off in a crappy old car like Kevin's and three people leaving the building would be less conspicuous than two. I could lend you an old tracksuit – just to make you less noticeable. If that's okay?'

'That would be fantastic.'

'And you'll just have to crouch down a bit, Dominic, so you don't look so bloody tall.'

'Are you sure your boyfriend won't mind?' asked Nicola.

'*Mind*? Rescuing a superstar from under the noses of the paparazzi? That'll keep him in drinks for a year. Besides, he's got fuck all else to do – he's on the dole.'

'Supposing they follow us?' said Dominic.

'They won't,' laughed Sandra, 'not the way Kevin drives.'

IV

The day after his interview, Ted left the caravan and walked along the beach to Wemborne then through the town centre and on to their house on the outskirts. It was early evening by the time he arrived and, as he entered the gate and heard the crunch of gravel under his feet, he noticed Anne's car was parked in the drive. The forget-me-nots had run wild again, their chalky-blue swathe of petals offsetting the yellow of late narcissi. Anne had liked to keep them under control but he had preferred to leave them be – probably because he disliked weeding. He walked past her car and Linda's, entered the red brick porch and rang the bell.

It was Linda who answered it. He remembered a time when she had been pretty but now she was a gaunt, pale woman with wispy grey hair and glasses. 'Hello Ted,' she said, rather guardedly.

'Hello Linda. Is Anne home?'

'Yes, she is. Come in.'

It seemed strange to be invited into his own house. There was the telephone on which he had received his first call from Nicola. So much news had entered the house through that phone line – Ben's announcement of his engagement, Jess's announcement that she had attained a First at Cardiff, the news from the hospital that the lump on Anne's breast had proved benign. A purse lay beside it on the hall table – one he did not recognise. The door to his study, with its view of the garden, was closed.

Anne was in the living room. She got up from the sofa where she was watching television and turned to face him. She seemed surprised and flustered. She turned off the television with the remote.

The three of them stood in a triangle, facing each other. Anne said, 'Linda, could you possibly …?'

'I'll see to the supper. It's almost ready, by the way,' she added as she withdrew to the kitchen, leaving the door open. Anne closed it.

'I came to apologise,' said Ted, suddenly feeling weak and foolish but determined to deliver the speech he had rehearsed. 'All those years we were together, I was selfish, self-pitying and egotistical. All you ever wanted to do was love me and support me and that was how I repaid you. I'm so sorry.'

She looked astonished. 'Well, I … don't know what to say. I saw her broadcast, by the way. I couldn't believe it when she just appeared like that, out of the blue, confessing everything.'

'I know. Amazing. Did you see mine?'

'Yes. And I don't have a clue what's going on.'

'I'm not sure that I do,' he answered with a brief laugh. 'But there's something I wanted to tell you. There's been a bit of movement on the publishing front. With *Summers*. I thought you'd like to know.'

'What kind of movement?'

'An agent has asked to see it. But I don't want to say too much in case it turns out to be nothing. For all it's a much better book, *Summers* is less commercial than *Tyranny*.'

'Still, it's a start, isn't it? I'm thrilled for you.'

'Thanks. It's important to me that you are. I just wish …'

'You just wish what?'

'Oh … nothing.'

'So this must have happened before her broadcast?'

'Oh yes, it's got nothing to do with her broadcast.'

She hesitated. 'Ted, if you do publish …'

'That's still a long way off,' he laughed.

'I know. But if you do, will you promise me one thing? That you'll move out of that bloody caravan. I can't bear to think of you living in those conditions.'

'Okay, if you feel so strongly about it. But I'll need somewhere quiet.'

'Well, we'll have to give that some thought …'

'I never slept with her, Anne.'

She stared at him. 'Ted, don't say that to me if it isn't true. Because you've already hurt me enough.'

'I know. But it is.'

'So why did you say you did?'

He looked pained for a moment. 'Well, I … to be strictly accurate, I didn't say I did. I just didn't say I didn't. I don't know why not. It was complicated. I just ... felt you wouldn't believe me. And I felt an idiot. But I never slept with her.'

'She was crying, and you comforted her. That's what you said.'

'Yes it was. And I did. But not like that.'

'Ted, I ... I don't know what to think ...'

Linda came back into the room. 'Your supper's going to be ruined.'

'Right! Sorry.' He launched forward and kissed his wife on the cheek. 'I'll go and let you get on. I've already ruined your life, I don't want to ruin your supper as well.'

Chapter Eight

NINETY MILE BEACH AND BEYOND

Nicola always swam in the afternoons. Sometimes she would pause above the tideline, glance around, then slip out of her bikini and go into the sea naked. She had no particular wish to be brazen, it was just that, since no living soul was ever visible for miles around – except, maybe, a tiny fishing boat poised on the skyline – there didn't seem much point in putting anything on. Traffic had been banned from that part of the beach as autumn storms and high tides had made the surface unstable. And even Dominic wasn't there to see her. He'd taken the jeep up to Baily's Creek to stock up on supplies.

He had told her never to go swimming alone but she ignored him. She walked into the foaming surf, feeling the waves lapping at her ankles, at her knees, at her waist. She loved to watch the walls of water rumbling towards her, to feel them crash into her and over her or buoy her high in the air, where she would spread her arms like wings and soar and spin to see them sweeping on towards the beach and the sullen cliffs beyond. She was no longer a superstar at that moment – she was free of herself, of everything – a tiny, pale organism like the fish and the eels and the prawns. To the sea, the sand and the silver void of the sky she was nothing.

She presently emerged, cursorily dried herself then slipped back into her bikini and flip-flops and started up the beach. A sandy path wound between scrub and thorn to the flight of steps leading to their little wooden house constructed partly on stilts in the lee of the hill. There, for the past month, they had lived the simplest of simple lives, Nicola going by the name of Louisa – her middle name. They had no television and no internet, partly to enhance the illusion that the wider world had vanished and partly to reduce the chances of being traced. Dominic was working on a novel, installing himself every morning on the veranda which commanded the entire horizon of the sea. Nicola spent her days swimming, walking, reading or just lying in the sun.

Sometimes, in the evenings, they would go for a drink or a game of pool at The Blue Lizard, the only bar in town, where they were greeted like old friends. The residents of Baily's Creek, far from the fast lane and concerned only with their own survival, had made them their own and seemed to take pride in their role as protectors from the outside world. Nicola wondered, from time to time, whether her publisher or Connaught International were pressing charges back in the real world, but they would have to find her first.

She stretched out on one of the loungers and sighed as she closed her eyes. She was just drifting into a doze when the mobile on the little wicker table beside her rang. It would be Dominic, since he was the only person who had her new number. He probably wanted to check on something to do with the shopping.

She reached out dreamily and picked it up. 'Hi-ya, babe.'

'Hi-ya, babe,' said a voice. But it wasn't Dominic's.

She sat bolt upright, grimacing. '*Bill?*'

'Hi Nicola,' said her agent, Bill Grainger.

'How the *fuck* did you get this number?'

'I've got some really clever friends in the *News of the World*. I'm afraid your secret's out. This morning's papers are covered with pictures of you and your boyfriend in your little hideaway.'

'*Ffffffffuck!*' she exploded, wondering which one of the cosy residents of Baily's Creek had tipped them off.

'And there are pictures of you ...' He paused.

'Of me what?'

'Of you swimming ... in the buff.'

She thought of that tiny boat which always seemed to be poised on the horizon.

'They're pretty vague – probably taken with an elephant gun. They could be anybody.'

'No they couldn't. You know damn well they couldn't or they wouldn't be able to sell them.'

'So how are you liking your little corner of the antipodes?'

'I'm not telling you. I just want to be left in peace.'

'Try telling that to the rest of the world. My phone hasn't stopped ringing since you made that statement on telly. And I've had enough offers of work to keep you going for years. That was the greatest performance of your career.'

'It wasn't a *performance*, it was a confession. It came straight from the heart.'

'I know. That was what made it was so moving.'

'It wasn't meant to be moving. It was meant to be honest – to tell the world what happened. Don't people believe me?'

'Nah, course they don't. Well, some may, but not the ones who count. It was like at the BAFTAs – people just put it down to you being a nutter who's got their finger permanently on self-destruct. Then your old mate in the caravan came on telly saying you didn't steal his novel and are delusional.'

'I know. I saw him.'

'And your publishers and the Connaught people are plugging that sentiment for all they're worth.'

'So they believed him?'

'Of course they believed him. They wanted to believe him. And since his novel doesn't exist, there's no way anyone can check.'

'Haven't they withdrawn *Loss* from the shelves and pulped it?'

'Are you kidding? It's back in the bestseller list. In a few weeks' time you'll be getting a royalty cheque that'll make your eyes water – if they can find where to send it. And they're making the movie.'

'Bill, this is a nightmare.'

'I know, it's great, isn't it? Then vanishing like that and having everyone wonder where you'd gone was a master-stroke. Everyone's talking about it. Has she topped herself? Is she living on some desert island? Has she joined a hippy commune on Vancouver Island? The BBC even wheeled out that old psychologist of theirs – the one with the silly moustache – and he reckons your vindication of Ted Whatsisface is a plea to your father to forgive you.'

'Fuck that. He should be pleading with me to forgive him. He's the one who walked out on us.'

'I know, it's all bollocks, of course it is. But there you go. That's show business.'

The line went silent for a moment.

'Well, whatever people think, I'm not coming back. It's over, Bill.'

'Nicola, for Christ's *sake*. You pay my children's school fees.'

'Bill, I'm ... I'm scared.'

'Of what?'

'I'm scared people will hate me.'

There was a silence.

'Listen. You're talking about real people living real lives in the real world. People who wake up with a hangover, have a row with their partner, a row with their kids, then sit in a traffic jam for an hour so they can have a row with their boss. And, once in a while, they need a bit of magic in their lives, something to lift them out of it all – and not any old rubbish, either. That's where you come in. You have the gift. You're blessed. But don't kid yourself they love you or hate you – they're far too busy loving and hating each other.'

'So what you're saying is, I don't matter.'

'Well, since you put it like that. No.'

She couldn't prevent a smile. 'You don't say that when you're negotiating my fucking contracts.'

'That's because I know your worth, even if you don't.'

She was gazing at a scarlet hibiscus flower which she had placed in a glass vase. It was already wilting in the afternoon sun.

'Are you still there?'

'I'm thinking.'

*

Dominic called out, 'I'm back!' but there was no reply. Surprised, he went out onto the veranda but she wasn't there. He scanned the beach, his hand shielding his eyes, but there was no sign of her. He glanced in the kitchen and living room then entered their bedroom. It was plunged in gloom, some splinters of light through the cracks in the blinds suggesting her form humped on the bed.

He sat down behind her, reached over and gently took her hand. 'Hey...'

'It's over,' she muttered.

'What do you mean? What's over?'

'This. Our little pretend paradise. We've been rumbled.'

'What are you talking about?'

'Bill phoned.'

He frowned. 'Bill who?'

'Bill Grainger. My agent.'

'How did *he* get your number?'

'I don't know. But it turns out one of the lovable residents of our little town has tipped off the tabloids. There are pictures of me swimming … in the nude.'

'Shhhhit! Shit! Shit! *Shit*. We'll have to go. We'll find ourselves somewhere even more remote. We'll go tonight. Right now.'

'There's no point.'

'So what are saying? That we stay here and face them down?'

'No, I'm not saying that.'

'Then what are you saying?'

'I don't know.'

They both sank into hopeless silence.

'You want to hear the crowning irony? I'm being swamped with multi-million dollar offers, and among them was one from some theatre company who want me to do Adela in *Bernarda Alba*. Although they did admit they probably can't afford me.'

'Why's that the crowning irony?'

'Because that was the part I'd auditioned for the day I met Ted. And I didn't get it.'

*

Dominic was sitting out on the veranda, smoking a cigarette and watching the sunset. Nicola presently emerged from the bedroom and flopped down into the wicker seat beside him.

'I've made a decision,' she said. 'I'm going to go back and get on with my job. It's been a fantastic holiday but that's all this can ever be. And it's over now – that's how it is with holidays.'

He was silent.

'Dominic, I love being here. I love being here with *you*. But I can't spend the rest of my life skulking round places like this, terrified in case someone tips off the press. It's crazy.'

'We're not going to skulk around here forever. This is just a breathing space. People will forget you in time – there'll be new stars and new scandals. Okay, maybe we can't find paradise, but when the dust's settled, we'll find ourselves and live like normal people. We even talked about kids. Don't you want kids anymore?'

'Yes ... yes, I do. Sometime. But in the meantime I want to work. I want to do what I do.'

He took a long, slow drag on his cigarette. 'And what about *Loss*?'

'Oh sod it, I'm sick and tired of that fucking book. I've made my confession. If people don't believe me, that's their problem. And neither Hale nor Connaught are pressing charges. They're going with the theory that I'm a raving lunatic. They're probably right.'

'You know it's not as simple as that. Some people may not believe you but there'll be plenty who do. There'll always be some smart-arse comic or gossip columnist who's got it in for you. They're not going to let you forget, and you don't need that pressure – not now you're so much better.'

'Yeah, but everything's changed, don't you see? It's not about what's out there – it never was. It's about what's inside. I feel clean inside now, and I feel strong. And there's no mileage in accusing me of plagiarism because I've already admitted it.'

Dominic went quiet again, listening to the perpetual roar of the waves as the crimson sky darkened over the sea. Nicola reached out and squeezed his hand. 'But I'll only do it if you're okay with it.'

He sighed. 'It's just been so nice here. With you and ... writing again. And I've felt ...'

'Felt what?'

'I don't know ... like your equal, I guess.'

'What are you *talking* about? You'll always be my equal, wherever we are. And you can still write back in London. We'll find somewhere quiet ... '

He considered the prospect. 'So which one of these mouth-watering offers are you going to take?'

'I'd like to do *Bernarda Alba*.'

'A play?'

'Yes, a play. I want to be a proper actress again. I want to stand there in the flesh and look a real-life audience in the eye and be myself – or, at least, myself being someone else.'

II

He gazed at one particular raindrop dribbling down the porthole as black clouds clustered round distant hills. Parting from him at passport control, Nicola – in jeans, a bomber jacket, sunglasses and a baseball cap – walked alone and unnoticed through the terminal building then took a taxi to Greenwich where they met up and checked into a small, unobtrusive hotel near the theatre. Two days later, they bought a new car – a Mercedes – and the old Cabriolet – battered and bruised but still faithful – was given away to two Pakistani brothers who ran a car lot in Leytonstone. When rehearsals began, Dominic told Nicola he was taking a drive to the country to clear his head.

*

He could just about remember the way. He parked by the pumping station, climbed out and stood for a while, gazing over the marshes at the corner of Ted's caravan protruding from its clump of bushes. Once again he was unsuitably shod but this time he didn't care. When he reached his destination, his knuckle hovered an inch from the door before he knocked.

It opened almost at once. Ted stared at him. 'Well, I'll be damned.'

'Ted, there's something very important I have to say to you.'

'Right. Well, you'd better come in then,' he mumbled, turning back inside.

Dominic clambered through the little door and glanced around at the cramped interior in dismay.

'Do you want some tea?'

'That'd be good. Thanks.'

He didn't really want tea but he thought, in the circumstances, that it might be politic not to refuse.

'I warn you, I use whisky instead of milk. It doesn't go off. At least, that's my excuse. Sit down.'

Unable to stand up straight anyway, Dominic was glad to be able to lower himself into the narrow bench seat behind the paper-strewn table. Ted struck a match and lit the gas.

'So what brings you to this neck of the woods?' he asked, filling the kettle. 'I thought this whole boring business had finally been laid to rest.'

'Ted, I'm not sure if you're aware of it, but I'm seeing Nicola.'

He laughed. 'I am aware of it. Despite my official designation as "hermit" I'm not completely out of touch. I dread to think how you pulled it off, though.'

He told him how he had pulled it off, describing – with some pride – the elaborate ruse by which he had gained access to Malvern Hall. 'I was hoping to get a confession out of her,' he said.

Ted turned to face him, the kettle dangling in his hand. 'You're just not going to let this go, are you?'

'I've let it go now but I hadn't then. I was going to write a book about it. That was my motive all along.'

'I always knew you had another agenda. So did you get your confession out of her?'

'Not then. It turned out she had an agenda of her own. She discharged herself and came and stayed with me.'

Ted responded with a laugh – or rather, a cynical rasp in the nasal passages.

'I know. Not quite the outcome anyone was expecting. Least of all me.'

'And has she confided in you now?'

'Yes.'

Ted looked at him for a moment, then turned away to search for cups in the little cupboard.

'I know the truth, Ted.'

'Oh? And which particular version of the truth is that?'

'The true one. The one where you meet a waitress and wannabe actress called Nicola Pearson in your local pub and you commiserate about your respective disappointments. And then, to cut a long story short, you propose to her that she submit *The Tyranny of Love* with her name on the cover, change that name to Nicola Carson and call the novel *Loss*.'

Ted lowered his eyes from the cupboard. 'That was her idea. I hated that title.'

'But the rest is true?'

'Pretty much.'

'So what you told me and Anne and the solicitor was all lies? And the court case, had it gone ahead, would have been based on a falsehood?'

Ted fixed him with a flinty stare. 'You wouldn't be capable of understanding how betrayed I felt. When we were in Richmond, we made a pact – to pool our resources and help each other launch our careers and get our revenge on those bastards who'd been knocking us back all our lives – people like your boss. But she never kept her side of the bargain. Okay, she *eventually* sent me some wads of cash but that was just to cover her back. She never put her weight behind *Summers* like she promised to do, and that was all I cared about. And when – after you turned up – I tried to contact her to warn her we'd been rumbled, she was too busy being a superstar to see me. I just had a message from her stuck-up secretary – "Miss *Caaarson* sends her best wishes and her sincere apologies." She wouldn't even deign to speak to me in person. That's why I did what I did.'

'So why did you back down?'

'I didn't. I withdrew the lawsuit because my conscience got the better of me.'

Dominic was not sure he could see the distinction. 'You probably won't believe me but she refused to see you because she was ashamed.'

Ted considered his words. 'You're right. I probably won't believe you.'

'And that's why she lied in her statement on television. I tried to persuade her not to, to protect her reputation, but she was adamant.'

'You mean, she lied to protect *my* reputation?'

'Exactly.'

'Well, that's great except that, thanks to her, I don't have a reputation to protect.'

Dominic's hand was distractedly fiddling with one of the sheets of paper on the table. 'Ted, the real reason I came is to ask you a favour. Quite a big favour. It involves yet more deceit, I'm afraid, but it's not deceit that's going to harm anyone.'

'Is there such a thing?' he murmured but Dominic did not respond. He was in no mood for Ted's moralising.

'Nicola's insisting on coming to see you. She wants to ask your forgiveness – to your face. And when she does ...'

'Oh *I* get it,' Ted laughed. 'She doesn't know, does she? She doesn't know you know me.'

'No. She doesn't.'

'Of course she doesn't. Because if she knew you were the one who'd unearthed our little secret and spent five months of your life obsessively trying to destroy her, she wouldn't be so in *love*, would she?'

'But I didn't know her then. And I didn't know the truth because you'd been lying to everyone. Once I got to know what she's really like, everything changed.'

'So why don't you tell *her* that? Why don't you try being honest with her?'

'I daren't. She's still fragile – physically and emotionally. I'm the one person in the world she trusts ...'

'You should tell her, Dominic. Get things out in the open.'

'I know. But then I think, why does she need to know? It's all over now and what really happened anyway? Nothing. The lawsuit was scrapped. And only you and Anne know I was involved.'

'So if you can square it with us, you'll be in the clear?'

'Something like that. But not because I want to deceive her. I hate lying to her. I'm just trying to protect her.'

'You never protect anyone by lying to them. Lies grow, they grow from tiny seeds of deceit until they acquire a life of their own and become monsters.'

Dominic snorted. 'With all due respect, Ted, I don't think you're in any position to lecture me on lying.'

'The lie we told was entirely different. It was a ploy. A marketing strategy, nothing more. It didn't hurt anyone. We weren't betraying anyone.'

'You betrayed each other. And you lied to Anne.'

'Keep her out of this.'

'Are you going to be honest with *her*?'

'It's none of your business.'

Dominic wanted to go. He wanted to get out of that tiny cage of a caravan and back to London.

'All I'm asking is that for the few minutes you and Nicola are together, you pretend I'm a total stranger. That shouldn't be too big a challenge to your celebrated acting skills.'

'What's that supposed to mean?'

'Oh come on, you've been performing ever since we met. Mystification. Righteous indignation. A sudden passion for justice. And those wads of cash you mentioned. How much did she send you? A million? Two million? Must have been quite a comfort while you were living the simple life – gazing at the sea and writing your poems about nature and the human condition. Oh, and since we're on the subject of favours, don't forget I can do one for you.'

'Really? What's that?'

'Not telling Anne the truth.'

Ted laughed. 'Are you threatening me?'

'No. I'm just pointing out that we're in the same boat. You know something I'd prefer kept under wraps and vice versa. So I think it would be best if we both keep our mouths shut, don't you?'

III

Anne picked up Ted and they went to The Lemon Grass – a Thai restaurant in Eastbourne which had a good reputation. They were greeted by a diminutive waitress who was exquisitely pretty but had rather limited English. 'Good evening, you are very happy nice day?' she said.

'Thank you, we're having a very happy day,' smiled Ted.

She showed them to a table by the window then brought them menus and crackers and took their order for drinks. When she left, Ted cast a glance at the other customers scattered among the tables. The place had a pleasant, peaceful ambience, enhanced by soft oriental music emanating from the walls. He briefly surveyed the menu, then laid it aside.

'I've been thinking about what you said the other day ... about me moving out of the caravan. I've had a look at the accommodation columns but ...'

'I've been thinking about that too. And I was wondering if it's maybe time to start afresh.'

He stared at her in stunned silence. He had been hoping against hope that the opportunity might present itself, sometime in the future, for him to make that proposition to her. He had never imagined it would be the other way around.

'What's brought this on?'

'It's got nothing to do with Nicola's confession, if that's what you're thinking. Or with the possibility of you publishing.'

'I didn't think it would have.'

He glanced down at her hand, which was touching the base of her wine glass. 'You've never stopped wearing your wedding ring.'

'I couldn't get it off,' she laughed.

After a pause, he asked, 'And what about Linda?'

'She's aware it's a temporary arrangement. And she needs to get herself sorted out.' She did not seem to feel that anything further needed to be said.

'You can't imagine how long I've waited for this moment. But ...' He adjusted the position of his fork, even though it lay precisely parallel to his place mat, which depicted a profusion of pink and purple orchids. '...there's something I have to tell you first.'

She withdrew her hand as the waitress reappeared with the drinks. Having carefully set them down, she asked, 'You ready order now?'

'If you could just give us a moment,' said Ted, whereupon she smiled and melted away, leaving silence in her wake.

'So what did you have to tell me?' smiled Anne.

'It's nothing. It doesn't matter.'

She squeezed his hand. 'Come on. Tell me.'

'No. It can wait.'

She met his eyes for a moment. 'Ted, what you said in that interview in response to her statement on television. I was thinking about it. I know what you said wasn't true but I still admire you for saying it.'

'Admire me?'

'Yes, because it was your way of saying that it's time to put all this anger behind us and focus on ...'

'Nicola never stole my novel, Anne.'

She was taken aback by his interruption. 'What?'

'She never stole it. What she said on television was no more the truth than what I said.'

She shook her head in bemusement. 'What on earth are you talking about?'

'I knew about it. I knew about it all along. In fact ... it was my idea.'

'*What?*'

'I was never going to break in on my own. You know I wasn't. Everything was wrong. With her, on the other hand, everything was right. She could be marketed. And she was.'

Slowly, haltingly, and frequently repositioning the cutlery, he told her everything. About Richmond. About Nicola meeting Tom Newcomb at the book launch. About Miranda Cole. 'We weren't working on *Summers* during that time. We were publishing *Tyranny* – or rather, *Loss*.'

Anne had gone pale. 'I can't believe what you're telling me.'

'I know. I'm sorry,' he muttered.

'And what about all the money that book must have made? And the Connaught Prize money?'

'We were going to go fifty-fifty.'

'And did you?'

'No. She took ages to send me anything, even though her agent had screwed a fifty grand advance out of Jonathan Hale.'

'Fifty thousand pounds!'

Her reaction attracted glances from other diners.

'That was entirely her doing. She was very pro-active. Finally, when she made it in films, she starting sending me wads of cash, care of the pub – just money stuffed into jiffy bags – no note with it, nothing.'

'So all this time you've been living like a pauper in that caravan, gaining all that *spiritual enlightenment*, you've been literally sitting on a fortune. All that stuff about inner peace and serenity was all … rubbish. It was all an act.'

'Well, not entirely. I'd have chosen to live like that anyway. Believe it or not, I've been happy out there in the wilds. I've been … '

'So where is all this money? Buried under your vegetable patch?'

'Most of it, yes.'

She snorted with bitter, ironic laughter. 'That was a joke.'

'I couldn't think what else to do with it. I didn't want to put it in the bank, where it would have attracted attention, and there's no security at the caravan. When the time's right, I'll give it to the children to help them pay off their mortgages, maybe get Jess a new car so she doesn't have to drive around in that banger all the time.' He smiled slightly. 'It'll make me feel better about having been such a lousy father. But I had to tell you first.'

'So how much money are we talking about?'

He thought about it. 'I'm not sure exactly… I suppose altogether… over the whole four and a bit years … and what I paid the lawyers … about a million.'

Anne was shaking her head in utter disbelief.

'But I hated the whole thing. I was coming to feel more and more like a cross between a charity case and a blackmailer. So in the end I tried to contact her. I wanted to tell her to stop sending me cash and start doing something about *Summers*. But she refused to see me.'

Anne's eyes narrowed. 'I might have known. I might have bloody known. You just can't help yourself, can you, Ted? You just can't help lying. And to think that I went along with all that righteous indignation, to think that I supported you and found you Bill Peach and nearly went to court to … do you have even the faintest idea what could've happened if the truth had come out? We'd have committed perjury and that money would've been incriminating evidence.'

'That's why I've kept it hidden …'

'I could've been suspended for assisting you. I still could be. And you could go to prison.'

'To *prison?*' he grimaced, rather uneasily. 'For *what?*'

'Tax evasion, for a start. People have to pay tax on large chunks of income back here in the real world. HMRC doesn't take too kindly to people burying it under their Brussels sprouts.'

'Of course I won't go to prison!' he retaliated in a hoarse whisper. 'Nicola will have paid tax on that money, it was sent to me in cash and hasn't been within sight of a bank account. No one knows it exists.'

'Of course someone knows it exists! A girl like that can't handle her own affairs. She'll have an accountant. A broker. Someone always notices when large sums of money go walkabout.'

'She could've spent it on designer clothes or fancy restaurants – you wouldn't believe the cash these people get through. There's no possible way it can be traced to me. And I haven't exactly been driving around in a Porsche.'

'It's a mercy you never told the truth in that bloody interview. God, I just can't believe you could be so *stupid*. And all just to get back at her for bruising your ego.'

He stared at her. '*Bruising my ego?*'

'Yes, bruising your ego! You were infatuated with her and when she left you behind, you couldn't handle it. You wanted the world to know you'd written that book because you resented all the adulation she was getting, in spite of your sordid little arrangement.'

'It wasn't like that. I genuinely wanted to help her. And all I asked in return was that she keep her side of the bargain. I was desperate, Anne. You know what it was like.'

'Oh, I know what it was like all right,' she retorted, her lips tightening. 'I've heard nothing but you whine about it ever since we met. How nobody appreciates your genius. How the whole world is conspiring against you. How all publishers care about is money. Well, I've got news for you, Ted, that's the world we all have to live in. Deal with it.'

'That's exactly what I was doing ...'

'And you slept with her, whatever you say. You've lied about everything else, so why shouldn't you be lying about that too?'

'I didn't sleep with her,' he retorted, then glanced around and repeated, more softly, 'I didn't sleep with her. It was just an arrangement.'

'You're pathetic,' she snapped, suddenly on her feet, towering over him, trembling with rage. 'Everything I said just now is off. Don't ever try to contact me. I don't *ever* want to see you again.'

She made to leave but he grabbed her arm and clung to it. 'Anne, please don't go.'

She murmured, through clenched teeth, 'If you don't let me go, I'll scream.'

'And if you don't sit down and let me say my piece, *I'll* scream. If we're never going to see each other again, at least allow me that.'

The waitress was there again, armed with her pad above which her pencil was poised defiantly. 'You ready order now?'

'No, we're not ready to order,' answered Ted. 'It all looks so delicious, we're ... having trouble deciding. Please just give us a moment longer.'

She sighed faintly and went away again. Anne glanced swiftly around at the other diners then resumed her seat. 'You've got one minute.'

'I did sleep with her. Once. Technically. When I got to Richmond, I knew she was somewhere in London, homeless and penniless, but nonetheless I spent a whole day in turmoil, trying to decide whether to invite her there. I never imagined for a moment she'd ... but I didn't think of it like that. I just thought that, since I had all that space to myself and she had nowhere to go ... But the first night she was there she became distraught, she was crying ...'

'Oh *please*. You seriously expect me to sit here and listen to this garbage?'

'Yes I do. Because it's the truth. And it's important.'

She remained seated, simmering in silence.

'She was crying and I ... I went to her bedroom to comfort her. I was sitting on her bed ... in time she calmed down and stopped crying. And then she wanted to ... But I told her I couldn't, I just couldn't because I loved my wife. And she was okay. She understood. So we talked into the small hours – about acting, about writing, about publishing – and this idea just came to me. I wanted to give her some hope, some encouragement. And eventually she fell asleep and I stayed there the rest of the night because I didn't want to risk waking her. So, yes. We slept together.'

Anne stood up. 'I'm going now. Don't try to prevent me and don't ever contact me again. Ever.' Then she left.

Ted glanced at the other diners, who were all scrupulously staring at their plates. He contained himself for a moment to give her a head start – he didn't want to run into her again in the street. Then he looked up and found his exit barred by the waitress.

'You ready order now?'

IV

'Nicola, there's something I have to tell you. Your boyfriend, Dominic. I know him. I've known him for months. And he's not what he seems. You may think he's your most loyal fan and unfailing support but when he came to visit you in hospital, it was to destroy you.'

Nicola's gaze travelled slowly from Ted to Dominic. Her face was a grimace of horror and incomprehension. Then she uttered the words, 'I think you just missed the exit.'

He was snapped back to the present. '*Shit*,' he murmured, glancing around. 'Never mind, there's another one a few miles further on. We can take that and double back on the Maidstone road.'

'Are you okay? It's like you're on another planet today.'

'It's just the prospect of finally meeting your Mr Haymer.'

'I did offer to go alone.'

'I know, but I want to be with you.'

She reached out and placed her hand over his on the wheel. 'That's what I love about you. You're always there for me.'

As they sped on along the motorway, Dominic's thoughts raced ahead. How would Ted react to him after their last meeting? Would he play the game? Or was his anger still so raw that he'd relish plunging the dagger into his gut whatever the consequences? Why had he been so sanctimonious that day? And then to *threaten* him. After all, if Ted did blow his cover, would he really go through with telling Anne and the rest of the world what really happened? Of course he wouldn't. What would be the point? If he had lost Nicola he would have lost everything. And there was the damage it would do to her since most of her fans still believed she *was* the true author of *Loss*. The ace of hearts he'd believed he held to his chest was nothing more than a two of clubs. And Ted knew it.

'There's something I have to tell you,' he blurted out.

She turned to him in surprise.

'When I said I'd never been to Whitesands Marsh, actually I have been there before.'

'Really? When?'

'When I ... when we were children. We went there on holiday.'

'To Whitesands Marsh? Jesus.'

'Well, not Whitesands Marsh. Whitesands Bay. My parents liked it because it was never too crowded. It's because there's no road to it – you have to walk from the car park ...'

What on earth was he talking about?

'Oh,' was her only response.

Even though he was driving a Mercedes instead of his ancient Golf, the journey was reminding him powerfully of the first time he had come to see Ted. Once again, the sky was obscured by a pall of grey cloud, promising rain, and once again the weather reflected his mood of foreboding.

'How the hell do we find this caravan?' he mumbled as they entered the gloomy wasteland presaging the sea.

'We need to go to The Queen's. Someone there's bound to know where it is. Ted might even be there himself – he practically lives in that place.'

He considered the prospect. If Ted were there, his unmasking would be made public. And even if he were not, the landlord might remember him. That was the problem with being built like a giraffe. People remembered you.

'You don't want to go in there. You know what it's like in these places – you'll be recognised.'

'I'm used to that.'

'Okay, we'll go there as a last resort, I promise. Just humour me.'

The Sat Nav was no help since Ted did not have a postcode. He pulled into a lay-by and consulted the map.

'Dominic, this is crazy. We could be driving round and round this place for hours. Let's go to The Queen's.'

'They definitely said in the papers that his caravan was on Whitesands Marsh,' he murmured, 'and as far as I can see there's only one lane – or track – going across it. And that branches off this road about a mile ahead.'

She sighed with resignation. 'Okay, Scott of the bloody Antarctic. Do your worst.'

They found the turning and advanced along the track, weaving slowly around the puddles, Dominic casting his eyes back and forth across the marsh like a radar scanner. When they reached the pumping station, he pulled into the gateway where he had parked his Golf.

'Why are we stopping?'

'I think I saw something.'

They both got out and gazed around. 'There it is, over there!' he cried, pointing triumphantly. 'In that copse of trees. I recognise it from the photos in the press. Those are alder trees, aren't they?'

'I've no idea what sort of trees they are. The only tree I know is the palm tree because it grows in *nice* places.'

'I'm sure this is right.'

On Nicola's insistence they had bought two pairs of wellingtons and some proper rainwear. The exercise had amused her. 'All we need now is a Range Rover and a Labrador to go with them,' she'd said. Now, as they got their brand new wellingtons out of the boot and put them on, she was in a less jocular mood. The ground was boggy after recent rain and, as they squelched along the path, they had to hold hands to keep from stumbling.

'Jesus,' she murmured when they arrived. 'Ted can't live here, surely? Not after all the money I sent him.'

'Maybe he likes living like this, if he's a bit of a recluse like everyone says.'

Dominic, his heart pounding, knocked on the door. There was no reply. He knocked again. Using his hands as blinkers, he peered through the window and his spirits soared at what greeted his eyes. Gone were the books, the papers, the dirty cups and glasses, the music stand and all Ted's other paraphernalia. The place was an empty shell.

'He's gone,' he said, striving to keep the note of jubilation out of his voice.

'Are you sure?'

'Take a look for yourself.'

She looked for herself. 'Maybe this is the wrong caravan.'

'No, I'm sure this is it. It looks exactly like the one in the paper. They made a big deal of how it was standing on its own in the middle of nowhere, not even on a road – part of their profile of Haymer the hermit.'

'A caravan in the middle of nowhere looks like any other caravan in the middle of nowhere. This could be the wrong one.'

'No, it isn't. I'm sure this is right.'

'Maybe it was the publicity that drove him away.'

'Whatever it was, he's gone. So I think we should forget him and head back to London.'

'No, Dominic, I haven't come all this way to give up so easily. I want to go to The Queen's. Ted's been a regular there for decades. Someone's bound to know where he's gone.' This time her tone brooked no objection.

Once they were back on the main road, Dominic let her direct him. As they entered the town centre, she glanced around at the picturesque but tatty buildings. 'Fucking Wemborne,' she murmured.

He pulled into the pub car park and switched off the engine and they sat for a while in silence. 'You were right,' she said. 'I can't face going in there. It'll be too weird. Would you mind going in for me? Just ask the landlord – his name's Ian. But don't mention I'm here. Unless Ted's there, of course.'

Once again his spirits soared – his spirits were on a roller-coaster that day. 'No, of course not,' he replied gently. 'You wait here. I'll be back in a jiffy.'

Alone in the car, her eyes wandered over the scene – the street to the harbour, the fish and chip shop, the little café called The Bosun's Bite. Then they came to rest on the back door of the pub from which she and Ted had emerged the night she had met him and she had lit a cigarette beneath the stars before setting off for Snetsham. She smiled faintly as she remembered the awkwardness of his embrace when she burst into tears and how warm and safe it had made her feel. Large raindrops were splattering on the windscreen.

Suddenly Dominic was back in the driver's seat. 'Nothing,' he said. 'Total blank. Apparently Ted came in to say goodbye and when they asked him where he was going, he just said "off travelling".'

'When was this?'

'A couple of days ago.'

'So no one has any idea where he is?'

'None at all.'

'No mobile number, contact details ... anything?'

'Nothing.'

She considered the situation for a while. 'Come on then. Let's get the fuck out of here.'

V

'Mrs Haymer? It's Frank. Frank Brewer.'

It took Anne a moment to register. 'Ah yes. Hello, Frank.'

'Yes, I just wondered if you'd care to pick up Ted's books when you're passing. It's not that I mind having 'em here, they're no trouble. But some of them old books are worth a few bob, aren't they, and I thought you might want them.'

She frowned. 'I'm not quite with you.'

'You mean you don't know?'

'Know what?'

'About Ted going.'

'No. Going where?'

'Dunno. Wouldn't tell me. He just gave me the keys and headed off with a rucksack on his back like some sort of student. Daft git.'

'So when was this?' she asked, after a moment's thought.

''Bout a week ago. Maybe more.'

'And he didn't leave any clue in the caravan? A note or anything?'

'Nope, nothing. He left the place spotless, I'll give him that.'

It was ten days since their trip to The Lemon Grass, ten days in which Anne had thought of almost nothing but that disastrous evening and the events leading up to it. On her way to the farm she called at the pub. Someone there would be bound to know Ted's plans, but Ian shook his head. 'You're the second person who's asked me that,' he said.

'Oh? Who was the first?'

'That tall lad. The one who used to come in here to see Ted. Hooked up with Nicola now, I believe.'

'Dominic? When was he in here?'

'Last Sunday, I think it was.'

'Did he leave a number or anything?'

'Nope. Just came in, asked for Ted and went out again.'

Perplexed, Anne drove on to the farm. As she pulled into the yard, she spotted Frank Brewer coming out of one of the barns. He turned and smiled and his trusty spaniel scampered over to greet her as she was getting out of the car.

'I'll bung the kettle on,' he said.

'That sounds like a good idea. Frank, can you remember Ted's exact words when he left?'

His furrowed face settled into thought. 'He just said you'd told him to move out so he thought he'd better do as he's told.'

She wondered if she detected a hint of resentment in his voice, but then he added, 'I'm glad. It wasn't doing him any good living in that place. He wasn't well.'

'I know. And it was very kind of you to store his stuff.'

He shrugged. 'The books are in the spare room and there's a few boxes and bags of rubbish in the barn. I'll put them out on dustbin day but if I do it any sooner, the foxes'll have it everywhere.'

'Would you mind very much if I went through them? There might be something. I won't make a mess, I promise.'

'Help yourself. And don't worry about the mess. This place is a tip anyway.'

He took her into the shed and switched on the light, showed her the boxes and bin bags ranged against the wall then shambled back to the house to make tea. She checked through the two boxes but they contained only copious drafts and redrafts of his novels. So, bracing herself and wishing she had a pair of Marigolds, she took the first bag of rubbish, untied it and tipped its contents onto the concrete floor. It comprised mainly sheaves of paper covered with typescript or scribbled notes, some irredeemably holey socks and a couple of torn shirts – one of which she remembered buying for him years before. She sifted through some of the papers but they consisted only of yet more discarded drafts of his novels or jottings connected with them. She sighed. Ted had always distanced himself from his writing – he recorded his observations but seldom his innermost thoughts, still less his plans. And he could be impulsive. It was possible he did not even know where he was going himself – as Frank had suggested – in which case it was unlikely she would find him unless he contacted her. But she had told him never to do that.

The second bag was even less promising, consisting mainly of household rubbish – plastic bottles, tins, cartons, vegetable peelings, yet more paper. But among it she spotted a white A4 envelope on which was scrawled the single word 'Miranda'.

She gingerly extracted it from the muck and shook it to dislodge a lump of squashed tomato. It was unsealed so she peered inside then pulled out the contents. It proved to be three letters joined by a paper clip. She detached the first:

Dear Mr Haymer
You do not know me but, as you can see from my letterhead,
I am a literary agent. I hope you will forgive me for writing to
you out of the blue but I received an email from Tom Newcomb,
the novelist, in which he expressed the absolute conviction that
you are the true author of Nicola Carson's novel, Loss. I still
find this hard to believe but, nonetheless, if you have written
any other novels, I would be interested to see them.

Tom gave me the number of the solicitor who contacted him
and I ascertained from him that you live near Wemborne
but nothing more precise. I am thus sending this care of the
Wemborne Post Office and hope it finds you,

Yours sincerely,
Miranda Cole.

She looked at the second. A certain familiarity must have developed between them in the meantime – possibly they had met – because it was far less formal:

Dear Ted
I hope you are well. Having now read the whole of Three
Summers by the Sea, I am tremendously impressed and deeply
moved – it is a multi-layered and beautiful novel which is crying
out to be published. It is a far more complex book than Loss, for
example, but also, sadly, in the present climate, less commercial
and may prove difficult to place as a first novel. Publishers have
all pulled in their horns and are taking on very few new authors
indeed. Please rest assured that this is purely a reflection of the
times and not of your work.

I will continue to try my utmost on your behalf and will contact you the moment I have any success,

Best wishes,
Miranda

Then she came to the third:

Dear Ted
Fantastic news. Nicola's dramatic appearance on television has completely reversed our fortunes. All the publishers I previously contacted have, without exception, got back to me, clamouring for the rights to Three Summers by the Sea and any subsequent novels you might produce. We need to go for a rights auction.
I am so thrilled to be able to share this news with you and look forward to hearing from you at your earliest convenience,

With very best wishes,
Miranda

Slowly, thoughtfully, she clipped the letters back together and set them aside. She then spent another hour going through her husband's detritus – reading notes, snatches of manuscripts and letters – then getting it all back in its bags (except the letters from Miranda Cole) and tying them up again. She had relived some poignant memories, had wiped away a tear, but was no nearer to finding out where he had gone.

Over tea and a slightly soggy chocolate digestive in Frank's shambolic kitchen, she tried to glean any further information that might be useful. Apparently they had got into the habit of opening a bottle of whisky and playing scrabble together on Friday nights. Frank suspected that Ted had usually let him win.

Despite his assurance that the caravan was an empty shell devoid of clues, she got the key from him and went to check for herself. She scoured through the drawers, opened the cupboards, looked under the bed. Nothing. It was as though the place had not only been vacated but had never been lived in. And what about the money? She gazed through the window over the patch of weeds and roughly-dug earth that Ted had glorified by the title 'vegetable plot'. She guessed his horde was still under there somewhere and, for the first time, it became a reality. She imagined it in a large tin box a foot beneath the earth – it couldn't be too deep as he would have needed to access it from time to time. No wonder he had a bad back. The money would be wrapped in plastic bags inside the box – wad upon wad of red and, maybe, some blue and orange notes. She smiled to herself. There was something about the whole performance that was typical of her romantic husband – like a pirate burying his treasure on a desert island – and, although that money's legal status was highly dubious, he had had no criminal intent. He had been naïve, and there was something touching about the way he wanted to keep it to help their children. And – morally, if not legally – he was entitled to it. That money was there because his novel had won an award, was about to be filmed and had been bought and read and enjoyed by millions of people. That money was there because *The Tyranny of Love* was good.

She sat down with a sigh and drifted into thought, gazing at the cheap vinyl walls and listening to the wind moaning over the marsh. She imagined his life in this place – his routine, his attempts to write, his drinking, his back pain. Then she thought of their lives together, of their meeting at Oxford, their courtship and marriage and the birth of their children. And there returned to her mind a question which had nagged her persistently since their final encounter. If he had never slept with Nicola, why had he not tried harder to protest his innocence, to save their marriage? Maybe she hadn't given him the chance, maybe she had been beguiled by Marie's and Linda's whispers in her ear. Maybe she had made the mistake as a frail human being that she never made as a lawyer – of going into trial with a preconception of the truth. Perhaps her fear of that seismic force that was Nicola Pearson – the first tremor of which she had felt that night he had gone out of the drawing room to take her call – had robbed her of her judgement. Or maybe, just maybe, he had needed to part from her at that moment. Maybe he had needed his time in the wilderness.

VI

After a great performance, the electricity seems to infuse the entire theatre, right down to its shabbiest corners. Dominic sensed it acutely as he edged his way with the excited, chattering crowd down the stairs towards the rear exit and the door marked 'PRIVATE' which yielded onto another, much narrower staircase leading to the dressing rooms. The crowd had momentarily jammed in the little vestibule before the street exit and, confronted by the obstruction, he made for the 'gents'. As the door swung open, he found himself face to face with the last person in the world that he wanted to see at that moment. They stared at each other in disbelief.

'Well, there's goes my evening,' said Ted.

'Look, this is ridiculous,' said Dominic. 'Let's get a drink.'

'I don't think we've got much to say to each other, do you?'

'I've got something to say to you.'

He hesitated. 'I've got a train to catch.'

'Ten minutes. There's a bar round the corner. I can afford to buy you that double brandy now.'

He considered his proposal. 'Won't your other half wonder where you've got to?'

'I'll tell her I've run into someone. She always takes hours to get out of costume anyway. I just need to pop in here and then I'll go and talk to her. If you wouldn't mind waiting a minute.'

'I'll have a drink with you on one condition. That you don't tell anyone you've seen me. Not Nicola and especially not Anne, if you're still in touch with her.'

'I promise.'

As he was hurrying up the stairs to the dressing rooms, he felt sure Ted wouldn't wait for him. But when he got back, he was still there – and alone – the crowd having now dispersed. Hunched in a battered old Barbour, he was shifting his weight from one foot to the other and looked as though he wished he were invisible.

The bar they went to was not around the corner at all – it was a good six minutes' walk – but at least it was in the direction of the station. At first they walked in awkward silence then Dominic said, 'It was good of you to come.'

'No, it wasn't. My motive for coming was entirely selfish.'

'Right. And what did you think?'

'I thought it was good. But then I knew it would be.'

'Just good?'

'Look, this is my thing. I don't want to ruin it by having to dredge up a load of inadequate superlatives.'

'No. Okay. Sorry.'

The lights in the bar were dimmed, soft music oozed from the walls and a residue of customers were scattered among the tables. When Dominic had bought the brandies and settled in his seat, Ted said, 'So what did you want to say to me?'

'I wanted to apologise. For the way I spoke to you. And to ask your forgiveness.'

He looked surprised. 'My forgiveness? For what?'

'For not getting *Tyranny* published all those years ago. I know I was only an assistant editor but I should have been more insistent, more confident of my convictions. If I had, you'd be an established author by now and none of this would've happened.'

No doubt feeling the warm glow of brandy doing its work, Ted seemed to relax a little and contemplated Dominic with a look almost of amusement. 'So, I gather you're a bit of a celebrity in your own right, now. As Nicola's latest "squeeze" – I believe that's the expression.'

'It's more than that, Ted.'

'Anyway, it should help get your writing career off the ground.'

'That would be a nice bonus, I suppose.'

'So how is she? Nicola.'

'She's fine. Great.'

'Good,' he murmured then took a sip of his brandy. 'She certainly looked pretty fine on stage.'

'Ted, I am aware of what a terrible thing I did. And not a day's gone by that I haven't regretted it.'

'Dominic, you were a rookie. And it was just a manuscript – one of hundreds you had to wade through every day of the week. You made a mistake. Forget it.'

'All the same, I'd do anything to be able to be turn back the clock and persuade Alistair what a gem I'd found in the slush pile, just like he was always telling me I might.'

'It wasn't a gem. It may have had its moment in the sun but it was never going to be a great novel. *Three Summers by the Sea*, on the other hand, that is a half decent novel, if I do say so myself.'

'That was the other thing I wanted to talk to you about. I'd like to help you get it published. I'm in a perfect position to do that now, if you'll let me.'

Ted looked up at him in surprise. 'Why?'

'To try to make amends for what happened.'

He sighed softly. 'Dominic, if you're going to be a serious writer, you have to stop using expressions like "if only this hadn't happened" or "if only that hadn't happened" or "if only I hadn't done what I did, things might have been different". What's happened's happened. What's going to happen is going to happen. That's how life is. That's what makes life extraordinary and that's what makes writing extraordinary because it's a mirror held up to life. If I'd had a positive response from Alistair Milner that day instead of ... okay, I'd have been feeling elated instead of suicidal. I'd have gone up to the pub and been patted on the back and bought lots of celebratory drinks. Chances are I'd never have noticed Nicola and, even if I had, I wouldn't have empathised with her the way I did. I've often looked back on that day and wondered if it was the worst day of my life. But, then again, it could've been the best day of my life because, when we were walking home together, she became upset and I connected with her in a way I'd never connected with anyone before because it was the first time in my life that someone needed me. Anne never needed me. She loved me but she never needed me. I never even felt my children needed me. I remember them, from time to time when they were little, asking where I was and Anne telling them I was in my study playing with my novel-writing kit. It became a kind of family joke – Dad playing with his novel-writing kit. She meant no harm by it, but somehow it summed up the way things were. She was the one who was out there dealing with real life, I was playing a game. But with Nicola it was different. So don't waste time trying to make amends or wondering how much nicer things might have been if you'd acted differently. You did what you did. And it's all right.'

'Ted, it's not all right ... there's something else ...'

'Well, it'll have to wait,' he responded, glancing at his watch, standing up and draining his brandy in swift succession. 'If I don't catch that train I'm going to be spending the night in this God-awful town and that's the last thing I want. Thanks for the drink.'

He held out his hand and saw a look of anguish on the young man's face. 'Look, Dominic, whatever's on your mind, forget it. I forgive you. Life's too short. It's time to move on.'

VII

'It's very good of you to see me at such short notice.'

'It's a pleasure,' said Miranda Cole, shaking Anne's hand. 'Do sit down.'

'The reason I came,' she began as she perched on the seat in front of the desk, 'is that I found some letters you wrote my husband. And I gathered from one of them that his work is suddenly in demand.'

'It certainly is. I must admit I'm surprised and rather dismayed that he hasn't got back to me. I've tried phoning his mobile but had no joy, and he doesn't seem to have an email address. He's a hard man to track down.'

'That's one of the reasons I wanted to see you. He's disappeared and I'm worried about him, quite apart from not wanting him to miss this opportunity.'

'Disappeared?'

'Yes, none of his friends have the faintest idea where he's gone. I know it's a long shot but I'm getting rather desperate and I wondered if he might have given you a change of address or mentioned anything about his plans.'

Miranda Cole shook her head. 'I'm sorry. I had lunch with him here in London and he just seemed delighted that someone was taking an interest in his work. But I've had no contact with him since I wrote him that letter.'

Anne became subdued and thoughtful. 'I'm sorry to have troubled you then.'

'It's no trouble. And I sincerely hope you find him. And when you do, perhaps you could ask him to contact me as soon as possible. It's a fickle market we're dealing with and the interest in his work won't last forever.'

Anne hesitated a moment. 'There is one other thing I have to ask you. Ted and I both know the young man who is now Nicola Carson's boyfriend. His name's Dominic and I happen to know he's also searching for Ted. I've been trying to contact him on his old mobile and landline numbers but both have been discontinued, as has his email address. And I just wondered, since your Nicola Carson's agent ...' Seeing a look of mystification come over the woman's face, she added, 'Perhaps I'd better explain.'

She then told her everything Ted had told her that night in The Lemon Grass, omitting only his nocturnal foray into Nicola's bedroom. And the jiffy bags stuffed with cash. The look of mystification deepened into one of consternation.

'That completely contradicts what he said when I met him.'

'I know. But he lied to you for a reason.'

'So it's true? Nicola didn't write *Loss*?'

'No. She didn't.'

Miranda Cole had gone pale and was slowly shaking her head. 'I was always in two minds. I suppose part of me clung to the hope that what your husband said was true. I should've listened to Tom. I thought he was just ... so she lied in her statement on television?'

'Yes. She lied to protect Ted's chance of success.'

Miranda Cole fell silent but Anne could sense, behind the delicate, intelligent features, a brain hard at work examining all the implications of what she had been told. 'Mrs Haymer,' she said at last, 'I really appreciate your sharing this with me. But I think it might be better for all concerned if we forget we ever had this conversation. Your husband's a fine writer. *Three Summers by the Sea* will establish his reputation. I'm going to make sure of it.'

Anne considered her words. 'I don't think Ted's going to forget, though. That's why he hasn't contacted you. I think that, after everything that's happened, he wants to try to achieve success without unfair advantages.'

'When you find him, you have to persuade him otherwise. In my experience one should never underrate unfair advantages – most people who've achieved anything in this life have had them and it would be a tragedy if his talent went to waste.'

'I couldn't agree with you more,' murmured Anne.

Miranda Cole observed her for a moment. 'I probably shouldn't be telling you this. But, as you pointed out, I'm still Nicola's agent and I do happen to know that she and her boyfriend are staying at the Cadogan Hotel in Greenwich.'

*

Anne went straight there from Miranda Cole's office. It was four-thirty in the afternoon and, since the performance wasn't until seven thirty, it was possible the couple would be in their room.

The hotel seemed pleasant enough but was not, she imagined, the sort of place Nicola was used to. The young man on the reception desk greeted her with a cheery smile but when she said the words 'Mr Seeley' he became distinctly cagey. Clearly the staff had been told to keep the couple's presence low-key. When Anne became insistent, however, he phoned through to their room. 'Mr Seeley will be down in a moment, madam.'

Some imitation leather sofas and armchairs were positioned around low tables in a bay to the left of the entrance and Anne perched in one of them. An empty beer glass stood beside a tumbler containing a twist of lemon. This was definitely not the Savoy.

A few minutes later, she spotted Dominic approaching across the reception area, looking awkward and bewildered. Though wearing only jeans and a T-shirt, he somehow seemed far better dressed than when she had seen him last. She stood up.

'Anne. What a lovely surprise,' he smiled, placing a hand on her arm and pecking her on both cheeks. 'Nicola's taking a nap.'

Why he had told her that, she was not entirely sure. 'I'll be seeing her tonight, anyway,' she said. 'I managed to get a ticket for the play.'

'Oh, fantastic. Would you like to go and get a drink at a pub? Or a coffee?'

'No, no, this is fine.'

He glanced around. 'Let's at least find somewhere a bit less public,' he said, then ushered her into the lounge where he chose a quiet corner near a fireplace.

'So you're going to be watching tonight too?' she said as they sat down.

'Oh yes, I watch it every night.'

'That's very loyal of you.'

'Well, I reckon if Nicola can act every night, the least I can do is support her. I guess you could say we're kind of a team,' he added with a short laugh. 'Ghastly expression.'

Anne contemplated him for a moment. 'So how are you?'

'I'm fine. Great. I'm working on a novel.'

'Not about plagiarism, I hope.'

'No,' he laughed. 'I've had enough of that subject to last me a lifetime.'

Despite the banter, the word created an awkwardness between them.

'Anne, I'm assuming you know the truth.'

'Yes, I do. Ted told me everything. And, as you can imagine, I was … well, anyway. And you do too, obviously.'

'Nicola told me a while ago, before we went abroad. Are you sure you wouldn't like a coffee? Or some tea? I could order some.'

'No, I'm fine, really. I have to confess this isn't a social call, even though it's great to see you again. Ted's disappeared. And I need to find him. He's not well and … I gathered from Ian at the pub that you were in there recently, asking after him, and I just wondered if you'd had any luck in tracking him down.'

Dominic was thoughtful for a while, slowly shaking his head. 'I'm afraid I have no idea where he is.'

'That's a shame. So why were you looking for him? If you don't mind my asking.'

He hesitated. 'It was Nicola. She wanted to see him. To clear the air.'

'I see. The thing is, I came across a letter from Miranda Cole, saying that the publishers were clamouring for his new novel after ... well, after Nicola's statement ... and he hasn't responded to it. I don't know how you feel about that, but I don't want him to miss this opportunity.'

'Oh no, he mustn't miss it. And Anne, I have this ... feeling ... that Ted's fine. And that you shouldn't worry about him.'

'You have a feeling?'

'An intuition. I get them.'

'Oh. Are they reliable?'

'Totally reliable. And I just know everything's going to be fine.'

She was scrutinising him through half-closed eyes. 'Dominic, is there something you're not telling me?'

'No. Absolutely not.'

'Well, I'll just have to trust in your intuition, then,' she murmured doubtfully. 'What I can't understand is why he didn't just tell me what he was planning with Nicola from the start. I would have thought it was stupid and I would have disapproved but I wouldn't have ... And I always sensed he was dissatisfied with *Tyranny*.'

'Maybe he didn't want you to think he was cheating.'

She did not reply and he knew she was considering the irony of his unfortunate choice of words.

'I do hope you find him, Anne. I really do.'

'So do I,' she murmured, then lapsed again into silence, thinking about what he had said. She was so preoccupied that she did not notice the young woman who had suddenly appeared by their table. Then she looked up and knew at once who she was, though in the eyes which were looking back she saw only a question.

'So this is where you're hiding,' she said to Dominic.

He was on his feet, aghast, and Anne followed suit, partly out of politeness but mainly because she wanted to be on a level with Nicola Carson. Dominic forced a smile. 'Darling, this is Anne. An old friend of mine.'

The two women surveyed each other. 'I'm delighted to meet you,' said Nicola.

Anne took the proffered hand. 'I'm delighted to meet you too.' Then she added, 'I understand congratulations are in order – on your return to the stage.'

'Thanks,' Nicola replied with a brief laugh, glancing at Dominic, 'I'm really enjoying it.'

'And I'm really looking forward to seeing you tonight.'

'Thank you. I hope I don't disappoint.'

'I'm sure you won't.'

Nicola turned back to Dominic. 'Honey, I'm off to the theatre now.'

'Okay, I'll catch you up,' he said and kissed her on the cheek.

As she was turning to go, she smiled again at Anne. 'It was nice meeting you.'

'And you.'

Her departure left a vacuum in the air.

'Well … that was interesting,' Anne murmured as they sat down again. 'Did she know who I was?'

'I don't think so. I thought perhaps it might be simpler if she didn't.'

'You're probably right. I have to be honest, Dominic, for the past five years I've … felt bitter about her. But I realise now that it wasn't her I felt bitter about, it was the Nicola I'd formed in my head out of all the lies I'd been told about her. I didn't know her. I didn't know anything about her. And I still find it hard to believe that …'

He knew what she was going to say. 'Anne, if it's any help, there's something I should tell you. When I first met Ted, when I turned up out of the blue with my piece of the jigsaw puzzle, he saw a way of establishing himself as the true author of *Tyranny* and all his other novels. That was all he cared about. I don't think he cared about the money. He wanted to be given the acknowledgement he felt he deserved for one reason only, to …'

'To what?'

'To regain your respect. He wanted you to be proud of him.'

'But I was always proud of him. I never allowed his failure to publish to affect my opinion of him as a writer.'

'No, but it made a difference to him. Even though every writer knows that a manuscript contains exactly the same words in exactly the same order as the published book, they also know, in their heart of hearts, that it's not the same.'

Anne responded with silence.

'And there's something else you should know. It was I who suggested we involve you. I thought your being a lawyer would give weight to our cause. He was opposed to the idea but, after he had been rebuffed by Nicola, he was angry and asked me to talk to you. That was why I came to see you at that coffee shop. But he told me not to pressure you. "I don't want you to coerce her in any way," were his exact words. "Just tell her the facts and see how she reacts. If she wants to have nothing to do with it then leave her be." And I think he said that because he didn't want to admit he was hoping that going after Nicola might … bring you closer … maybe even bring you back to him.'

Anne thought for a long time about his words then snorted once with hollow amusement. 'It would have done if only …' She left the sentence hanging in the air.

'If only what?'

'If only he hadn't told me the truth.'

*

The stage was bathed in turquoise light – the light of an Andalusian farmhouse on a summer evening. Adela, the youngest daughter of Bernarda Alba, was centre stage, in copious red and orange skirts, yelling at her sister Martirio, 'I can't stand the horror of this house a moment longer, not after knowing the taste of his mouth! I will be what he wants me to be! With the whole town against me, branding me with their fiery fingers, persecuted by people who claim to be decent, I will put on a crown of thorns right in front of them, like the mistress of any married man!'

A few minutes later she would hang herself, for the love of Pepe el Romano, the man to whom her elder sister is betrothed, the sister with the dowry. But she has been with him – her petticoat is covered with straw and she has brought shame on the household. Then comes the showdown with her mother, Bernarda – she seizes the old woman's cane, snaps it across her knee and tosses it aside. 'This is what I do with the tyrant's rod! Don't take one step more! No one gives me orders now but Pepe!'

From time to time during the performance, Anne had glanced among the darkened faces of the audience, trying to spot Dominic but he was nowhere to be seen. Perhaps he was watching from the wings. She found herself thinking about Ted, about Ted and Nicola, and about how this girl striding about the stage before her could so easily have turned the head of a disenchanted middle-aged dreamer. Then she thought about Nicola and Dominic and his weirdly meandering route to the fulfilment of his dreams. But then, as Adela's hanging corpse was displayed as a stark shadow slanting on a wall, she thought about Nicola and something happened to her which took her completely by surprise. Her eyes filled with tears.

Nicola, smiling and radiant, appeared second to last in the curtain call, to cheers and thunderous applause. Anne wondered if she would upstage Dame Helen Mellon who was playing Bernarda herself and who finally walked from the wings into the centre of her line of daughters. But the applause which greeted her – which greeted the entire performance – was tumultuous. It was as though Nicola, as the daughter who had committed suicide for love rather than be constrained by a tyrannical mother and a tyrannical society, had bestowed a kind of benediction upon the play by being alive for love, by being spared.

*

'*No corner of the human psyche was left unexplored,*' one critic would write of that acclaimed performance. '*No woman will ever feel the same about being a woman after seeing Nicola Carson in that role,*' wrote another. Dominic, who had been watching from the wings, knew it too, though he didn't need critics to tell him. As soon as the curtain fell, he made his way through the barrage of excited chatter, trying to avoid getting caught in conversation. Anne, he noted with relief, was nowhere to be seen – she must have already left to catch her train. He made it to the back stairs marked 'Private', ran up them into a narrow corridor and, seconds later, was greeted by the spectacle of his beloved resplendent before him, still in costume. 'You were amazing!' he cried, crossing the room and taking her in his arms. 'Absolutely bloody amazing.'

'Just doing my job,' she said, detaching herself.

'That wasn't a job. That was passion. You're so inside Adela now, you've almost become her.'

'Oh, bollocks. It's a job. A job I have to work bloody hard at it. Especially tonight.'

She turned away to begin the tedious business of disrobing and removing her makeup. 'So who was that woman you were talking to?' she asked, unpinning her hair.

Dominic was pulled up short. 'What woman?'

'You know perfectly well what woman. The one you were in a huddle with at the hotel.'

'She's just ... someone I knew in publishing.'

'Really?' She did not meet his eyes in the mirror. 'It's just that I've got this weird feeling I've seen her somewhere before ... in Wemborne.'

Dominic's heart was thumping. 'Wemborne?'

'Yeah, Wemborne. I did spend six years in that dump, on and off, and in a place like that, you notice people – in the bank, in the chemist – especially classy people like her – they stick out like a sore thumb. And when she was shaking my hand there was ... something, something in her eyes, as though *she* knew *me* or had some connection with me. Then it struck me. She'd be about that age. And she's called Anne. I may be putting two and two together and making five but I don't think so. That woman's Ted's wife.'

Dominic was silent for an age. He breathed very deeply and exhaled a trembling breath. 'It's no good. I can't keep this up any longer.'

She turned to face him for the first time. 'Keep what up?'

'Let's go back to the hotel. There's something I have to tell you.'

'If you've got something to tell me you can tell me now. What's going on, Dominic?'

He sank into the chair beside the dressing table. He looked down at his hands. 'Nicola, everything that's happened since you met Ted ... and I mean everything ... has been down to me. You may think it's been down to him but it hasn't, it's been down to me. If I hadn't done what I did, none of this would've happened. You would never have got involved with him and *Loss* would never have existed ...'

She was standing over him, leaning against the dressing table, staring at him. 'I haven't the faintest idea what you're talking about.'

'You told me, the night we first made love, that when you met Ted he'd just received a letter ... from a publisher. It was from The Dragon's Head – the firm I worked for and which he'd had high hopes of. It was a letter of rejection but it also contained some sarcastic remarks about his work which, in his depressed state of mind, he found hard to take.'

'I know. He told me. But how do you know so much about it?'

'I wrote it.'

There followed a stunned silence.

'Well, strictly speaking it was Sonia, one of the secretaries, who wrote it. But I was behind it.'

She was slowly shaking her head. 'But why would you *do* that? I thought you loved *Tyranny*.'

'I do. But I hadn't read it then.'

'*Dominic?*'

'It was all a horrible, horrible mess, jumbled up with my weakness and immaturity and cowardice. I'd just shown Alistair my pile of infantile crap I called a novel, assuming he'd recognise it as a work of genius and publish it instantly, instead of which he told me the truth. He let me down very gently but I'd worked on that novel for eight years – I'd put my life and soul into it – it *was* my life, and I was devastated. I just wanted to lash out at something, at someone. And the first thing I saw when I came out of his office was Ted's manuscript. Or, at least, not the manuscript but some marketing thing he'd concocted.'

He paused a moment, not daring to look up and meet her eyes. 'I never even glanced at his sample chapters. In my distraught state I just shoved them aside ...'

'Go on.'

'We attached a slip to every submission which went back to Sonia so she could write to the author telling them whether the book had been rejected or whether they wanted to see the whole manuscript. I just wrote on his slip ... well, something very offensive, I'm afraid, then chucked it in the box, thinking it was the actual sample. I was in such a state I didn't know what I was doing.

'Then I forgot about it, I was so busy feeling sorry for myself. But later that day, Sonia came over with the slip I'd defaced and asked me what I was playing at. When I told her about this guy's proposal – how he'd given *everybody* as his target readership and *originality* as his USP – she just smiled and said, "We've had submissions from people like that before. Too high and mighty for a bit of self-promotion. Don't worry. Leave him to me." I felt uneasy about it, even then, but she signed for Alistair all the time, so, in theory, he'd never know. Then, as she was leaving, she turned back and said she'd better return his sample chapters.

'I went to give them to her but they weren't there. They'd just vanished. I searched all over my desk but I couldn't find them. So I told her he couldn't have his sample chapters back and it was no big deal.'

'So your boss never saw them?'

'Yeah, he did, but much later. Our office was small and cramped, with too many desks and too many people. There was stuff everywhere – books, papers, manuscripts, computers, you name it ...'

'Okay, I get the picture.'

'So more than a year later, Alistair's edging past someone to get to his office and brushes against my desk, causing an avalanche. He crouched down to help me pick the stuff up – in a right tizz – and then something caught his eye ...'

'Ted's chapters.'

'Exactly. Ted's chapters. I must have thrust them away so roughly that they'd slid off the pile on my desk and got stuck down the back, behind the column of drawers. "What's this?" he says and yanks them out and starts reading them. "This looks intriguing," he said. Then he took the file into his office, re-emerging about an hour later, all fired up. "Who *is* this Edward Haymer?" he kept asking. "Has he published?"

'I was frantically thinking on my feet so I said I didn't know but I'd thought it looked promising too and had been meaning to run it past him. He asked me how long I'd kept it stuck down the back of my desk and when I said only a couple of days, he gave me an old-fashioned look and the standard lecture about finding a gem in the slush pile. He told me to get onto him right away. Then he said no, better still, he'd call him himself.

'I practically yelled at him not to phone him, and he asked why not. I came up with some feeble excuse like I'd lost the cover letter – I only had the address on the manuscript. He looked daggers at me and said he'd write to him then.

'He dictated a letter to Debbie – Sonia was off that day – and I watched her print it out and shove it in an envelope along with his chapters, then put it in her out tray for posting. A few minutes later, she went to the loo and I nipped over, swiped the envelope and stashed it in the bottom of my bottom drawer, under a heap of other stuff. I suppose I should've destroyed it but somehow I just couldn't bring myself to. But I knew it was only a matter of time before the shit hit the fan.'

'And did it?'

'No. I just waited. And hoped. And prayed. Nothing happened and, after a couple of weeks, I began to think I'd got away with it, that everything was going to be okay. Then Alistair collared me in the corridor and told me he still hadn't heard from Haymer and to get his number from directory enquiries, using his address. I made out I'd already tried and looked on Google and Facebook and Twitter and all over the place but had no joy. "You know what's happened, don't you?" he said. "He's gone somewhere else. I tell you, Dominic, if this author turns out to be another Ian McEwan, I'm going to string you up by the balls."'

His story left a silence in the air.

'I can't get my head around this. He liked *Tyranny*.'

'He was crazy about it. He'd have published it like a shot.'

Nicola sank down into the chair opposite him as she began to fully comprehend what was being said to her, the burgeoning skirts of Adela spewing over the sides. 'So why didn't you track him down and tell him?'

'I couldn't. I knew if Alistair found out I'd let Sonia write that letter under his name then lost his manuscript for more than a year, he'd have fired me.'

'So you shafted Ted to save your own skin?'

'Pretty much,' he muttered.

'So, if you'd fessed up like a man, he'd be an established novelist by now. He'd have self-respect. He'd still be with his wife and living in a proper house instead of that fucking caravan. And *Loss* would never have ...'

There came a knock at the door. 'Who is it?' she snapped.

'Sorry, Miss Carson. Security. I wasn't sure if you were still in there.'

'Well I am!'

'Okay. No hurry.'

It took her a moment to recover from the intrusion. 'It still doesn't explain what you were doing with Anne Haymer.'

'Well ... there is more.' Slowly, awkwardly, not meeting her eye, he went on to describe his momentous discovery and all the events leading up to his meeting with Ted at the pub.

Her eyes widened. 'You've actually *met* him?'

'Well, I thought if I could find out what had happened, maybe establish the novel's true authorship it would help to make amends for what I'd done.'

Gradually, little by little, it came together inside her head: his wish that they hide away in some distant land for the rest of their lives; the ease with which he found Ted's caravan on Whitesands Marsh; his reluctance to go and look for him at the pub, where he would have been recognised.

'It was you,' she murmured. 'It was you who persuaded him to sue me. It wasn't his wife at all ... it was you. That's what your book was going to be about. You weren't planning some arse-kissing biography, you were planning to expose me ...'

'No. *No*. It wasn't *like* that.'

'That's why you put on that shy, gormless act and lied your way into Malvern Hall. That's why you were so nice to me all those weeks. You were trying to sweet-talk me into confessing.' Her voice hardened and she looked up at him. 'You insisted on giving me that Dictaphone – you wanted to get it on tape. The proof you needed in court.' Her mouth was hanging open, her head swaying helplessly from side to side. '*Jesus* ...'

'No! The Dictaphone had nothing to do with it! I just use it as a memory aid. Okay, I'll admit when I first came to Malvern Hall it was to get a confession but things changed when I got to know you. I came over to your side. I ... fell in love with you. And I didn't know the truth because Ted had been lying to *me*.'

'Get out of here!'

'Nicola *please*. Let's just talk about this! It's not as though you didn't have an agenda yourself. You wanted me to help you confess. You admitted it. You were going to stage your own death, remember? Then disappear. And I was the one you'd chosen to help you. Anyway, if that *was* my motive, why didn't I write the book and use it?'

'Because you had me by then! Who needs a golden egg when they've got the whole fucking goose?'

'Nicola ...'

'*Get out of here.*'

*

He went back to the hotel, not knowing where else to go. And there he waited, wandering between the rooms, waiting for her to return, knowing she would not return. His phone vibrated, announcing a text. It said simply:

Staying with friends

At least she had sent him that text. He tried to derive some comfort from that. But he knew in his heart that it had not been sent to comfort or reassure him, it had been sent to tell him to leave her alone.

He didn't even try to sleep. He could not stay in their room, surrounded by her things, by the scent of her, by the sound of her voice echoing in his brain. He wandered the streets of London, hour after hour, returning finally to their room where he sat in a chair, staring into space.

You have to stop using expressions like 'if only this hadn't happened' or 'if only that hadn't happened' or 'if only I hadn't done what I did, things might have been different'. What's happened's happened. What's going to happen is going to happen. That's how life is.

There came a knock at the door. Emerging from a medley of nightmares featuring Nicola – furious, vengeful, betrayed – he was surprised to discover he was lying fully clothed on the bed. He glanced at his watch and was even more surprised to find it was twenty past nine. Then he remembered he had found her Nitrazadon and taken two of them. The knock came again, more timidly. He hauled himself up, swayed and stumbled then went to answer it, finding himself staring at a dark, curly-haired woman of about forty. She seemed very awkward.

'Hi. You must be Dominic.'

'Yes.'

'I'm Rebecca. Rebecca Goodman. My husband's a friend of Bill Grainger, Nicola's agent. Nicola stayed with us last night and she ... she asked if I'd mind calling round to collect her things. But if it's not convenient ...' she added hastily.

Dominic looked around in bewilderment. 'Um ... I've only just woken up. I was about to take a shower.' His appearance must have corroborated his words, even though he was dressed.

'Yes, of course. I can call back.'

'Give me an hour.'

'And I was told to say...'

He waited for her to finish her sentence.

'I was told to say that the bill's been paid up to today – the hotel bill.'

'Right.'

He closed the door and rested his forehead against it. He had no intention of taking a shower, he just needed some time to orientate himself, to try to come to terms with the situation, to accept that this pleasant, polite woman had been sent not only to collect Nicola's things but to inform him – in code – that it was over.

He was unclear whether he was supposed to pack her stuff himself or whether she was going to do it. He found himself fondling her clothes, the delicate scent of Chanel evoking the memory of the day he had first met her, the day he had gone to Malvern Hall and they had sat together on the terrace that mild March afternoon, smoking his cigarettes. Then he opened another cupboard, crouched down and gazed at her shoes and boots and sandals, his eye drawn to her red shoes nestling among their companions – her beautiful Ralph Lauren shoes – simple and stylish but getting a little old and scuffed in places now. He smiled faintly as he thought of how she loved those shoes with a passion that was almost childlike and had to have them with her everywhere she went. He reached out and picked them up and gazed at them, then his awkward body folded around them like a mother's around her dying baby, his shoulders heaving and trembling as the tears poured down his cheeks.

Finally, angrily, he got out his own suitcase and threw the red shoes into it, along with his own things. He zipped it up, collected his jacket, wallet and keys and left the room.

*

The hubbub of conversation died as the lights were dimmed and the audience turned its attention to the curtain which was about to open. They waited. They whispered to one another. Then, to their surprise, a spotlight swung stage right to reveal a silver-haired man in black tie emerging from the wings. It followed him as he walked briskly centre stage and turned to face them.

'Ladies and gentlemen,' he began, 'it is with great regret that I have to announce that Nicola Carson is unable to take part in tonight's performance ...' The end of his sentence – '... due to illness' – was drowned in a howl of disappointment bristling with anger. Nicola Carson was the reason most of them had bought their tickets. He held up his hands in a gesture of conciliation, beseeching calm, forbearance and forgiveness. When the outburst had subsided a little, he added, 'However, we have a superb understudy in Hannah Jameson, so the show will go on!'

*

Dominic unlocked the door, knowing the emptiness which awaited him. He tossed the keys onto the kitchen table and stood in the middle of the room, gazing around. The place was exactly as they had left it the night they had fled in Sarah's boyfriend's car. One of Nicola's cigarette packets lay empty on the counter, some dishes were stacked in the rack on the draining board. It was as though time had frozen – a time when everything had been different, when planet Earth had been a billion miles from where it was now.

He grabbed the kettle and filled it even though he did not want coffee. He moved to the little table and sat down to wait for it to boil. If he could just address himself to small tasks, one after the other, maybe he could keep going, at least for the moment.

He reached into his pocket, pulled out his mobile and gazed at it. He scrolled through the numbers, selected the one he was looking for and pressed dial. His heart was pounding as he lifted it to his ear. A woman's voice said, 'Malvern Hall Mental Health Clinic.'

'It's Dominic Seeley. I wonder if I might speak to Dr Lennox.'

'Hold the line a moment.' He waited – his heart in his mouth –

then the woman came back and said, 'As a matter of fact, he wants to speak to you. Is it possible you could get down here?'

'You mean, he wants to speak to me in person?'

'If you wouldn't mind.'

'So Nicola's with you?'

The woman hesitated. 'I'm afraid I can't divulge that information.'

As far as he was concerned, she just had.

'When shall I come?'

'As soon as possible.'

It was five past eight in the evening and he set off at once in the Mercedes they had chosen together. Nicola had insisted it should be a convertible. And white. Her scent lingered there too, in the sumptuous leather upholstery. As instructed, he announced himself through the intercom and the electronic gate buzzed and swung open. The receptionist was off duty at that hour and the woman who unlocked the door and asked him to sign in was a stranger to him. She wore a grave expression – whether it was habitual or for his benefit he was unsure.

They walked to Dr Lennox's office, she knocked, admitted him and closed the door behind him. Dr Lennox was seated at his desk, writing something on a form, and gestured to him to sit down. They did not shake hands. Finally he set down his pen, sat back and stared at him.

'So. Here we are again.'

'Dr Lennox, is there any chance at all I can see her?'

'None whatsoever. She was in a bad way when she arrived but one thing she was quite coherent about was that you shouldn't be allowed anywhere near her. She's a little calmer now and I've spoken to her at some length. But I need to get as complete a picture as possible of what's been going on, so I'd like to hear your version of events.'

Dominic opened his mouth to speak then closed it again. He was silent for an age. Dr Lennox did not hurry him. 'You remember that morning Nicola left here and came to stay with me?' he said at last, 'and you asked me if I was worthy of her trust?'

'Yes.'

'Well, I wasn't. I was lying to her – and to you – from the start. I never ran a fan club website. That thing you saw on the internet was a fake.'

A fake. By the time he had finished relating the saga of his deception and its consequences, he felt drained but also oddly unburdened. Dr Lennox had not interrupted him once.

'I should have told her the truth, I know I should, but I was just so amazed that a girl like that should be interested in me and I was terrified she'd turn against me. And I was concerned for her. I remembered what you said about how easily a bipolar sufferer can be pushed over the edge.'

Dr Lennox was still staring at him. 'And what about the other lies you told?'

'I'm sorry?'

'That morning you referred to, you claimed to be taken completely by surprise when she announced she was coming to stay with you. And yet I now know that it was you who persuaded her to leave here and help you write the very book that was going to destroy her...'

'No. That's not true.'

'... and that it was you who persuaded her to go on television and make that statement.'

Dominic grimaced. 'What? Why would I *do* that?'

'To corroborate what you were going to put in your book before the storm of protest it would've unleashed. Not to mention a barrage of lawsuits. You knew you had no proof. So what better substitute for proof than to get the accused to go on national television and confess? Then, on the back of the scandal, you were going to come out with your book – the inside story.'

Soundlessly Dominic mouthed the word '*What?*'

'Everyone now agrees that Nicola did write *Loss* – her publisher, her agent, Connaught International, academics, critics. The truth is what Haymer – whose conscience presumably got the better of him – said in his statement – that he showed her his manuscript and she was influenced by it. The allegation of plagiarism was nothing more than a scandal you whipped up out of that to launch your pathetic career.'

Dominic was shaking his head. 'I don't know what she's been telling you but she's clearly delusional. Or she's punishing me. She admitted to me she didn't write that book. She wanted to admit it. She *needed* to confess.'

'Of course she did. Because you'd convinced her that the influence she'd received from Haymer's manuscript amounted to full-scale plagiarism. It's a common phenomenon among patients in a vulnerable condition. They meet someone who makes them feel safe and secure and they fall entirely under their spell. And it makes them very easy to manipulate.'

'Oh ... *crap*. I never manipulated her. And I never persuaded her to go on television. I tried to *dissuade* her. *She* had to persuade *me*. That's the truth.'

'The truth?' Dr Lennox laughed. 'After what you've just told me, I'm supposed to accept what you say as the truth?'

Dominic was lost for words.

'By the way, do you know what's happened to her red shoes?'

He couldn't negotiate the change of subject. 'What?'

'Her red shoes. They weren't with her luggage and she's very upset about it. They're her talisman.'

'I've no idea what's happened to her red shoes. Some woman came to our hotel room to collect her stuff. Maybe she stole them.'

Dr Lennox sighed. 'I think I've heard enough. All I know is that before you appeared on the scene I had a patient who was steadily, if slowly, improving. Now, thanks to you, she's back to square one – or even further back. And I've only got myself to blame. You took me in – hook, line and sinker – and that takes some doing, I can tell you. Whether Nicola ever trusts anyone after this remains to be seen. All I can say is that, as long as it's within my power, I'll move heaven and earth to make her better. And I'll also move heaven and earth to ensure she never lays eyes on you again.'

Dominic fell silent. Then he raised his eyes and said defiantly, 'There is one thing I'm not lying about, that I've never lied about. And that's that I love her.'

The doctor's stare was relentless, seeming to probe into the deepest recesses of his being. 'I'm sure you do,' he said. 'Her mistake was loving you back.'

*

'I can't believe it,' Anne murmured, slowly shaking her head, 'I just can't believe it. I mean ... she was there, right before my eyes, just hours before. I shook her hand. And she looked so ... *well.*'

Linda was standing behind her where she sat at the kitchen table with the day's copy of *The Times* spread before her – the poignancy of the story enhanced by a four-year-old shot of Nicola receiving her Oscar for *All about Me.*

'Have you any idea what caused it?' she asked.

'None whatsoever.'

*

The wind was rattling the tiny window that never quite shut properly, though the rain had ceased and the clouds had parted to bestow a few final bursts of sunshine on the little Devon town. Ted left his caravan and set off under tossing, swaying trees and scraps of paper flying on inky skies like tiny, demented seabirds. He crossed the patch of grass behind the sea wall then made his way through the sloping streets towards The Mariner's Arms. Passing the petrol station, his attention was drawn to the newspapers stacked in a row of plastic compartments beside the door, one of which – *The Evening Star* – bore on its front page the words:

NICOLA CARSON BACK IN REHAB

He crossed the few yards of concrete, lifted the lid and grabbed a copy:

Troubled superstar Nicola Carson (28) has once again stunned the show-business world by dropping out of the production of 'The House of Bernarda Alba' at the Rondel Theatre, Greenwich, which she had single-handedly turned into a box-office smash.

Sources close to the star have revealed that she has suffered a mental breakdown and returned to Malvern Hall, the rehab clinic where she was previously being treated for depression. She is reported to be on twenty-four hour suicide watch. The cause of the crisis is as yet unknown but it is believed that her boyfriend – wannabe writer Dominic Seeley (29) – is heavily involved.

Adrian Miles, director of 'The House of Bernarda Alba', told The Evening Star, 'We are stunned by what's happened. Naturally we are very concerned for Nicola and hope she makes a speedy recovery. In the meantime, her role is being taken over by her understudy.' When asked if the company was considering legal action, he said, 'I cannot comment at this stage.'

Ted did not go to the pub. He couldn't face that bright, cheery environment nor could he face his caravan and the relentless loneliness of his own company. The sea lay across the road beyond the car park and the parade of shops and he felt drawn towards it. The sea was the edge of everything, the end of everything, the boundary at which all human life has to cease, especially on a night like this. He battled over tarmac and concrete, then picked his way through the ragwort-infested wasteland above the beach and kept on going until the shingle was slipping and sliding under his feet. The tide was in and the first cool mists of spray were sprinkling his face. He edged down the bank of clattering pebbles towards the surf line, slid into a sitting position and remained there, hunched in his battered Barbour, gazing at the rays of burnished sunlight touching the heaving, thundering walls of foam. As the hours passed and the darkness folded around him, he relived in memory every moment he had spent with her – their first inauspicious meeting at The Queen's, their time in Richmond and the night she had nestled under his arm and he, like a father comforting his frightened child, had caressed her hair until she had fallen asleep. And he had maintained his vigil until the morning, giving himself to her because she needed him, just as he was giving himself to the wind and the waves and the roaring sea.

VIII

Far away in London, Dominic was slumped on his sofa watching what might have been moving, speaking wallpaper on the television screen. His mobile rang and, since it was on the sofa arm, he grabbed it. Had it been out of reach, he wouldn't have bothered.

'Is Nicola with you?' said Dr Lennox.

He sat up, instantly alert. 'No. Why?'

'She's gone. But she's in a critical state and I'm very worried about her.'

'*Gone*? You mean she's just walked out?'

'Yes.'

'And what makes you think she's here?'

'Her red shoes. She's obsessed with them. She won't eat, can't sleep. And she's convinced you've got them. Dominic, I want you to be honest with me for once. Have you got them?'

'No. I haven't.'

The psychiatrist responded with silence, as though challenging him to tell the truth.

'Maybe one of the hotel staff took them. That woman I told you about. They could've gone into the room before she got there.'

'It's possible, I suppose. Though it's unlikely they'd own up. More likely they'd just get rid of them if they thought the pressure was on.'

'How long has she been missing?'

'Since about five.'

'Well, if she was coming here, she'd be here by now.'

'I know.'

'So what you're saying is that she's somewhere in London, in a suicidal state, and no one knows where.'

It was now Dr Lennox who was on the defensive. 'Look, I can't force people to stay here against their will. This isn't a prison. And I don't actually believe she's suicidal, not at the moment. But, thanks to you, she's completely lost faith in humanity and those shoes were the one thing she was clinging to ...'

'Have you tried her mobile?'

'Of course I have. It's switched off.'

'You have to call the police.'

'I already have. She's not officially a missing person yet but I've explained about her condition.'

'And she's a celebrity.'

'Well, officially that's not supposed to make any difference but we all know it does.'

'I've just had a thought. She may have tried to contact Ted. Ted Haymer.'

'Does she know where he is?'

'No, but she may contact the pub in Wemborne where they met, to see if he's back or if there's any news of him. It's a long shot, I know, but anything's worth a try. I'll get onto them.'

'Let me know if you have any luck.'

He found the number on the internet. The lad who answered went off to ask around and he could hear hubbub in the background. Then he returned to inform him that no one had spoken to Nicola Carson that evening. Nor to Beyoncé, for that matter.

'Very funny.'

'Is this about that broadcast?' he asked with a laugh. Dominic knew it wasn't the landlord.

'Indirectly.'

'We're still getting mileage out of that. It's been great for business. Really put the place on the map.'

He was about to respond to that remark but restrained himself. He couldn't afford to antagonise anyone – not that night. Instead he gave the lad his numbers and made him promise to call him at once if Nicola phoned or appeared.

'And I suppose you've heard nothing from Ted? Ted Haymer?'

'Nah. Ted's vanished off the face of the planet.'

Dominic was falling prey to the sense that it was all just activity for activity's sake, to keep himself from confronting the despair which, deep down, was already seeping into his being like icy water into the hull of a sinking ship. And her red shoes? What the hell was he supposed to do with her red shoes? He'd felt angry, felt that, in spite of everything, he was entitled to one small part of her, one tiny consolation prize. But if not having them was deepening her anguish, even pushing her over the edge, he had to give them back. But how could he give them back if no one knew where she was?

He went to the bedroom and fetched them, as though holding them might somehow provide an answer. He fondled them, skimming his fingertips over the vamp, caressing the sides, the soles, the heels. He remembered her telling him about them once, in New Zealand, after he'd joked that her attachment to them was almost unhealthy – about how she'd bought them in San Francisco when she was shooting *All about Me*. 'They're magic,' she'd told him with a disarming giggle. 'At least, one of them is.'

It had struck him as odd. If she'd said 'they're magic!' as in 'they're amazing' or 'they're fantastic' it would have been understandable, even though he had never heard her use that adjective about anything. But why should she say only one was magic? He held them together, trying to spot a difference, but both looked an exact mirror of the other. He turned them over and inspected the soles and heels. Then he noticed something – the left heel was less worn and of a different consistency – it was not leather like the right one but made of some composite material. Maybe it had been re-heeled at some stage. He touched it, fingered it, grasped it and waggled it and found that it wobbled as though it might come away in his hand. Perplexed, he gripped the shoe in his left hand, pressed the heel in hard and felt something click, then he turned it and – sure enough – it revolved on a thread, just like the lid of a coffee jar. He unscrewed it and removed it and stared at what lay in the shallow recess within.

He was back on the phone to Dr Lennox. 'I know why she's so obsessed with those shoes. It's not the shoes at all. There's a blade hidden in one of the heels.'

There followed a silence. 'So you have got them?'

'Yes, I have. I just needed a keepsake. Something of her.'

'It's a shame you couldn't have made do with a hairclip.'

Dominic knew what he was thinking and he didn't care. Anxiety for Nicola was now eclipsing every other emotion and he guessed the same was true of Dr Lennox.

'But why does she need those particular shoes and that particular blade? If she can walk out of your gates at any time and buy another blade, or a knife or ...' The end of the sentence was too horrible to form into words.

'It's complicated. As I said, the shoes are a talisman – a lucky charm, if you like – a lot of actors have them. The blade may be too. Habitual self-harmers often use the same blade.'

'So she's more into self-harm than suicide?'

'It's a grey area. But every time she's tried to take her own life it's been in a context where she knows someone can prevent her, which may suggest she doesn't really want to succeed.'

'You mean, it's a cry for help?'

'Possibly. But things can go wrong.'

His words sent a chill down Dominic's spine. 'So, in a sense, being denied her shoes is a good thing?'

'In a sense. But she needs them psychologically.'

'What should I do, Dr Lennox?'

'Stay put in case she turns up there. We'll keep in touch.'

He didn't have as much faith as the doctor in the belief that she wasn't going to kill herself. He may not be a psychiatrist but he knew Nicola. She didn't cry for help. He found himself thinking the unthinkable but he had to think it if he was ever going to find her. Where would she go if she wanted to take her own life? A hotel room? Somewhere where she could lock the door on the world and dispatch herself in peace?

He tried her mobile again. It was switched off. Had it been switched on, it might have been possible to locate her. He sighed with exasperation.

He tried Ted's mobile. Anne would have already tried it, of course, but anything was worth a shot. 'I'm sorry, the person you are calling is unavailable.'

He switched on the television as well as the internet. He wanted as much life as possible in that mausoleum of a flat, as much contact as possible with the outside world. Nicola was a star after all. And she'd be in people's minds after dropping so dramatically out of the play – the story had been in all the tabloids. If she checked into some hotel in a distraught state, she would attract attention. If people spotted her in the streets or at an airport or railway station, they'd notice her. If anything happened to her it would make the news in an instant – especially as the paparazzi and half the hacks in London were on her tail. But there was nothing. He was determined to draw some comfort from that.

The television was playing some American sitcom, each line greeted by gales of pre-packed laughter. Angrily, he grabbed the controls and switched to the rolling news channel, lowering the volume in case he missed the phone ringing. Not that he would. But there was no news. Everything in the world was normal.

He thought of ringing Dr Lennox again. But there was no point. He knew he would call the moment there were any developments at his end and he didn't want to make a nuisance of himself. He checked the internet again; he checked his emails and voicemail. Nothing.

Suddenly exhausted, he took his laptop to the bedroom, sat down and zapped his other television which also served as a computer screen on his desk. Wednesday drifted into Thursday. He switched to News 24. As the news droned on and on, the same stories repeated over and over again – an earthquake in Japan, a sham election in some African state, a rail disaster in Romania – his head began to swim. For an instant he forgot where he was. A voice was saying, 'We're now going live to Waterloo Station.' Waterloo Station? 'The toilet cubicle where the girl's body was found has now been cordoned off ... the police cannot release her identity at this time but foul play is not suspected ...'

He sprang forward and groped for his mobile, his fingers trembling so violently he could barely connect to the number. The ringing went on and on. There was a click.

'Dr Lennox?'

'Your call is being forwarded to ...'

'Oh for fuck's *sake*. Don't tell me you've gone to bed!'

Then his voice came on the line.

'Dr Lennox. Thank God! I've just seen the news ... a girl's ... a girl's body's been found in a toilet at Waterloo Station ... suspected suicide ... they haven't released her identity but you have to phone the police and find out if it's ... maybe use your influence ...'

The doorbell rang, making him jump. It rang again, longer this time, more insistently, its jangle echoing around the flat. It would be the police, of course, to confirm what he already knew. He tore out into the hall, snatched the door open and there she was standing before him. Nicola. Alive. Unharmed. He wanted to grab her and crush her in his arms but he could only stare at her.

'Give them to me,' she said icily.

'Nicola ...'

'*Give* them to me.'

Trembling with relief, fighting to maintain his composure, he went to the bedroom to fetch them. She came after him into the living room. He returned and gave them to her. 'There are your shoes.'

She dropped the right one, unscrewed the left heel and stared into the empty compartment. She sank down onto the sofa. 'You've stolen it. You've fucking *stolen* it.'

'I haven't stolen it. I got rid of it. I wrapped it in toilet paper and flushed it down the loo where it belongs because I didn't want you hurting yourself. Why have you still got it anyway? All the time we were together ... all the time we were in New Zealand ...?'

'It was my insurance policy.'

'*Insurance* policy? You had me, for Christ's sake!'

'Why do you think I needed an insurance policy? I never trusted you. Never. Not for one second!'

'So why did you come and live with me then?'

'Because ... you were a sad, pathetic loser, like me.'

'Bollocks!'

He lowered himself to the edge of the armchair. He drew a deep, trembling breath. 'Look, I fucked up. I know I did. And I'm sorry. But you know what it was like – you were there yourself, that's why you cooked up that scam with Ted. I just wanted to be a writer. A real writer. I didn't want to spend my life stuck in some office ploughing through other people's manuscripts. And when I saw that copy of *Loss* it was like … a door opening onto the future, it was like my passport out of there. You were the last thing on my mind. You were just a celebrity, an image on a screen. You weren't the person I met when I came to Malvern Hall, the person who smoked my cigarettes, the person I fell in love with. And when we got together, I wanted to tell you all that but I couldn't because I was scared I wouldn't be able to convince you. And I didn't want to lose you.'

'Well you've lost me now anyway.'

'I know,' he cried, pressing his hands over his face. 'I know.' He was suddenly sick of fighting the inevitable. 'Maybe you'd better go,' he said.

She turned and stared at him. 'What do you mean … *go?*'

'I mean go. You've got your shoes, which is what you came for. So go.'

'Look, I decide when I fucking go. *I* dumped *you*, remember, because you turned out to be a lying piece of shit, whatever pathetic story you dream up to justify yourself. So don't tell *me* to go. And, by the way, there's no comparison with what I did with Ted. We may've lied to the world but we didn't lie to each other.'

'You betrayed each other, which is the same thing. But it's different rules for you, isn't it? So take your brand new Mercedes and go. The keys are in the hall. I was never more than an appendage to you, anyway. Your chauffeur cum sex slave.'

She stared at him, speechless. Then she grabbed her shoes and shot to her feet. 'Okay. Fine. I'll go.' And she strode past him towards the door.

'And if you're thinking of topping yourself, don't expect me to have it on my conscience for the rest of my life. You're old enough to take responsibility for your own stupid decisions.'

She paused and turned back. 'You really think I care? Don't flatter yourself.' Then the door opened and slammed.

He clasped his hands over his ears to block out the sound of her leaving. Then he released them and gazed around in disbelief. What had he done? What the *hell* had he done? He sprang up, rushed out through the hall and onto the landing, grabbed the railing and peered down the dimly-lit stairwell. 'Nicola! Wait!' he shouted. But she had gone.

He tore down the four flights of stairs and out into the night where he stopped and gazed around. She was nowhere to be seen. He frowned, baffled. How could she have got away so quickly? It was as though she had vanished into thin air.

There were two streets she might have taken. The larger lead to the shopping centre. And there was an alleyway, though it was unlikely she would have taken that. The Mercedes still stood serenely in its bay.

He ran along the larger street as far as the first crossroads then halted again, gasping for breath in the cold night air. The way into town lay to the right and another street had opened to the left but all he could see in every direction were parked cars and terraced houses, silent in steady lamplight. His mobile rang.

'I've established that the girl at Waterloo isn't her.'

'I know. She was here.'

A silence. 'She was there? With you?'

'Yes.'

'What do you mean, was?'

'She turned up, we had a row, and she left.'

'You mean ... she's just wandered off into the night?'

'Yes.'

'For God's *sake* ...'

Dominic ended the call.

He ran back to the building and up the stairs – taking two at a time – but at a loss what to do. Should he call the police himself? At least he now knew roughly where she was. Unless she had found a taxi and vanished again. He re-entered the flat, went back into the living room and stopped dead. He could have sworn he heard something. And it came from the bedroom.

He opened the door and saw that it was there she had gone, that it was that door she had opened and closed, not the door to the hall, which was beside it. She was curled up on his unmade bed, hugging a pillow and rocking slowly to and fro, her cheek grinding against the pillowcase as though it could offer some comfort, her mouth wide in a silent cry of anguish, her eyes tight shut and tears pouring down her cheeks.

He sat down beside her, took her gently about the shoulders and eased her into a sitting position. 'Hey... hey, I'm sorry,' he murmured as he slid his arms around her, 'I'm so sorry,' and she clung to him as though she were drowning, her face pressed into his neck, her tears warm against his skin.

IX

Anne and Linda were having breakfast at the kitchen table when the phone rang. Linda got up and answered it. Anne, her thoughts miles away, was aware of her saying, 'No, it isn't. I'll fetch her.' She cupped her hand over the mouthpiece. 'It's for you. A hospital in Barnstable of all places.'

She darted across the kitchen and took the receiver. 'Yes?'

'Am I speaking to Mrs Haymer?' said a woman's voice.

'Yes.'

'The wife of Edward Haymer?'

'Yes.'

'We have your husband here, Mrs Haymer. He was brought in late last night, suffering from hypothermia. A dog walker found him on the beach, soaking wet and almost unconscious. There'd been a storm and torrential rain and he must have been out in it.'

'Oh my God. Is he all right?'

'He is now. The doctor will check him later this morning and then he should be fine to go home. He asked us to call you.'

'Can you keep him until I arrive? I'll leave straight away and should be with you sometime this afternoon.'

'That'll be fine.'

When she had received directions, she rang off and reported the gist of the conversation to Linda. 'Had he been drinking?' was her reflex reaction.

'Probably. But on this occasion, he may have had reason to.'

'Maybe. I'm sorry. Is he all right?'

'So they say.'

Ten minutes later, having phoned her secretary to explain there had been a family emergency and that all her appointments would have to be cancelled, she went upstairs, took down her overnight bag from on top of the cupboard, packed some essentials into it and zipped it up. Then she paused a moment, glancing around the double bedroom which, for nearly five years, she had occupied alone.

Linda was waiting for her downstairs and Anne squeezed her in a tight, protracted hug. 'I may stay over in a bed and breakfast or something. I'll see how I get on.'

'It's okay. I'll go and stay with my sister while I look for a place of my own. I need to get on with my life.'

'Linda …'

'It's okay.'

They went outside. Anne stowed her case and got in her car and Linda hovered by her open window discussing the various routes to Barnstable. She knew that part of the world quite well as she had a cousin in Biddeford. But the A303 was to be avoided at all costs – it was a horrible road, full of lorries and speed traps, although the views of the downs were stunning.

Anne smiled patiently as she reversed out of the drive and waved as she set off. Glancing in the rear view mirror, she saw Linda still waving, her slender, fragile figure fading into the distance.

Then she lowered her eyes and focused on the road ahead.